THE SCANDALOUS VIXEN

#2 The Duchess Society Series

BY

TRACY SUMNER

WOLF PUBLISHING

The Scandalous Vixen by Tracy Sumner

Published by WOLF Publishing UG

Copyright © 2021 Tracy Sumner
Text by Tracy Sumner
Edited by Chris Hall
Cover Art by Victoria Cooper
Paperback ISBN: 978-3-98536-036-9
Hard Cover ISBN: 978-3-98536-037-6
Ebook ISBN: 978-3-98536-035-2

Also by Tracy Sumner

The Duchess Society Series

The DUCHESS SOCIETY is a steamy new Regency-era series. Come along for a scandalous ride with the incorrigible ladies of the Duchess Society as they tame the wicked rogues of London! Second chance, marriage of convenience, enemies to lovers, forbidden love, passion, scandal, ROMANCE.

If you enjoy depraved dukes, erstwhile earls and sexy scoundrels, untamed bluestockings and rebellious society misses, the DUCHESS SOCIETY is the series for you!

#1 The Brazen Bluestocking

#2 The Scandalous Vixen

#3 The Wicked Wallflower

Prequel to the series: The Ice Duchess

THE
SCANDALOUS
VIXEN

Love and scandal are the best sweeteners of tea.
Henry Fielding

Prologue

Where a Duke is Charmed Without Words

Dorset, England 1813

He'd almost missed meeting her.

Or *could* have missed her, should he have chosen another locale in which to flee a dukedom.

There were a thousand possibilities; so bloody many, he was blinded by them. A thousand parlors were begging admittance, cloying spaces he'd been barred from when he was an impoverished baron. A thousand adoring mothers showcasing their remarkable daughters; what he'd come to understand were auditions for the role of duchess. Balls and musicales, theatre, the opera, which he especially loathed.

Prinny had even invited him to Carlton House, a palace in all but name.

The scrap of embossed royal vellum sliding across his desk had sent him packing his scarred portmanteau, escaping the pandemonium that was his new life. He'd not taken a full breath until he hit the borough of Surrey Heath, and the stink of Town softened to a serene remem-

I

brance, much like a woman's scent drifting from his sheets hours after she'd departed.

Not that there'd been *so* many women, not yet, but there'd been a few. Well, two.

From his perch on the outcrop high above a rocky seashore, Roan Darlington, seventh Duke of Leighton, watched the young woman whom fate had deposited before him traverse the pebbled shore. Her step was tentative on the slick stones, the wind ripping at her clothing as it ripped at his. A chaperone, her maid perhaps, sat on a stone crag farther up the beach, looking like a drab dot of paint on an otherwise vibrant canvas.

This daily observance, almost religious in nature, had become his favorite pastime, aside from exploring the beach for riches. Better than Drury Lane, this production. Much better than the procession of eligibles paraded past him at the standard intervals.

That kind of theatre he could live *without*.

As if she heard his thoughts, the beauty on the beach released a smile that Roan would have traded his entire ducal kingdom for. She dropped to her haunches, and snatched a stone from the frothy tide washing in around her. With a burst of laughter, she presented her prize to the leaden sky in triumph. The hem of her gown and the spencer topping it, exact details of each lost to the distance, dragged sorrowfully through the briny sludge with her movement.

Yet, she gave her attire less than a moment's consideration. She simply passed her wrist across her cheek and chin, leaving wisps of sea foam dotting her creamy skin. But of course, he only imagined this, as the distance was too far to see *precisely* how lovely she was.

Nonetheless, her sheer joy and abandon were a delight, and he was delighted. With his ascension, he now moved through a world inhabited by the most circumspect of acquaintances. Similar in composition to the sculptures he'd seen at the Royal Academy's summer exhibition. Each and every soul he encountered made of marble until he despaired of turning to marble himself.

Roan's impulsive flight had started out as a modest fossil-hunting voyage to the Lyme Regis coast in Dorset. The logic was sound.

Everyone knew he was mad about relics. Mad as in, the Duke of Leighton is interested in *what?*

He made a dart thrown at a target kind of decision to get away. A great aunt on his mother's side he'd not visited since he was a boy, combined with his search for remnants of the Jurassic period that routinely washed up on shore less than a mile from her dower cottage. A restful endeavor. Peaceful, soothing, a prescription for fresh air, long walks and solitude. Doctor's orders. He'd added this justification when asked where he was haring off to. Played the card, so to speak. Because he could. Weak lungs that weren't as weak as they'd once been, but still a grand excuse when he needed a grand excuse. He'd removed himself from many a lifeless ballroom with a delicate cough or two. Those voracious *ton* mamas appreciated the thought of their darling daughters becoming duchess to a duke who might not make it long in this world.

A rather perfect scenario if one was not in love with the duke.

None held a torch for the duke. They were in love with the *idea* of the duke.

Although Roan had been all too willing to evade the responsibilities lumped on his broad but untested twenty-one-year-old shoulders. Even for a fortnight. His apprehension was significant enough to induce panic, which brought breathlessness not created by ballroom tedium. After a childhood spent watching his father lose every farthing five times over and then again, there was no hope for *ever* feeling secure about money. This crystallized nicely with his current situation. Because no matter how much blunt he'd inherited with the role, there wasn't enough to support the duchy. Estates, tenants, domestics. The burden sucked the life—or the breath in his case—from one to imagine it.

There were disastrous scenarios written in the shadows that graced the ceiling of his Mayfair bedchamber, an expanse of plaster he stared at nightly, his heart racing. His name, his title were stamped across each and every one. Philippa's as well because she was now the sister of a duke. And there wasn't a girl alive who was less equipped to play the role.

Sister of a lowly baron? *That* Pippa could have pulled off, perhaps.

Sibling to a duke? They were going to be doomed by his temper and her rebelliousness.

Remembering he was supposed to have left his angst and his little sister temporarily in London, Roan drew a breath of salty air and let it rip free.

It had always been a possibility, of course. The duke bit. Remote, like a lump in the nether region you ignored until it became a raging problem. He'd known it might happen—just hadn't thought it *would*. If the two men standing between him and the dreaded occurrence had only (a) lived longer or (b) procreated appropriately, he would've remained a penurious, interested-in-relics-and-little else baron. A brother who tried his best while raising a girl on this side of wild, all the while hopeful Pippa at least married someone she loved. As he felt couples *should*, though he'd never seen a happy union himself.

But he and Pippa weren't blessedly insignificant any longer.

Now, his significance *stunned*. A parish in Derbyshire was waiting for him to coordinate the repair of a church roof. Another—the estate in Northumberland or Hertfordshire?—urgently needed refurbishment of the main lane in their charming hamlet. As the village was named Leighton, like the castle Roan owned five miles down the admittedly pockmarked thoroughfare, he felt it his duty to prioritize this on his list of responsibilities.

After the church roof, that is.

He could have told the multitude of people awaiting his return— solicitors, stewards at three estates scattered across England plus a crumbling cottage in Scotland, Mayfair staff, tenants, domestics, supposed friends, and hopeful lovers—that the title was choking him, not London's putrid air.

His rather finicky lungs notwithstanding.

No matter. The journey had brought the unearthing of another treasure entirely. Spellbinding for a man who dreamed of making discoveries but had not, as yet, lived long enough to make any.

She was his first.

As he stared, the mystery woman nicked another prize from the sea, her sodden skirt washing away from her in the rolling surf. Fascination gripped him as a feeling, the cavernous kind he believed one must pay attention to, twisted in his belly.

Roan took a faltering step down the path, his mind thrumming. What had she found? A brachiopod? A crustacean? It could be either. He'd found incredible examples of both yesterday.

Yesterday had been a marvel. A non-duke day. He'd heard only three "Your Graces" from sunrise to sunset and those from his valet, Graves, an aging retainer who'd unfortunately come with the title.

Today, however, he had another objective aside from fossil hunting.

Today was the day he *talked* to the young woman on the beach.

With a stretch and a languid rise from her crouch, an innocently erotic move that did little to alter his captivation, she dropped her prize in the leather pouch hanging from her shoulder, slid her bonnet back to reveal hair an indescribable shade caught somewhere between ginger and auburn, and continued her adventure down the shore. If he'd been able to hear her over the waves exploding against the rock, Roan would have sworn she was whistling.

He smiled, his heart giving a trilling skip. This woman, *ah*, she had no care for him. Likely had known he was there, but tolerating faraway flirtation was in actuality no flirtation at all. With the ocean unfurling behind her in a sapphire flood, she appeared distinct from any female of his acquaintance. Any female in England.

After withstanding the treachery that was London society for the past year, the genuflecting and duplicity, the fences Roan had been made to vault, someone not caring about him simply enthralled him. This girl's indifference was sketched in every slender line of her body, every careless toss of her head. Older by a few years perhaps than his sister— but she reminded him of Pippa. It was the hint of bravado in her step, bonnet tapping her back with her stride, hair as feral as she was coming loose from its fragile mooring and springing around her face.

He admired strong women.

Loved his sister to pieces, and she was nothing *but* challenging.

Now they both lived in a world where all that mattered was how one was viewed and, consequently, how precariously one viewed himself. Your standing, your *class*. The number of family generations stacked, one atop the other. He'd had no horse in the race before his ascension to the duchy. A disparaging remark, the reason he'd tossed the Earl of Hamblen in the river running behind Cambridge's Trinity Hall, then being discharged from the university for his trouble. Hamblen's whispered comment about Roan's father owing most of London by the time he was found floating in the Thames, debts not only of credit but honor, the sum having accumulated beyond what any mere man could correct, were entirely true. However, tales of a peer of the realm being cut off from credit—and his subsequent mysterious demise possibly at the hand of the underworld characters he was dealing with—were not to be uttered, especially to his son.

So, Roan had done what he must by tossing the earl in the River Cam, *glad* he'd done it even if furthering his education had been erased from his plans in seconds. With a shrug, he gulped in the sea air, his gaze traveling to the misty horizon. He'd barely been able to afford tuition, anyway.

As he moved down the bluff's precipitous footpath, he wondered what the Cambridge administration would think to know they'd dismissed a duke. It would have been lovely to drop *Cambridge* into conversations, especially with those in the *ton* who'd graduated from Oxford. Alas, a single semester with mediocre marks didn't allow for that.

Roan hated this about himself, but he wasn't above wanting to be thought of well. The last year had been spent desperately trying to salvage his family name from the jumble his father had crushed it into with a careless turn of his boot. Leighton, he cared little for, but the surname Darlington he *did*. He wasn't above planting a facer to defend himself either, be it earl, viscount, marquess, or duke.

His obstinacy was, at times, an issue. As was his pride.

And his temper.

He was in awe of those who didn't suffer from these weaknesses of character.

"How did I know I'd find you here gazing at the sea from this rather daunting spot? I can see why archaeology fits you. I truly can. Disciplined nature and an inquisitive mind. The brawling is the challenge. Someday, we must solve for your fierce temperament." The interloper flicked his cravat from his face and peered apprehensively over the edge of the cliff, evidently not a devotee of high perches from the way his cheeks paled. "What is it they've started calling you? The Defiant Duke?"

With a sigh, the breeze buffeting him filched before it formed a sound, Roan turned from his study of the young woman to find Dexter Munro, the Marquess of Westfield, standing beside him. They'd met in a calculus class at Cambridge and became fast friends not long before Roan's dismissal. Last week, Dex had made an impromptu visit to his ancestral home during a break in the school term and had a vicious row with his father. Thus, his inclusion on the journey. His expectations *were* grandiose. However, his father's opinion was reasonable.

While Roan dreamed of being an academic, Dex planned on it.

He wished to be a geologist when a lord daring to have a profession was intolerable. To make matters worse, to make them unbearable, Dex was the only child of the Duke of Markham. So, he was set to manage his own kingdom someday. Become a *real* duke, to Roan's way of thinking. Which would leave time for little else. Nothing smashed dreams to bits like ascending the throne, but Roan hadn't had the heart to share this fact yet.

Roan's gaze strayed back to the shoreline. "It's paleontology, Westfield, as you well know. Although after landing the lifelong gig of ducal horse trainer, I can in all sincerity tell you my interest has been relegated to a hobby. An expensive one I likely can't afford."

Dex walked back two steps from the cliff's edge. "Doesn't sound very defiant to me."

"Perhaps I'll become so soft, like the buttery insides of a scone, they'll change the moniker to the Docile Duke."

Dex slipped a flask from his coat pocket, glanced over his shoulder to make sure they were alone when there was no chance of them being anything but, then gave the dented silver carafe a fast pull. Wiping his mouth with his gloved fist, he wagged it at Roan in invitation. When they discussed their futures, liquor always seemed to make an appearance. Dex's angst was equal to his.

"Docile Duke doesn't have the same ring. I say leave the nicknames in the salons and parlors where they are cheerfully birthed. Along with the horrid watercolors and ragged needlepoints you go cross-eyed looking at, but every chit in the *ton* produces by the thousands. But those are some of the only accomplishments afforded women, I suppose. That and playing the pianoforte."

Roan grabbed the flask, took a sip, then wished he hadn't when the rotgut brandy hit his tongue. "Just you wait," he said in a choked voice. "Once you're admitted into this elite club, they'll find a name for *you*. Maybe I'll even float a few suggestions out there like a bit of flotsam in the Thames."

Dex frowned and tipped his head back to stare at the ponderous clouds, the sky indeed threatening to release a deluge at any moment. Westfield desired his duchy about as much as Roan desired his. The only difference? His father was healthy, so Dex had *years* before he was forced to make the leap. "I won't go easily into the great beyond, Your Grace. Fighting it tooth and nail, as evidenced by my leaving Derbyshire in a black rage. I'm not giving up the only thing I love in this world for that bloody title."

Roan handed the flask back and inhaled sharply, salt stinging his nose and his tongue. The honorary still shocked. And smarted. *How in the world*, he wondered, *did I get here?* "Possibly, but you'll go into the beyond, willing or no, Dex. Society will demand it. Every person depending upon you for their existence will demand it. Trust me, they'll keep you up at night, those charges. See their expectant smiles just once, and you're caught. No two ways about it. You'll want them to have a decent roof over their heads and food in their bellies."

"Let's talk of simpler things. Or things not so simple." Dex nodded to the woman on the shore who'd circled back to her maid. They were having an animated conversation, shaking out damp skirts and knocking sand from their boots, buttoning the frog closures on spencers and wrapping scarves around their throats.

The sky was a dark menace separating him from her. They were leaving, and he'd yet to talk to her.

Roan's panic was sudden and sure.

"I have to go," Roan whispered and started down the path.

Dex caught his coat sleeve, halting him. "I know who she is. The focus of your keen interest these past days. Silent interest, I should add. Never would've guessed that the Defiant Duke, aside from being defiant, was also shy?"

Roan ripped his beaver hat off his head and whipped it against his thigh. "*Who?*"

The word held more weight, more importance, more *impatience* than it should. How could it truly matter who she was? He was leaving in two days, bound for a thorny life, far from a girl searching for fossils on a lonely stretch of sand. She was probably a governess or a house-keeper, a modiste or a milliner. Engaged to be married or with a babe currently sleeping in a snug cottage in the village. Although she looked young for it, everyone knew they started early in the country.

Dex released Roan's sleeve and stepped back. Tipping his flask high, his throat pulled as he swallowed. "Helena Astley," he finally said, his reluctance clear.

Roan's mind spun, his gaze recording the girl's bold march down the beach in the opposite direction of the cliff he stood motionless upon. Hair whipping about her face in a crimson fury, the end of her scarf dragging out behind her like a cat's tail. The tips of his fingers tingled inside soft kid, this newfound knowledge burning a path through him. Heat pulsed through his veins until he saw only her. *Helena Astley.* Not married. Not a governess, housekeeper, modiste, or milliner. She didn't live in a snug cottage in Lyme Regis. She wasn't impoverished or silly, brainless or fearful.

She was a hellion. And a woman grown. Or as much as he was a grown man.

He'd been right; she didn't give a shite what anyone thought of her. She was a chit who wouldn't *ever* be placed agreeably in a duke's path.

"Don't smile," Dex warned, "because it can't be. Not her, not this one. Fall in love in one glance with an earl's daughter or something." He gestured wildly with the flask, his overcoat flailing about his knees. "Lady Hildegard Templeton, possibly. She's just polished off her first season, and she's quite attractive. Gorgeous even. Maybe out of your league, come to think of it."

"Not interested."

"You're a peer of the realm, remember? The highest peer if we're being precise about it. There's only so much scandal you can create and have your dominion survive, Roan. Even I know this. Open *Debrett's* and pick blindly, but your duchess needs to come from those exalted pages."

Roan snorted out a laugh. "Who said anything about a duchess?"

Dex rocked back on his heels, his smile crooked. "Well, then, a lark is it? I suppose a lark is always in order."

He didn't think talking to Helena Astley, because he was damn well going to speak to her, was a lark—but he wasn't telling Dexter Munro this noteworthy tidbit. "As if *you* should be advising anyone on decorum."

"True, I'm the last man to conform to society's dictates—"

"The *very* last."

Dex stared into the narrow spout of his flask, his argument wilting like a petal on a dying rose. "There's a girl. In Derbyshire, where I grew up. Georgiana. Little sister of my closest friend. Astley reminds me of her. Force of nature and all that." He cursed beneath his breath and gave Roan a heated side-glance. "Now you've got me thinking about *her*. Thanks a lot, friend."

Roan watched Helena grow smaller in sight but not presence as she tramped along the shore, heading for the trail leading to the eastern fork of the village, her maid ten steps behind. "You know I'm no good when told not to do something, Westfield." He sank his hands in his trouser pockets and drew a feeling of confident inevitability around him like a coat. "Makes me want to do just the opposite. I'm stubborn that way."

Dex sighed and tapped the flask against this hip. "Yes, yes, I recognize the look. Same one you were wearing when Hamblen got his arse tossed in the drink. She's a demon and not yet twenty, Ro. Gone through a governess a week since she was born, if you believe the rumors. Worth more blunt than ten dukes put together. An heiress to end all heiresses. She won't need a husband, won't want one. Hasn't been brought up to require one. Father's said to leave her the shipping business, proving he's as cracked as she is. Mother died when she was young, so he raised her like a son. Haunted his warehouse since she was in leading strings. Rides her mare through Hyde Park like a maniac.

Seventeen hands at the withers, the beast. Truly, is this who you want to be smitten with?"

Roan's smile grew. Decided, he reversed course and began to climb the cliff.

"Perfect for a lark, but nothing else." Dex rushed to keep up, his boots skidding across the pebbled path. "It's time to secure a mistress, that widowed countess you mentioned who's been sending you peony-scented notes. Because Helena Astley can never be more, and she's too young yet to be anything else."

Roan could only think with a fateful echo he realized might spell his doom: *She sounds perfect.* "Call it a lark, then, my meeting her, if it makes you feel better."

"Hold up, dammit. This crag is bloody steep." Dex bent at the waist and slapped his hands on his knees, releasing a frantic breath through his teeth. "There's a musicale tonight. Fringe of society affair, likely to be godawful. Word is, the Astley chit will be in attendance."

Roan ran his finger around the fossil in his pocket and hummed softly. In response, the sky split, and a ray of sunlight pierced the thunderous clouds, scattering light across their path. "Can you get an invitation?" he asked, his words carried away by a fierce gust tearing off the sea. He repeated the question just to be sure.

Dex wrapped his arms around his chest as a shiver rolled through him. "Christ, Leighton, you've got to be the most naïve duke ever."

Roan grinned and continued his trek. Tonight would be the night his life changed.

He could just feel it.

Chapter One

Where an Heiress Seethes Over a Race Lost

Epsom, 1823

She wished she'd never met him.

Arrogant, contemptuous *toad*.

Helena Astley blew out an aggrieved breath and scrubbed her hand down her filly's neck, murmuring soft words of praise at her valiant effort. Keeping her gaze anywhere *but* on the Duke of Leighton standing a mere ten paces away, his smile so wide it looked ready to crack his granite cheeks. Not a winner, either of them, but of course, his horse had edged hers out by a nose. *Of course.*

"There's always next year, gel," her trainer, Murphy Donovan, said as he grabbed the reins, prepared to lead Nike from the cooling pit and into a stall behind the track. "I have my eye on a colt that'll be of age next year. Three on the dot. Fastest mount you've ever seen. Oh, now don't go looking vexed. Red cheeks to match that hair of yours. We can't win *every* race. Not with that blasted horseshoe bend Epsom is known for. A challenge, it is, for any thoroughbred. Even with, if I do say so myself, the best trainer in England running her."

She gave her filly another buffing rub. "I know, I know."

"Can't top a duke most days, miss. Best to not put your happiness on such a feat. Not in this world. *His* world." Murphy wrenched his shoulder in the toad's direction and wound the scuffed leather leads around his hand. "November's the start of fox hunting season, what with fields lying fallow and frost months away from making the ground too hard for hooves to stick safely. Leighton's sure to go tearing off to some estate or another to try his luck, waste his days as only men of means can. You won't have to see hide nor hare of him, I reckon."

Murphy looked back to find the duke's smile tilted in their direction. "Cheeky bastard. If I do nothing else in this life, I'll make sure he doesn't get that colt."

Patience, Helena's weary companion since she was a child, stepped in and shooed the trainer away. "Your direction is *not* required. Keep it to what you know, horseflesh and manure."

Patience, who had little of it, and Murphy got along as well as Helena and the Duke of Leighton did.

Which was not well.

"I hate him," Helena whispered as Murphy stalked away, leading Nike from the courtyard and grumbling beneath his breath.

Patience dusted straw from Helena's sleeve and gave her employer's cuff a straightening yank. She always seemed to be searching for ways to make them both fit in. She as a ladies' maid, Helena as a lady. When there was no hope for either. For once, however, Helena looked adequately put together in a stunning crimson gown that brought out the ginger streaks in her hair, as Patience had noted.

She hadn't worn the new garment or the elegant plaid bonnet to impress anyone. She *hadn't*. Considering her profession, and society shunning her because of it, she didn't have many opportunities to dress the part. *Any* part, aside from the owning a shipping enterprise that could buy and sell most of London.

"Mr. Donovan is hard to manage. Routinely oversteps his position, and you let him," Patience murmured. "His language is appalling, and yours isn't much better. I thought to expose you to a better set, to get you away from the docks for one afternoon. Your da made me promise to try to smooth off a few of your rough edges. To make life simpler. Women don't have it the easy way of men."

Helena kicked her boot through the soiled straw covering the ground, a frown tugging her lips low. "I didn't mean Murphy when I said I hated someone. And I don't want these people's acceptance or an easy life. I have a life, a fine one. *My* life." Her focus wandered in the duke's direction. Turned away from her, he didn't see the way her gaze drifted from his glossy Wellingtons to his equally glossy mahogany hair and back.

It was a beautiful journey, even she was forced to admit.

Seeing a diversion was needed, Patience linked her arm through Helena's and guided her toward the barroom, where women were, thankfully, allowed. Expected even, if they had a horse in the running. "That little tiff at Lyme Regis years ago has grown like a weed into the mishap we have now. Lady Hell versus the Defiant Duke. The two most stubborn people in London putting on a show they think only they're watching. When we're all watching. And some are rightly enjoying it."

Helena yanked her arm from Patience's as they stepped through the barroom's entrance, the sound of hushed laughter and subdued conversation circling them like a cloak. "Tiff? He stated publicly that my father should be considered for Bedlam if he left me the shipping business upon his passing. Everyone heard him at that horrid musicale you dragged me to. Although Leighton had no idea who he was speaking to, three business associates of my father's were in the parlor. The brandy talking, as I recall. As if it isn't hard enough to navigate a man's world without those same men knocking me down. When a duke has everything at his disposal. Including respect he's never had to *gain*. I had to work twice as hard when I got back to London to recover my reputation. When I know the shipping business better than any man in England!"

Helena left out the worst part, the part that sent a dart of embarrassment straight through her. The part she hoped only *she* had heard.

Remember, Helena Astley is nothing but a lark.

The words had been the Duke of Markham's, *yes*, but they'd been directed at the Duke of Leighton.

When he'd finally come off that cliff of his and approached her, she'd rudely rebuffed him. Two strikes were one too many. Nevertheless, the anger she could manage. Managed the emotion every day, in fact. What she *wouldn't* accept was that the Duke of Leighton had stuck a needle in her vulnerable core, a piece she violently protected.

To think, she'd once thought him the most attractive man she'd ever seen.

"Maybe it'd be easier for everyone if you forgave him. Quit playing games with those pricey trinkets he seems to love. Unlike any nobleman I've ever seen, collecting anything aside from light-skirts and blunt. You buy his treasures before he gets a chance to, then you turn around and sell them while making sure he knows about it. All to pay him back for that incident at Lyme Regis when he was practically a boy?

"Couldn't have been more than twenty, Hellie. And a foolish young bloke at that. As I've said a hundred times, I always thought he was trying to impress you in some misguided way. Insolent pup. Now he's merely an insolent man. As if we need another one of those."

Patience gracelessly elbowed her way through the crowd, leading them to a vacant table in the back. "Grew up more like you than not, handed that godawful title for next to no good reason. Only his wits to sustain him. Why we have titles and such in this country, I can't fathom. Isn't the monarchy enough? The Americans have it right. My cousin married a tobacco farmer and lives somewhere in the southern colonies. She's thought of quite kindly where here she'd be less than less."

Helena settled at the rickety table, flounced actually, feeling cranky and churlish. But somewhat mollified to hear Patience thought the Duke of Leighton had been set on impressing her. She never tired of being told this, although she didn't agree and never would. The man was a cur, a rake, a coxcomb. "I don't care. It's old news, what happened at Lyme Regis."

Patience tilted Helena's bonnet until it sat just so. "Oh, you *do* care. Don't sass me. Who do you think attached your leading strings and dried your tears when your papa didn't come home for weeks because the weather had delayed his ship? You stir the pot when Leighton can ask Tobias Streeter for anything he needs in the way of artifacts and pottery and such. Make him angry. What does he care? Your father would never agree with letting spite overrule business. You're turning away good money, a nobleman who'd owe Astley Shipping a favor if you gave him what he wanted now and again. You never know when you'll need to call in those markers in life."

Oh, Patience mentioning Tobias Streeter's friendship with the Duke of Leighton was a low blow. Streeter & Macauley Shipping was Astley's main competitor. They were thick as thieves, Streeter and Leighton. Besides, she would never give the duke what he *wanted*.

Aside from a trilobite fossil she'd gotten her hands on recently, a fossil the duke had inquired about twice so far, she'd no idea what the man wanted.

She might have argued with Patience. Should have argued. She wasn't spiteful. Wasn't a sore loser. She didn't act like this. She was a competent businesswoman. Perhaps the only woman in all of England who could call herself thus. Only, the combination of a maid who'd changed her nappies, giving her advice she didn't want, and the man who made her skin itch when she looked at him edging her horse out on the track was a foolproof recipe for bringing out the pouting girl in her.

"He's been nothing but despicable since the day I met him. Condescending lout. I'm glad I sold that hunk of rock to Viscount Davies-Finch before I gave the duke a chance to purchase it. I hope Leighton never finds another fossil he admires as much."

She wasn't going to enlighten Patience about the trilobite.

"You can't divine what the upper classes contend is valuable, dear heart. You'll drive yourself mad if you attempt it." Patience gave her beaded reticule a pat and held out a staying hand. "Don't cause any trouble until I get back. No arguments, no business transactions, no horse trading. I'll locate Henry, then we're going home."

Helena laughed into her gloved fist. The smell of damp leather was more soothing than the scent of horseflesh and spilled whiskey soiling the air. "Henry's likely in a storeroom helping someone relace their bodice."

Patience's cheeks lit, her lips forming an outraged O. *"Helena Blythe Astley!"*

Helena shrugged and traced a gash in the table with her pinkie. Henry, part footman, part protector, his family employed by Astley Shipping since before she was born, had the tendency to disappear at events only to return with rouge on his collar or his cheek. Buttons mismatched, cravat crumpled, a dazed expression on his face. He put his good looks and strong back to use and then some.

Helena admired his resourcefulness.

The burst of laughter rippled over her like a sea current, lush and deep, a shiver skimming her skin. She couldn't stop herself from searching the room until she found him, and when she did, the impact stole her breath. Lit her temper. Both common occurrences.

Taller than almost anyone in the barroom, the Duke of Leighton was easy to locate. A secret she'd hold as her own until the day she died, that she'd *always* been able to locate him. Across a crowded theatre, ballroom, or opera house, sweet shop on Bond Street, or while passing each other on a busy lane. If the Duke of Leighton entered a space, *her* space, her body, much against her will, let her know it.

His features weren't as youthful as they'd once been, the startlingly handsome face that had stared down at her from a seaside cliff. He'd settled into his chiseled looks as skillfully as he'd settled into his dukedom. A pleasing mix, everything about him, like a biscuit with a creamy center. Hair the color of an elm trunk darkened by rain curling about a firm jaw. Cunning green eyes bounded by lashes so thick they should have been outlawed on a man. Controlled in dress and manner. Dark colors *and* moods. He was fabled for both.

Predictably, he was surrounded by the usual suspects. A group she'd come to think of as the Leighton Cluster. The Duke of Markham and his duchess, Georgiana. Tobias Streeter and his new wife, Lady Hildegard. Xander Macauley, Streeter's partner in trade and constant companion. Competitors of Astley Shipping, although the rivalry was civil for the most part. Helena and Streeter's most heated discussions regarded trade routes and tariff payments. Amazingly, he spoke to her as a rival, even going so far as looking her in the eye. Which she appreciated. His regard made sense because his wife wasn't a modicum of decorum herself.

Lady Hildegard Streeter and the Duchess of Markham were partners in their own enterprise, The Duchess Society. A consortium known for taming wild chits and buoying improbable marital matches. Matches beneficial for the female participant. Streeter was a by-blow only months ago acknowledged by his father, Viscount Craven. Part Romani, too, if one believed rumors. That he'd married an earl's daughter was quite the mission statement for the miracles the Duchess Society could accomplish.

Another predictable stroke of the painting was the woman clinging to Leighton's arm like a poisonous vine. Or two clinging vines, it looked like on this day. One on each side of him, the lucky devil. Helena checked them off like items on a shopping list. Daughter of a marquess, sister to an earl. She repressed the urge to yawn into her fist even as her heart gave a *thump* she ignored with everything in her.

Leighton smiled down at one of them. The marquess's daughter. A blonde bit of fluff who tittered sickeningly and bumped his broad body with her own. He made no effort to push her away.

Blackguard. Flirt. Libertine.

Helena heaved a lament, her finger jamming so hard in the table's gash that a splinter slid through her glove and pricked her skin. *Attracted.* She was attracted to the Duke of Leighton.

There, she'd admitted it. No reason to lie to herself when she was busy lying to everyone else.

The man made her melt when his gaze met hers; mysterious feminine nonsense warming nooks no one had ever warmed. A powerful yearning swirled through her after the melting, every time. She lived in a rough world, was not wholly inexperienced, and knew what her body hungered for. Unfortunately, the Duke of Leighton had presented possibilities. Possibilities that had her aching, but she didn't *want*.

Not with him.

The situation was abhorrent but unavoidable—and had been since the day she'd felt his stare burning through her spencer as she walked a lonesome stretch of beach. Hadn't her father always told her that one did not choose who warmed their toast?

Although she wished any man aside from the bloody Duke of Leighton could warm it.

Jerking her glove off one finger at a time, she cursed her foolishness and Leighton's inaccessibility. When it didn't matter that he was far above her reach because she was never going to reach for him.

"Well, if it isn't London's brightest scandal."

Blast, this day was getting worse and worse, Helena reflected.

The duke's voice was low, private harassment of the cruelest kind. Hypnotic, burrowing like that splinter beneath her skin. Inevitably, his leather-and-brandy scent galloped in behind his softly spoken rebuke. The indefinable aroma that was simply *him*. A scent she recognized instantly. Another secret yanked from the chest she kept buried deep. A chest filled with hundreds of impressions of this man—and this man only.

Drawing strength before she stepped into battle, Helena took a fast breath, then glanced up from her injured fingertip to find him looming over her. He'd easily stepped into her space, a distance she didn't care to close. Hard to imagine that in all the years they'd waged verbal war, she'd yet to touch him.

"Leighton," she replied, thrilled his name came out as steady as it did.

She'd whispered it in the darkness of her bedchamber two nights ago, and it had *not* been calm. That her pleasure featured him should have alarmed her more than it did. But she'd become used to picturing him when she came.

His eyes seized hers, and the air around them sparked like magnesium had been lit. Helena feared she wasn't the only one to recognize the change.

Placing his hand on the chair across from her, his fingers circled the top spindle and clenched tightly. Then with an expression she couldn't decipher crossing his face, he sent his blistering gaze to the muddy hem of her gown and back. Ceaselessly, he caught her looking flushed or mud-spattered, out of breath or speech. Leaving a shop with arms loaded with packages, scurrying into a carriage to escape a sudden burst of rain. On the docks, on the street outside her warehouse. She was as far from the woman he would choose to be his duchess as any in the world.

Although this was undoubtedly true, Roan Darlington, Duke of Leighton, never made her feel *less*. Honestly, he never acted as if he disapproved of her or her choice to assume control of her father's business when he'd died three years ago. This confused her extraordinarily after he'd made such a show of publicly cutting her low all those years ago.

She frequently had to remind herself.

They dealt with each other because he desired antiquities, and she supplied them on the rare occasion. End of story. Business arrangements of the sort she negotiated every day.

She shook her head, breaking the spell he'd cast, the present—ribald laughter, the clang of crystal, the aroma of tobacco, hair oil, and scented bosoms—recapturing her consciousness.

For a moment, it had merely been the two of them.

Leighton gestured with his glass, his magnificent lips parting to say something sure to send her temper soaring. Then, realizing she had no drink, he leaned across the table, his gaze never leaving hers as he placed his before her.

She fidgeted in her chair and set it wobbling, wondering if he could feel the heat radiating off her skin. *Lud*, she hoped not. With a weak swallow, she stared at the glass as if it were a live pyrotechnic he'd placed before her.

His mouth kicked up on one side in a devilish tilt, close to a smirk. He had a tiny scar that cut faintly into his top lip, a perfect imperfection she wished she'd never noticed. "I only took a modest sip if you don't mind sharing. It's quite the best whiskey to be had if I do say so myself. You won't find it at Epsom. My own label as I'm a partner in a malt brewing venture with—"

"Tobias Streeter," she interrupted and, daring herself, grabbed the tumbler and threw back the contents. It was smooth, creating only a soft burn as it spiraled down her throat. She was the lone daughter of a man who'd started his career as a sailor. She could handle her liquor, thank you very much. Feeling a moment's liquid courage, she glanced up to find him unprepared.

For once, the saber in her hand, *his* back to the wall. His emerald gaze exploded with the same ferocity likely blasting from hers. She licked her lips and watched with genuine joy as a muscle in his jaw started to tick. Take *that*, Defiant Duke.

There was an elemental reason they'd circled each other as adversaries for years.

And they both knew what that reason was.

"Congratulations, by the way, Your Grace." She saluted him with the glass, his whiskey warming her tongue, his dazed expression twisting her belly into a fierce knot. "Your colt made an excellent show on a muddy track."

He blinked as if she'd yanked him from a trance, proving the day wasn't entirely shot to hell. Color rose high on his cheeks before he took control of himself. Then he laughed and, delighted with life, the capricious bounder swiveled the chair around and collapsed into it, stacking his arms along the top rung. "Nike. Goddess of speed, am I right? Typically drawn with wings, daughter of Ares and Styx. An unusual name for a horse. But you are, Helena Astley, an unusual woman."

"Pallas," Helena whispered and wished silently for more drink. "Her father was thought to be Pallas." Why did Leighton have to go and prove he had a brain in that pretty head of his?

He smiled, his eyes glinting in the muted light piercing the windowpane above them. She curled her hand around the glass until she feared it would crack. She was having particular trouble today ignoring that enticing scar on his lip.

"Ah, Pallas. I get the gods confused. Just diving into Greek mythology when I was asked to depart Cambridge."

"How rude of Cambridge to eject a scholar. Eject a *duke*."

He shrugged gleefully, his broad shoulders straining against his superfine coat. "Quite. I don't know why they were provoked. What's another earl tossed in the River Cam anyway?"

She drew the glass in a tight circle on the table, wondering what topic would provoke *him* enough to leave. Unfortunately, she could only handle close proximity to the Duke of Leighton for so long and keep her wits about her. It's why she limited their infrequent business dealings to written correspondence. "Did you stop by for a reason, aside from congratulating me on *my* filly's excellent run on a muddy track, Your Grace?"

"Oh, yes, that." His fingers did a teasing dance where they were hooked around his elbows. "Congratulations on Nike's excellent run. Well done. Your trainer should be very proud."

She inclined her head as regally as possible when she was not a regal girl. It felt dishonest but served as well as any gesture in society should. She had closely observed the way they dealt with each other.

"Although it wasn't enough, was it?"

Her heart gave a hard thump in her chest. *Of all the—*

"Now, don't get angry. Nike did fabulously well, close to perfect but not. As is life." Suddenly, he leaned over the table as if she were a refreshing rain shower he wanted to step into. "What's that smear of blood on your finger?"

She glanced down, her stomach dipping. Never, ever a lady around this man. Muddy, bloody, woefully inadequate. "A splinter." She dropped her hands to her lap and twisted them together. "It's nothing."

He extended his arm, wagged his fingers. "Give it here. I'm skilled at splinter removal. Ask the Duchess of Markham over there. She'll attest. They have two young ones I'm around more often than I'd like. They call me Uncle, even. I suppose it's rather sweet. And surprising us all, I'm quite good with them. Splinters and children."

Helena caught his gaze and the mischief shining like a beacon. She shook her head. *No.*

His gaze lifted over her shoulder, his straight, white teeth coming out to catch his lip as he pondered. "I didn't figure you for the apprehensive type, Miss Astley. We've battled over antiquities four times, with my losing the battle twice. A dead heat. You're a fierce competitor. Hence the label the *ton* has saddled you with. So, a silly sliver of wood is causing you hesitation? Consider me shocked."

Her hands tangled in the folds of her skirt. "I'd love to know when you've beaten me even *once*, Leighton."

"The Dutch East Indies urn."

"I sold that chipped jug to you if you recall. How do you consider a standard business transaction besting me?"

He dropped his chin to his hand, his smile dreamy as he gazed across the table at her. The distance narrowed until she felt as woozy as she would sitting on his lap. "It's worth twice what I paid. I turned around, sold it for seventy pounds, then purchased a coprolite from Streeter with the profit. He, unlike you, drove a hard bargain for what is, if you don't know the term, fossilized dung. Can you believe it? Your middling negotiating skills in the world of antiquities helped finance my next purchase. I thought you should know. As you can likely guess, most of my funds are tunneled back into the duchy like filthy rainwater down a street drain. I don't have as much supplementary blunt for my passions as I'd like. One must become adept at the game."

"You cheat. Conniving, thieving—"

"Give me your hand, Hellie," he whispered in a brutal tone that, instead of making her angry, thawed her ire. Lit a fire inside her. Raised the hair on the back of her neck. An inferno heating her skin in places she sheltered from view.

For perhaps the *first* time, the Duke of Leighton wasn't joking. He was renowned for having an uncertain temper, for being the crossest man in the ballroom. Although she'd never seen it, she only read about the explosions in the scandal sheets.

Honestly, she didn't know the man that well.

After all, he was a duke, and she a sailor's daughter. Two people who'd had a fraught interaction years ago at a tiresome musicale on the coast. Then went on to do business with each other on several inauspicious occasions. It didn't amount to much.

Then she realized what he'd called her.

"Hellie. Only Patience calls me that." And her father had, of course. But so long ago now, the memory was as faded as a painting left in the sunlight.

Leighton wagged his fingers, impatient. "I overheard her at the opera last month. We were in line waiting for our carriages. It was starting to rain, and everyone was crowding in." He frowned, possibly revealing too much. "Standing close enough, I suppose, for me to have heard."

Gambling, she made the mistake of thinking it was nothing and gave him her hand, knocking fate in the jaw. Arrogance overriding good sense. His hands were bare, she realized when his skin touched hers. Smooth skin, calloused fingertips. With a quickening pulse, she belatedly remembered seeing fawn kid gloves of excellent quality protruding from his coat pocket.

He brushed his index finger over the location of the splinter, and her breath seized. She emitted a hushed, uncontrollable gasp, desire settling in every hidden nook of her body.

His gaze caught hers and held. It was then she grasped his eyes weren't solidly green but an indescribable mix midway between jade and light brown. Changing even as he stared, leading her on a quest to solve the puzzle of them. Brown, green, brown again. Then he lowered those long lashes enough to hide from her and glanced at her hand captured firmly in both of his.

She wondered at her certainty that he'd done this to test himself as well. And that they'd both failed the test.

"I'm writing an article for a scientific journal," he began and proceeded to tell her a tedious story meant to soothe while he finessed the splinter from her skin.

It wasn't painful. Well, rather, *nothing* could intrude upon what was happening to her with his touch. The sound of his voice moving through her like butter oozing through toasted bread. The cascade of sensation drowned her senses, dissolving the sights and echoes in the room to faint pinpricks of awareness. Recognition of *him* vibrated like a strike of lightning, shaking the ground beneath her and charging the air. She'd never been this close to him, not even at that horrid musicale. But then, they'd only argued across a table much larger than this one.

A distance so vast she'd understood then they had no chance of bridging it.

She recorded it all—because she *could*. Tucked the details away for future review. Tiny grooves shot from the edge of his mouth as he focused on his task. Stubble dotted his hard jaw, the muscle beneath it flexing in time with his thoughts. Leather and a subtle kick of bergamot washed lazily between them, a river of delight. Enticement. Wonder. He was, quite fantastically and perhaps only to her, a most appealing man. *The* most.

A quandary, as she interacted with men daily. Business partners, employees, clients. She wasn't a highborn debutante stashed in a dusty parlor corner awaiting matrimony, but a businesswoman roaming London's docks in an era when this kind of behavior was social suicide.

They were a bomb set to go off and destroy everything.

"There," he murmured and lifted his head. "Got it." Then he made a move to bring her hand to his lips—unconscious on his part—and her heart dropped somewhere within the vicinity of the straw-covered planks beneath their feet. Her tenacious heart gave a twist at the adorably perplexed look on his face. Then her body betrayed her, a shiver she thankfully contained racing through her body. Want, need, *desire*.

Dear heaven, I shouldn't have let him touch me.

"Your Grace, so nice to see you," Patience murmured in a tone that was worse than a shout as she entered a scene that was as unseemly as it appeared. "I've just returned from trying unsuccessfully to locate our footman."

Leighton dropped Helena's hand like it was on fire and scooted his chair back with a skidding motion, rising instantly to his feet. Yanking his sleeves taut, he grabbed his gloves from his pocket and muscled them on his hands. She could see from his bewildered expression that he genuinely hadn't known what he was about—almost kissing her fingertips in front of half of London.

Then he made matters worse, his gaze instantly dropping to her lips, affecting them like he'd done something wicked like actually kiss her. An event she'd only dreamed about. But she *had* dreamed about it. More than once.

He swallowed hard as if he'd had similar dreams.

"Helena, dear, you remember Sir Reginald, don't you?"

Helena exhaled miserably, the day entirely without hope. Rubbish, sheer rubbish Epsom, 1821. She swiveled in her seat to find the man who'd asked for her hand in marriage—*twice*—standing just behind her companion. A tricky situation, as Sir Reginald had told her following each detailed rejection that he wasn't giving up until she said yes. He looked immaculate and soldierly, as if he'd just stepped away from a thorough review of his stylish rig in a mirror. "Of course, Sir—"

"No sir, please, as I've insisted. The gesture was the queen's verdict, not my wish. The battles in India would've been fought and won with or without me," Reginald Norcross humbly intoned and, reaching theatrically around Patience, slid a drink on the table in front of Helena, knocking aside Leighton's empty vessel with a clack. The scent of cinnamon and clove rose to sting her nose, steam to dot her cheeks. This man, a valiant knight to his core, whether he appreciated the recognition or not, would never have offered *whiskey* to a woman.

Leighton coughed under his breath, audibly enough for everyone to grasp his derision. "Norcross," he finally said when it became apparent he had to say something.

"Your Grace," Reginald returned, equally obliged. He added a charming tug of his gloved hand through his golden hair, a feature she suspected he liked to call attention to.

Helena glanced between them, captivated despite herself. Their masculine bluster illuminated the space and secretly did pleasing things to her insides, like children fighting over a toy. But of course, she'd never once been any man's toy.

Despite the allure of the scene, she refused to *be* any man's toy.

Helena cast her gaze at the duke, taking a sip of spiced wine, her smile firm, all business. If her hand trembled to find he was a head taller than Sir Reginald, his shoulders a hand wider, that was her... little... secret. "I'll look for the piece for you, Your Grace. Ammonite, did you say? When I find it, I'll send a note round to Mayfair. I fear I've already sold the trilobite to a higher bidder."

The duke's lips pressed tight at the dismissal, a muscle in his jaw jumping.

Embedded in hazel eyes that had flooded with a varied mix of color, there was a challenge she should have been smart enough to register.

Chapter Two

Where a Duke Fights With His Friends

Six Weeks After the Splinter Removal
Gentleman Jackson's Boxing Saloon, 13 Bond Street

Roan never saw the punch coming.

There were multiple reasons for his failure to incorporate Jackson's principles into his weekly boxing match. Nimble footwork was key, which Roan clearly didn't have this day. And judging the distance from the object when throwing a punch or, in this case, when receiving one.

His first mistake was spending the previous evening in a misguided quest for entertainment with the Duke of Markham, Tobias Streeter, and his partner, Xander Macauley, that had left Roan with an aching head, a parched throat, and a less than steady gait.

Hence his lack of nimbleness and inability to judge distances.

Problem number two was Helena Astley.

He'd not seen her once since their row at Epsom weeks ago. Or their flirtation at Epsom. Not really a row when you almost kiss a chit's hand before a roomful of people who would have been keenly interested in the gesture. A significant blunder on his part should his lips have brushed her petal-soft skin. It had been enough to touch her at all, a blazing path of need washing through his veins from the first moment. *This...* he frowned, unsure what to call their interactions when he always knew with other women. Although those situations were admittedly more blatant, his intent clear. The game begun, decision made, invitation accepted, an adjournment to a bedchamber, vacant parlor, or a time or two, a linen closet. Tight spaces and the risk of being discovered drove creativity to new heights, he'd come to find. Especially when neither party was truly invested in the other.

However, Helena was nothing like the women he'd dallied with in spaces smelling of laundry soap and linseed oil. In carriages bumping along, throwing two people who sought nothing more than the appeasement of a nagging hunger together. Oddly, bouts of abject loneliness always followed those episodes. Leaving him feeling as if he were searching for something more than a moment's release but not finding it.

Lady Hell, as the *ton* called Helena, mystified him and always had. He was haunted by her, and he wasn't a man accustomed to being haunted. Moreover, her motives were ambiguous when women in society usually advertised theirs as cleanly as chalk markings on a blackboard. So here he was, having finally, *finally* touched the object of his adolescent desire, and he was no further along in his decision about what to *do* with his emotions than he'd been ten years ago in that damned parlor in Lyme Regis. When he'd opened his mouth, poured brandy in, then let things he shouldn't have said about a chit he fancied spill out.

Time was passing, more quickly the older he got. Pressure for him to find a duchess mounted with each tick of the ancient grandfather clock guarding his vestibule, an imposing piece that had come with the duchy. Already, the weather had turned, a fierce, frosty bite signaling the arrival of winter. He'd settled Pippa and her maid at the Hertfordshire estate last week, and he planned to join them once he finished up the few business dealings that would not wait until the new year.

There would be no brief, pulse-drumming sightings of Helena

Astley in Hertfordshire. Outshining every woman he'd ever known without trying.

In preparation for this absence, if he'd passed Astley Shipping's warehouse more times than required these past weeks, it was because it was the fastest route through Wapping, where he had business to conduct. Which sounded like a legitimate excuse if one didn't know Wapping in the least.

He was still infatuated after all this time. When he could have any woman he wanted, he wanted *her*. It made sense. He'd always felt possessive, a nagging sense of ownership. Ridiculous, but the word *mine* chimed through his head like a bell whenever he saw her.

Roan was pondering this rather dismal development when Xander Macauley's fist smashed into his face.

Roan saw stars, but only for the half-minute it took him to rise from the knees he'd momentarily fallen to. He ignored the Duke of Markham's rabid burst of laughter from somewhere behind him and wiped his wrist across his mouth, staring at the smear of blood on his cuff before lifting his gaze to his sparring partner. "I'll give you that one for my tossing you in the drink last year, Mac. But there won't be another. Trust me on this."

Xander, a handsome brute of a man and Roan's new partner in shipping, now that Tobias Streeter was putting more time into his architecture business and his new family, grinned and took a challenging step closer. "You certain about that, mate? Let's go another round. See where we land with it. Limehouse versus Mayfair. Now *that's* a ticket I'll buy any day of the week."

Dexter Munro, the Duke of Markham, always the coolest head in the house, stepped between them with an angelic expression Roan didn't buy for a damned minute. Dex gave them hard shoves in the chest that sent both men stumbling back. "We call it when someone bleeds, remember? The ladies can only kiss and make so many bruises better. So, why give them more than one to choose from?"

"Pansies," Macauley muttered and turned to rip off the linen strips wrapped about his wrists with his teeth. His hair, dark as the coal dust that coated London's streets, hung in a damp tangle across his brow. "By some foul means, I find myself surrounded by posh toffs. Weak lungs on this one, innit? I have to go easy. If he coughs, he well may be dying right here before us. An ordinary man can't kill a duke. That's my worry when sparring with him, truth be told."

"My lungs are *fine*." Roan yanked his boxing gloves off and tossed them to the floor. Now he remembered why he'd thrown the cur in the Thames last year. The man was an excellent business partner but a devil of a rival in life. Everyone knew Macauley had grown up in the rookery with a chip the size of Wales resting on his shoulder. He didn't trust anyone in society. The higher the title, the greater his suspicion. Roan often felt like Macauley was a dog he fed every morning, a campaign he never won. Left begging when he wasn't a man who *ever* begged.

Tobias Streeter yawned from his sprawl in the scuffed leather chair wedged in the corner of the only private boxing parlor in Gentleman Jackson's establishment. A tight space reserved for royalty, Lord Byron, and on certain days, dukes. Tobias's wife, the former Lady Hildegard Templeton, had recently given birth to a baby boy, and Tobias slumbered in any place they let him. He was hungry for sleep but so delighted with his existence that it was sickening to watch. It was an amazing transformation for a man once thought of as the king of London's underworld.

"Never mind him, Mac. The duke's mad about that idiotic sketch in the *Gazette*." Tobias mimed drawing, then suppressed another yawn. "Of him knocking the Marquess of Gadsden on his arse before all of parliament. Hell's teeth, I wish I'd seen that. But the House of Lords is too fine a place for a viscount's bastard, I suppose." He pretended to straighten a cuff that didn't need straightening, his smile incandescent. "What was that argument over again? Or better I should ask, *who?*"

Roan plucked his damp shirt away from his chest and gave his hair, equally drenched with sweat, a swipe off his cheek. "No idea what you're talking about, Streeter."

Macauley shook the scraps of linen from his hands and watched them flutter to the floor. "He's hung up on Helena Astley, and everyone in Town knows it. Everyone except Helena Astley. Popped that blighter a good one for saying something contemptible about her is the going story. Knocked him flat out, didn't you? Hit his wee head on the corner of one of those uncompromising church pews you're forced to sit on in the main chamber. Bled like a stuck pig. I heard all about it." Macauley glanced over his shoulder with a partially impressed expression. "Your temper is the thing I like best about you, Your Grace. That and your inclination to let yourself be well-used by someone wearing a revealing frock on the occasional reckless outing."

Roan shrugged into his coat, these topics older than that grandfather clock in his Mayfair manse. His temper, his obsession with Helena Astley, his status as a rake. All true, but one of those facts known only to the men in this room. In a city where many had no friends, he considered himself lucky to count these three as his, despite their tendency to taunt him until he blew. Which wasn't, perhaps, the hardest of feats to accomplish.

Dex tucked his shirttail into his trousers and buttoned his brocade waistcoat, bottom to top with composed precision. "Better pick a duchess soon, Ro, or the society mothers are going to expire. Have my wife help you. Matchmaking is what the Duchess Society does best, although my darling duchess, Georgie, claims they're *not* matchmakers. Rather, she likes to call them marital managers. A better option than another trip to Almack's. I think you're the only available duke left aside from Rothers. Who's so old he gads about with a cane. And even *he* gets invitations from eager mamas."

Despite the chiding words, the look Dex threw Roan was sympathetic. He'd been there when Roan had spoken out of turn and ruined his chance with Helena. What had his friend called his infatuation with her back then? A *lark*. When Roan's feelings for Helena had never felt like a lark. In any case, Dex had been right. She was a hoyden fit for ships and the high sea, and she would never make a proper duchess.

Even if, when he dreamed of one, Helena's was the face in his dreams.

Roan had tried to make it right, tried to apologize to her upon their return to London years ago. Sent notes round until it was apparent Helena had either forgotten about the musicale incident or was never going to get over it. From the way her lilac eyes blazed when she looked at him, not always but often, he was betting on the latter. He could be a difficult man, uncompromising and obstinate, but he was never cruel. He didn't like imagining that he'd hurt her, or worse, made her business dealings trickier with his pointless comments. If she only knew. Most men were intimidated by her when he found her strength and independence magnificent.

Of course, he wasn't going to risk another pummeling by admitting this.

Because he and Helena were not to be, and he needed to accept that. Find some impeccable society chit to marry and move on. Who met their soulmate sitting across a dinner table at a horrid musicale anyway? No one he'd ever heard of, that's who.

Macauley huffed a breath through his teeth and dabbed at the spot of blood tucked neatly in the corner of his mouth. "Take her if you want her. She's a bit rough around the edges, but that should make it more fun."

"It isn't that easy," he snapped. Roan didn't think Helena liked him, for one. A major impediment. Another? Top to bottom, they lived in different worlds. He wasn't blind to that fact.

"Isn't it, with a title as weighty as a king's?" Macauley yanked the ends of his cravat in annoyance, the seams of his coat tested by his broad shoulders. "You crook your finger, women come crawling."

"She's not duchess material," Dex chimed in, his tone implying that was a *good* thing. "Temperamental. Beautiful. Fiercely independent. Wealthy as Croesus. A handful for any man to manage. Hmm, describing her reminds me of a defiant duke I know."

"Stop with that damned nickname, will you?"

Macauley snaked his fingers through his hair, his lips kicking up on the side. "True, she doesn't need a husband with that pot of gold she's sitting on. A fleet of five ships, number six being built in Portsmouth as we speak. Good for her, good for you if you can find a way inside. If you get my meaning." He dusted his hand down his chest with a flourish. "I'll never get married myself. Not with so many options. Why settle on one slice when you can have the entire cake?"

Roan glanced at his fists, curled his fingers until his nails cut into his palms. Macauley's words echoed through his mind, accompanied by a fierce, pointlessly male desire to tame an untamable woman. Still, he couldn't get past a straightforward belief. Helena was nothing like she pretended to be—and he didn't know why his lenses let him see her differently. He honestly didn't. Traces of her perfume, something light and exotic, a scent he couldn't quite place, fluttered through him like mist while he daydreamed. Despite his reluctance, he stepped into the memory.

"There's the sentimental simper again. I can't take you three much longer." Macauley stomped out of the small square serving as a ring, yanked his greatcoat from the peg, and jammed his arms into the sleeves. "This love business has got to *stop*."

"Wait until it happens to you, my friend. I'm going to laugh my arse off," Tobias murmured sleepily from his chair. "Love arrives much as your fist did against Leighton's jaw. Without notice. I hope you have ten children to keep you up at night. You'll worry your damned life over them, let me tell you. But be happier for it, I promise."

Macauley pointed, a vicious jab directed at each man in the room. "Never. Never, *ever*."

Dex saddled up beside Roan and lowered his voice. "Are you well? I know today is a difficult day."

Roan uncurled his fingers, then dropped his arms by his side. The concern in Dex's voice caused a slight ache to erupt in the pit of his stomach. "I haven't thought too much about it."

When he had. Twelve years prior, on this very day, his father had been found floating in the Thames. It was kind of his friend to remember and brave of him to comment. And Dex only knew part of the story.

Dex's elbow bumped his, a male version of a hug. "I know all about surviving legacies, Ro. You can talk to me."

Roan shook his head, rolled his shoulders. *I'm fine*, he thought, when he didn't feel fine. But men were taught to, above all, carry on. "What do you know about Reginald Norcross?" he asked instead of remarking upon the tragedy that was his father's demise. Some secrets were best *kept*.

Dex tilted his head, his gaze narrowing thoughtfully. "Cherishes that knighthood, though he humbly says the war could have been won without him. Always the same. I think I've heard his reply a hundred times myself, and I hardly know the man."

"Weak-chinned blighter," Roan murmured, vexed for no good reason. But when did a man need a good reason if a woman was involved?

"It's been years since Lyme Regis, Ro." Dex sounded genuinely baffled, though he'd run his own heartfelt race and then married his childhood love, Georgiana. After letting her marry someone else *first*.

But not everyone believed in second chances. And a duke, after all, could have anyone he wanted. Why pine away for an unsuitable woman who didn't want *you*?

The realization crisped his mood around the edges.

Unexpectedly, Roan felt the breathlessness brought on by angst, not asthma. Reaching for his hat, he shoved it on his head and stalked from the room.

Chapter Three

Where an Heiress Lets a Duke In

Thought the Duke of L *is rumored to have caused an uproar in the main parliamentary chamber last week over a loathsome comment by the Marquess of G about a certain shipping heiress. What is one to think about this development when the duke needs a duchess, but the heiress doesn't need a duke?*

Dazed, Helena lowered the broadsheet to her lap, her gaze tracking the narrow band of light breaching the velvet curtains adorning her coach's rain-streaked window. Her head felt light—and in the distance, the sound of the Thames slapping the wharf pounded in time to her heartbeat. Was the man *demented?*

She inhaled air redolent of roasted chestnuts and coal smoke into her lungs and focused on her outrage, ignoring the flicker of awareness that streaked through her.

Insufferable cur. Gorgeous, stubborn wretch. Rake. Bounder. She didn't need defending. She wasn't one of his society marzipan sweets.

She didn't want to be connected to him outside that locked chest wedged deep in her heart. If the thought of him lit a fire inside her when other men left her cold, that was *her* business.

Life was full of many modest misfortunes.

She had freedom unlike any woman in England. Freedom she'd paid *dearly* for. The Duke of Leighton wasn't going to come in and rob her of her direction in life with those lazy smiles of his. Eyes that changed color with his mood, so much so that she found herself laying odds on green or brown. That enticing scar cutting into his top lip. His sleepy, smoky voice.

The image of him high atop a sea cliff swept through her like an unwelcome gust. Her body reacted, as it always did. She ran her finger along a stitched braid in the velvet squab, fighting with herself. But it was of no use.

She shifted, crossing her legs and pressing her thighs together. Her skin hummed beneath her silk shift, her fingertips beneath delicate kid. Her breasts felt heavy, her knees weak. The crisp burst of air shooting through the crack in the windowpane danced across her cheek and propelled a tremor down her body. Something had happened when he'd touched her at Epsom. He'd ignited a hunger that had been dormant. Or repressed was perhaps the better term.

Awareness. Need. *Curiosity*.

Helena could fight off most things in life—deny, refuse, reject—but curiosity was a hard sensation to conquer. She was a curious woman. And everyone knew that inquisitiveness had the power to kill.

It was her cursed luck that when her carriage halted in front of her shipping warehouse, who should have been standing on the curb outside but the blasted Duke of Leighton.

Helena catapulted from the vehicle as if she'd been shot from it, the stunned coachman only halfway down from his elevated perch. Her heart turned over at the equally stunned look on the duke's face as he turned to her. He had a bruised eye turning all sorts of blue and black, his hair wildly escaping the brim of a hat cocked at just the proper angle. Despite the flutter in her chest, she didn't stop until her boots nearly smacked his.

He glanced at the gossip rag wadded in her fist, his lips tilting crookedly. Adorably, damn him. "Oh well, too late for apologies as you've already seen it. I don't know if you have had a chance to review the sketch in the *Gazette* yet. The portrait is decent, actually. Better of me than the marquess. He looked like a starved chicken. I almost feel bad for the poor sap."

"*Sketch?*" She shoved the broadsheet into his chest, trying diligently to ignore the heat seeping from him like a blazing hearth fire. Ignore the lush scent of leather and man that for one brief second erased the choking smell of burning coal. A monumental feat in London, defeating the stink. "You... I'm... this—" She gave up, blowing out a harsh breath and knocking her bonnet back on her head. *Of all the...*

Her gaze caught his as the realization of how close they were standing finally thrummed through her. A mere heartbeat away. A single, breathless sigh, a shift, a stumble, and they would have been pressed against each other. She blinked, unable to move, recording the specks of gold in the outer edge of his eyes. Her lips moved, but no sound came out. No thought escaped. When her mind was full. Of sensation, images, impressions built on her overzealous imagination and her secret fascination with an unsuitable man. The crisp hint of winter against her skin, a child's laughter in the distance.

While he watched her watch him, a muscle in Leighton's jaw flexed, his mouth compressing into an unflinching line. His eyes turned as green as the shipment of jade she'd imported from Asia last month. All highlighted by his terrific bruise. The eye color meant something, but she didn't know what.

She would have given half her empire to know what he was thinking.

When she knew what *she* was thinking.

Attraction. Dense and impenetrable. Indescribable, written in the steady beat of her heart. Her nipples pebbled beneath her shift. Hidden triggers, points of information for her and her alone.

She was on the verge of ordering him to leave because he *needed* to leave when the spark of anguish lighting his gaze reached her. Something aside from his stellar decision to knock a marquess on his arse in her defense had brought him here.

She tilted her head, searching. What could that be?

With a whispered curse, he took possession of her arm and the broadsheet, propelling her into her warehouse and through the open double doors. Then he let her go, folded the sheet into a neat tuck, hiding it away in his coat pocket. As if this solved the matter entirely, when it solved nothing.

Speechless, Helena turned and made her way across the vast main floor, winding around stacks of crates and open boxes, stepping over a bundle of rope and a hammer, uncaring if he followed but knowing he would. The scents here were familiar, welcoming when the rest of London wasn't, calming her rioting senses. Spices, raw timber, dust, sweat. The aroma of labor and commerce. Success. A distinctive life. Courageous choices. Empowerment.

Loneliness. Isolation. Dread.

The warehouse was thankfully deserted on Sunday mornings, which was beneficial. It was enough to put one foot in front of the other and hope to make it to her destination after her mind had sent Helena the clear directive to pop up on her toes and press her lips to the Duke of Leighton's. A sailor's daughter kissing a duke on a London street would have been a fitting ending to a day that had started with her being featured in the scandal sheets through no fault of her own. The duke in question proving a point when there was no point.

If the dwelling smelled good, her office smelled even better. A tray of lemon scones sat on the corner of her desk, blessedly filling the room with the bracing scent of citrus. Her factotum, Hansard, had accepted the delivery from the bakery as he usually arrived earlier than she did. Though she wished it were not the case, she didn't enjoy getting up at the crack of dawn even if her business demanded it.

The Duke of Leighton's step was a resounding tread behind her. His footfalls echoed off the plank floorboards, then were silenced by Savonnerie as he entered her private domain. She circled behind her desk without taking her eyes off him. Keeping him in check should he decide to make a sudden move she was unprepared for.

Instead of taking a seat in one of the leather armchairs sitting before her desk, he stalked the space. Halting at her bookshelf, tilting his head to read the spines, poking inside an open crate he passed, looking at each piece of artwork gracing the walls as if he was set on offering to purchase one.

Taking measure. Of her. A restless tiger on the prowl.

And because of that blasted flare of grief in his eyes, she let him roam. Like the rest of the world, anything to please a duke.

Frustrated with herself as much as him, she sank into the chair behind her desk and tugged off her gloves as slowly as possible while wondering who would break and speak first.

Apparently willing to lose this battle when he routinely won many, Leighton halted by the door and leaned out, glancing down the hallway. "I don't suppose your companion is around to act as a chaperone? Prudence, is it?" He glanced over his shoulder, his brow winging high over his bruised eye.

He looked restless and reckless. Perturbed and amused.

His gaze dusted her bare hands before lifting to her face. "Or that brute with the missing teeth acting as your coachman? Can we have him come in and sit on the crate of vases in the corner, maybe? Merely to keep this above board."

Helena's temper sparked. Niles had wretched teeth, true, but he'd been with her family for years and was one of her most trusted employees. Almost family. When she had little family to spare.

"You've some nerve requesting anything of me after you've caused my name to be splattered across the gossip rags. I'm not sure what you think might happen in this office, aside from my asking why in heaven's name you'd knock a marquess to the ground in defense of me when *many* things are whispered about me daily. Why waste your time or the skin on your knuckles?"

After shrugging out of his overcoat and folding it neatly over the armchair she wished he'd deposit himself into, Roan took another turn about the room, this time stopping at the sideboard to pour a drink. At eleven in the morning, no less. Dissipated duke, like the scandal-mongers said. She might appreciate his *looks*, but his nature would be nothing she'd ever admire or respect.

Roan wedged his hip against the sideboard and sipped slowly. She had a nagging sense that he didn't want to get as close to her as he'd been on the sidewalk. That he wished for an argument for reasons other than the ones he was going to settle before her like a cup of tea.

"A banal disagreement in parliamentary chambers. Besides, the gossip sheets only said shipping heiress. Hell, they only said the Duke of L. Could be any one of us scattered about Town." He swallowed, and she watched helplessly as his long throat pulled beneath the folds of his cravat. "Thankfully, you weren't included in the sketch. Happens all the time to me. One gets used to it. For some odd reason, I've started saving them. A fat file of souvenirs for me to review in my old age."

"I've seen them. Entertaining, I suppose, for the bored masses. However, this banal snippet would only have been written about two people, which you well know. One of them being *me*. Find another shipping heiress running amok in London, and I'll eat my bonnet." Helena frowned because this didn't sound right the way it had come out, her treasonous stomach choosing that moment to growl loudly enough for him to hear.

His lips folded in to hold back the smile. He gestured to the plate of scones. "No need to eat your bonnet when you have those. They smell divine, by the way." He laughed then, his face lighting with his amusement. "Go on. Don't stop yourself because I said you should. Only a genuinely obstinate chit would react thusly."

Helena reached for a scone. Because she *was* famished. Not in any way because he'd told her she should. "Care to tell me why you've shown up on my warehouse doorstep this morning?" she asked, chewing deliberately, careful of the crumbs that tended to end up stuck to her lips. No licking of lips allowed with Leighton in the room. If his eyes heated even a fraction, she would herself combust. "Because I feel like it's not the public embarrassment you've subjected me to. And I can't imagine Wapping is your favorite place to spend the morning."

She took a moment to swallow, breathe, prepare to enjoy this next bit. "Public embarrassment you've subjected me to once again, that is."

He slapped his glass on the sideboard and crossed to her, his shoulders going high and back, a fighting stance. He braced his arms on the back of the armchair and leaned in. Still not as close as before. But getting closer. "Now, we finally get to it. After ten bloody years. You're a patient woman, Miss Helena Astley, I'll hand you that."

Helena flicked crumbs from her fingers while questioning what she'd left on her lips. "We have nothing to *get* to. You said something remarkably foolish, apologized, and I accepted your apology. Encounter put to bed. I'm merely pointing out that this is the *second* incident, not the first. Saints above, I wasn't asking to rehash Lyme Regis."

Roan laughed roughly and circled the chair, collapsing into it, long legs sprawled wide. He snatched his hat from his head and dropped it to her desk, right beside the scones. A teasing fragrance drifted from the fine felt, mixing wonderfully with the tang of lemon. His hair shot in unkempt tufts, and she had to quiet the impulse to straighten the overlong strands into submission. Because he didn't seem to care to.

"I apologized multiple times if we're conscripting the narrative surrounding my adolescent foolishness. Unfortunately, I never got the notification that you'd accepted any of them. In fact, your gaze slicing me into pieces whenever we happened to stumble upon each other over the years gave me the impression you had not." Grabbing a scone off the tray, he took an enthusiastic bite and settled back in the chair. "Hell's teeth, these are good," he said around a mouthful.

"That's a perfect example of my issue with you. With our association, which is no association at all."

He stilled, the scone lifted halfway to his mouth. He swallowed carefully, and she knew, *knew* from his intense expression, that he was keenly interested in what she had to say. His attentiveness sent an undeniable bolt of pleasure down her spine. *This* was the trap with the Duke of Leighton. She could see it now. Men rarely paid close attention to her unless shipping routes were being discussed. Merchandise being traded, bills being paid. That a man would care what she *thought* or *felt* was devastating.

And addictive.

Lowering her gaze to the partially eaten scone in her hand, she cursed herself for starting this conversation. But 'in for a penny, in for a pound' or so they said. She was not a woman who ran when faced with a troublesome discussion. "Your language around me..." She shrugged and took a petite bite of the scone, feeling foolish at exposing what might sound like a vulnerability. When she revealed herself to no one.

"You wouldn't speak to one of"—she glanced up to find his gaze focused on her lips and confusion swam inside her head—"the society dolls clamoring around you at Almack's like that. You've even used my nickname, one you heard from a woman who's been with me since I was in leading strings. But with me, it's fine. All of it. Because we're not on the same level, in society or life. We both know this."

His mouth opened, closed, opened again. He looked genuinely astonished, as if she'd pointed out a door to a room he'd not known was there. His lips curved after a moment, bringing her eye to the scar cutting into the top one. That tantalizing imperfection. The faintest hint of a flush drifted into his cheeks, and her heart sank. He was vulnerable. And hiding it all the time, just like she was. What a time to find out the man was human.

"You're right. I wouldn't. Not with anyone but my friends. The swearing and the nicknames. People I feel comfortable around, for whatever inane, chemical reason that is. The Duke of Markham, Tobias Streeter—"

"The Leighton Cluster."

His laugh sputtered forth, unexpected delight. "Excuse me?"

She smiled then. It spilled out like sunlight puncturing a cloud. She felt her cheeks lift and saw the way his chest rose and fell as her pleasure hit him. Watched the pulse kick just beneath his ear. "Markham. Streeter. Xander Macauley. The two women who run the Duchess Society. The Mad Matchmaker and... what do they call the other one?"

"The Ice Duchess," he murmured. "*Before* Georgie was Duchess of Markham, which is coincidental naming."

Helena snapped her fingers. "That's it. Anyway, you're a pack. Always together, a cluster. Impenetrable." She hoped her tone didn't voice her envy. She'd never had a pack of anything in her life.

A tiny crease worked its way between his brows as he contemplated a truth he hadn't clued her in to. "I have a cluster because I can't abide anyone else. I'm not myself around anyone else. I've sold enough of my soul for this title, given away parts of myself gradually, over time, until I wonder what's left. I've earned the right to befriend those I actually *like*. And wriggle my way through society as best I can with the rest."

He popped the remaining scone in his mouth, his tongue flicking out to lick his lips. A sensual bit of nonsense, doing to her what she'd promised *not* to do to him. The action erased any opposition she felt about sitting in her office alone with the Duke of Leighton. She wasn't going anywhere.

"You must have someone you feel this way about."

She paused, recalling the reticent figure standing high atop a sea cliff, the wind yanking at his clothing and his hair, a blazing sun setting behind his shadowed form. A slender young man compared to the strapping aristocrat sitting before her, but he was indeed the same person. Any other titled gentleman would have strutted down that gravel path like a peacock and talked to her, yet the Defiant Duke had not.

Could he be *shy*? Was that possible? She pulled herself from the fantasy of creating a better man than the one sitting before her, remembering that he'd asked a question. "I have business associates. Employees. Partners in trade. Merchant associates. Skilled craftsman. I'm refitting a brig that's docked—"

"*Friends*, Miss Astley."

Lowering her gaze, she stared intently at the plate of scones, noting that the duke had selected the largest, then consumed it in three huge bites. *Friends?* She was primarily shunned in society. Who did the Duke of Leighton think would befriend her? She was too low for the blue bloods and too high for everyone else. Sometimes when a person needed a loan, they were rather friendly, but she didn't think that counted. "No, nothing like your cluster."

"What happened? The shards of broken glass we crossed over in the main room?"

Helena drummed her fingers on the desk, an itch starting at the base of her spine. He didn't miss much. "A minor concern. A burglary last night. They broke a window in the alley, but my guards scared them away before they could filch me blind. Likely desperate children. Or hoodlums. The risk of working in the stews, isn't it?"

His gaze hardened like the jade vases she'd imported last week, an item no one in London needed another of. She knew that look. *Men.* They wanted to control everything. "I don't need help protecting my business if that's what you're thinking. The sentries I employ come from the roughest areas of this city. They'd make anyone on your crew look like marionettes. They strike first, ask questions later. Their loyalty, because I pay them exceedingly well, is unassailable."

"My dear Miss Astley, of this, I have no doubt. Although they weren't watching closely enough to keep glass from breaking." He reached for another scone, then fell back in the chair. An elegant slump befitting a man of his station. "Let's get down to business. Our business. Did you keep the fossil?"

Slyly, she let confusion mar her features when she wasn't confused.

"The one I gave you at the musicale. Before I uttered my ridiculous comments."

Her pulse quickened, tapping out a frantic rhythm through her veins. Why, with the thousands of questions he could have asked, did he ask *this*? Beneath the desk, her leg shifted to brush the drawer that held her treasures. Things she didn't want her meddlesome maid, Olivia, to find in her bedchamber wardrobe or her escritoire. Her father's handkerchief, her mother's brooch. A fossil a young man had given her in what felt like a whispered promise. Then, he'd turned around and ruined everything.

She shrugged, flicking a stray crumb from her fingertip. "I don't recall."

He took a bite, chewed, thoughtful. A gleam entered his gaze that she didn't trust. Light from the lamp on her desk that Hansard lit each morning when he delivered the scones turned Leighton's eyes the dewy green of spring leaves. "I have a sister. Did you know that? Philippa. Pippa for short."

Should she tell him she had a sister as well? Half-sister. Newly arrived in her life, a secret family her father had not disclosed to her. But, for some reason, she chose not to. Theodosia was the first person Helena had fallen in love with on sight, and she wanted to guard that feeling a little longer.

"Pippa's first season was this year. But a minor incident made it into those broadsheets you so love, halted her presentation in its tracks."

Helena searched her memory. *Ah.* She did recall. "Something about a viscount and a glass of champagne she dumped on his head at a masquerade ball. Or was it a baron?"

Roan bit down hard on the scone. "An earl. And it was ratafia. Pippa's too young for champagne." He curled his fingers in tightly without purpose. A natural reflex, like the ruffians guarding her warehouse, was to use his fists first. Which was *very* unlike any toff she'd ever known.

She wasn't about to underestimate this facet of his personality.

"And in return, you offered the earl what someone this morning"— she gestured to his bruised eye—"offered you."

Roan touched the mottled contusion with a rakish grin. "This was a gift from a friend. Mine was no gift. The man Pippa tangled with got what he deserved from *both* Darlingtons that night. Although I admire her pluck, she created a mess for herself."

Helena slipped her pocket watch from the fob she'd had sewn into her gowns and made a show of checking the time. The duke seated before her needed to leave before she got to know him better. Like him, just a little. Want him more than she already did. His fossil was burning a hole in her desk drawer, a life force of its own. A memory she wished to erase but could not.

Leighton took her gesture in stride, popping the rest of the scone in his mouth, then dusting his gloved hands together. "Let me guess. You have a meeting in fifteen minutes."

She slid her watch into her pocket. "Ten."

He scooted forward in his chair, crossed his arms over the top of her desk, leaning into the fold. "You also have a charge. A new addition to your household."

Her head came up, her spine locking. A maternal desire to *protect* roared through her. These society snips wouldn't involve Theo in their poisonous games. She would die before allowing it. "Word travels fast in this town, doesn't it? My half-sister, Theodosia. I didn't know about her until six months ago. My father had a relationship with her mother at some point. When her mother died, a friend of the family contacted me. She's fifteen and has no one else."

I have no one was left unsaid.

Theo was delightful. Winsome. Beautiful. Intelligent. Gifted with languages and mathematics. She desired an education, which wasn't part of the world's plan for women. She was the sister Helena had secretly longed for. But she was also curious to a fault. Defiant when challenged. A girl with expansive dreams and enough fortitude to imagine she would secure them.

Helena worried over her future and how to protect her. She'd had tutors, could read Latin and Greek, and present a very detailed accounting of expenses—and was fully capable of hiring the best for Theo. However, Helena had failed the test of navigating society. Success without setting fire to each and every bridge she crossed. They called her Lady Hell not because she was a lady but because she was a ruffian in a skirt. The exact *opposite* of a lady. A female terror with blunt and brains.

Theo had *more* brains and a fat dowry to boot. So how was Helena to cast the girl in a mold entirely different from the one she'd happily cast herself in?

Leighton rotated her inkwell in a sluggish circle on her desk, his gaze releasing its hold and giving her a moment to breathe as he checked his own watch. "I'm leaving for Hertfordshire after a business meeting next week. The Leighton Cluster"—his grin intensified, emphasizing his delight at the moniker—"will be there too. The Duke of Markham, his duchess and children, Tobias Streeter, his wife, Hildy, and their infant boy. Pippa, of course. Xander Macauley. A family affair. Doctor's orders, a bit, on my part. Which Lyme Regis was back in the day, though you had no way of knowing it."

Her breath caught. "Doctor's orders?"

His head tilted, the lightest of flushes again sweeping his cheeks. He was pleased about something, her concern, perhaps.

The *rat*.

He drummed his fingers atop his chest and gave a gentle cough. "Dashed spot of asthma, though it's much better than it used to be. Why I was on the coast years ago, a recipe for health. London's foul air for months on end aggravates my lungs, and the peerage aggravate my psyche. I have to take a recess from both now and again. In any case, the estates require periodic visits. Management beyond belief to keep a duchy afloat. Maybe similar to a shipping empire. Hertfordshire is genuinely lovely, my personal favorite among the nooses looped around my neck."

No. He wasn't—he couldn't. "Why are you telling me this, Your Grace?"

He growled faintly, almost a purr, the first flicker of anger all morning. "*Roan.* Or Leighton if you wish to stand farther away. Duke two steps behind that, nearly across the distance of a ballroom. But drop the bloody 'Your Grace' if you please."

She held out her hand in entreaty, hushed in voice but not thought. Asthma. Sister. Hertfordshire. The details were stacking up, a real man stepping from behind the façade. Sensation flooded her, terrifying in its intensity. Emotions she was afraid to examine. She didn't want to *know* him, only gaze in minor obsession from afar. The distance of that ballroom he'd mentioned, should she ever be invited to a ball where he was in attendance.

He gave the inkwell another rotation at her continued silence, a surprising show of nerves. "You take a holiday, yes? Streeter, Macauley and I"—he looked up, met her gaze, dipped those long lashes low over his emerald eyes in subtle retreat—"we're in business, I think you know. I'm a silent partner, for the most part, but a partner."

She nodded, releasing a spent breath. *Of course, I know. You roam Limehouse like a feral tiger. Much like you roamed this space earlier.*

"Part of our fleet is preparing to moor until January. Those ships remain on the sea with extra pay for the days not spent with family during Christmastide. Everything's slowing on the docks, our mercantile exchanges, so I can leave for a fortnight. Streeter and Macauley as well. I feel the need to escape the city. The Leighton Cluster is hoping this sojourn keeps my brawls inside Gentleman Jackson's."

He reached to touch the bruise circling his eye and winced endearingly. "Part of my plan for Pippa, following a rather disastrous first season, are lessons in comportment and the like with Hildy and Georgie. I don't care what they teach her as long as she doesn't dump ratafia on anyone's head *next* season. The Duchess Society prepares women for marriage, true, but they also educate them in how better to traverse the world they'll be forced to. With regard to the complexities involved. I can't change that Pippa is a duke's sister even if I wished I could."

Helena's stomach gave a slight twist. How did he know her this well *without* knowing her at all? "What can this possibly have to do with me?"

His gaze roved over her, sharp as a rapier. Pricking her skin, creating a bubbling sensation in her chest, belly, knees, one still pressed firmly to the drawer holding his fossil. She'd be foolish to underestimate his intelligence. When strangely, he seemed the rare man who didn't underestimate *hers*.

"Your sister could benefit from this tutelage as well, could she not? Chaperoned by an earl's daughter who challenged the *ton* by marrying a hoodlum-cum-architect and a former countess who grudgingly pleased society by marrying a duke. Society skirmishes, you can't win them all. These ladies, especially Tobias Streeter's wife, Hildy, understand where your sister is coming from and going *to*."

The shameless boor yawned and stretched his endlessly long legs out as if he'd proposed a superb plan, sinking into her armchair like it had been crafted for his broad body. "And then there's me, duke number two, definitely the lesser, rounding out what can only be a bounce in standing for Theodosia should she associate with us, the Leighton Cluster."

Helena blinked four times until she recaptured her negotiating tone. "Why would I do this? You and I don't even *like* each other."

"Is that right?" He gave her desk another arrogant pop with his boot, cocking his head as he considered the question. He was a cool-headed bounder, *oh*, he was. She bet he won at the hazard tables every blasted time he rolled the dice. "You'd do it for the same reason I would, Miss Astley. For your sister's future. Keeping company with two dukes and a duchess is a boon in this town. A melancholy fact, mayhap, but a factual one. What if, just what *if*, she comes out of the experience better prepared? I'm hoping like hell that's the case for Pippa."

Helena untied the satin ribbon beneath her chin and slid her bonnet free. They'd gone past any hint of propriety the moment he'd walked in her warehouse door. Bare head, bare hands, what did it matter now? "The scandal rags will rip us apart. Rip me apart. They'd love to, you know."

"We'll break no rules, not a one. In fact, I'll plant the romantic tale that I'm courting you in every broadsheet by tomorrow morning. It will sprout like a healthily watered seed. You and Theodosia will have my protection, the Duke and Duchess of Markham's protection, for as long as you need it. After the debacle I caused in Parliament and the comment the marquess made about you—because he did make a comment I objected to—the *ton* will bite. They already believe there's a connection between us, which confounds you to no end, I recognize."

"Wait, I can't, that is," she argued breathlessly when she realized he was getting the better of the conversation. Her bonnet slipped from her fingers to the floor. She had work to do. Shipments were arriving three times a week, depending upon weather and navigation. And the series of burglaries that Hansard was investigating needed attention, didn't they? She couldn't simply leave town like she had no cares in the world.

Unfolding his broad body, he reached for another scone and took an enthusiastic bite. "I've created an awkward situation for you where none existed before. For me, vexing situations are customary. I suppose creating them is one way I keep myself awake. However, you're not saddled with this damned title. That's my unfortunate luck. This holiday will simply be a continuation of the rumor that I fancy you."

"Fancy me? You don't fancy anyone." She picked up her bonnet, placing it on the desk between them, an ineffectual chaperone. "You don't even keep a mistress of late. The Defiant Duke is known as a one-night wonder. Although the ladies wish for more."

His lips twisted as he chewed, but he didn't disagree. Couldn't disagree. He'd likely never discussed his 'one-night' wonderfulness with a woman he wasn't intending to show the wonderfulness to.

Helena watched his eyes change color in the lamplight. It was a fascinating show. "If I accept this mad proposal of yours, how would we end our association?"

"You return after the new year and say to the world, *I rejected a duke.* I will concur." He popped the last of the scone in his mouth, his grin positively savage. "Blimey, it may even help business. Yours, I mean."

"Your Grace—"

His brow winged high, displeased.

She twisted the bonnet's ribbon around her finger. "Leighton, why would you make this offer? The truth, please. I have no time for society games. I never have."

The duke paused long enough that she knew he was going to tell the truth. Finally, he murmured, "Because *this* is the apology, after years of giving them, that I want you to accept."

Helena sat back with a sigh, the ribbon slipping through her fingers. He negotiated from the heart, a hard place to deny. It wasn't like she and Theo had nowhere to go. Hansard always invited her to his cottage in Shoreditch for Christmas dinner. Although she'd despaired over having little family to offer Theo, and Hansard and his wife had no children. No laughter in their small but lovely cottage. If she were being honest, as she'd asked Leighton to be, she would admit that she and Theo were lonely, stumbling around in the Mayfair manse Helena still thought of as her father's. She felt more at home in this warehouse than anywhere else. She'd grown up sitting on the edge of this desk, watching her father work his shipping magic. Those few days he'd acted like an actual father.

Inside this room is where she'd decided to challenge a group that thought women should be, well, nothing.

"Yes," she whispered before she had time to refuse his farfetched, temptingly seductive offer of a fake courtship and a holiday spent in the country. "If you believe you can convince the *ton* and help my sister, I'm willing to let you. Truthfully, you owe me after dragging my name through the muck on two occasions."

"Even if I didn't mean to drag it anywhere."

She snorted an unladylike murmur. But better he knew what he was getting, even if for only two weeks. Nothing could damage her reputation any more than it had been damaged—and this *would* make a world of difference for Theo. Helena hated it, but Leighton was right. Society acceptance and friendships were invitations to a better life. The only way for advancement when what Theo really wanted, an education, may not be possible.

But Helena had a little secret.

Aside from helping her sister, she'd agreed to this charade because she wanted to know why grief had colored a duke's eyes so sorrowfully on a beautiful winter day.

Chapter Four

Where a Duke Realizes He's More Than Mildly Infatuated

"Let me get this straight, Leighton. You used the Duchess Society to lure Lady Hell and her half-sister to Hertfordshire for Christmastide? Lessons in social etiquette with a bogus courtship thrown in for kicks?" Tobias Streeter sawed through the cedar limb he held wedged in place beneath his boot, then rocked back on his heels with a grunt when it finally gave under pressure and snapped in two. He shoved his hair from his eyes with a careless swipe, his smile as sharp as his saw's blade. "Have you informed my wife about her new student? Hildy was only counting on one rebellious young woman. I believe your contributions to the Duchess Society's scholarship fund just tripled."

Roan looked up from his spot hunkered down before a pile of branches, his mind half on Helena's impending arrival, half on decorating an archaic, rambling ducal estate for Christmas. Something he had never in his *life* contemplated doing. He hoped these were the right evergreens for beautifying railings and hearths and such. Mrs. Meekins, the housekeeper who'd been with Leighton House since the dawn of time, had ordered the restless group of men from the house with instructions to collect greens, holly, ivy, and mistletoe.

"It sounds worse when you say it than when I proposed it," Roan murmured. "Since I dreamed up the grand plan, I thought to leave the telling-to-the-ladies part to you. Hildy's so smitten, she won't say no if you ask anything of her."

Tobias flashed an equally smitten smile, adoration for his wife softening his chiseled features. "She is, isn't she?"

Macauley stretched, reaching high into the branches of the towering oak he negligently leaned against, yanking down a copse of leaves he'd been told was mistletoe. As the tallest among them, he had been informed he was the man to secure it. "I'm bloody sick of every soul around me falling arse over kettle in love. Deuced freezing out here too, and no hope of a plump, willing chit waiting for me in my bedchamber. London's never been this bloody cold, even the time I crawled from the cut in the middle of winter. Thanks to you, Your Grace. The lesser Grace of the two in attendance."

Roan grunted, refusing to be baited into the scuffle his friend wanted.

Macauley stuffed the greenery in the leather pouch hanging from his shoulder and sent a scathing glare in Roan's direction. "How do you even know this is mistletoe? Hope it's not poisonous. Had that happen once after a spur-of-the-moment adventure with an enthusiastic widow behind her gardening shed. Don't dip the wick in anything out of doors is my advice. Or you may end up with blisters in maddening places." He exhaled a frosted, crystalline breath that circled merrily around his face. "And I do mean maddening."

"Why do we always end up talking about wicks?" the Duke of Markham asked as he strolled into the middle of the gathering. Dex had gone off on a jaunt into the woodlands surrounding the estate and found what looked to be a fine assortment of ivy. He was resourceful in almost any situation. The calmest head in the bunch. Roan quite admired this talent.

Tobias rolled his shoulders and pushed to his feet, cracking his back with a pop. "Because we're fascinated with them. Especially our own."

"Who said anything about falling in love? I'm not in love. And when do wicks equate to love? Rarely, if ever." Roan wrapped a length of twine around the branches he'd assembled and tied the ends in a neat bow. "I'm righting a wrong. In the only way I know how. A way that matters. At least to her." He nodded to the satchel hanging halfway off Macauley's shoulder. "Everyone knows the cluster of white berries marks it as mistletoe. See the forked branches, the symmetrical leaves? It's partially parasitic, attaching to a host, the oak you're leaning against. Fairly basic as plants go. The wallflower of the plant world, I'd say. It finds a wall and binds."

"At least our wallflower mistletoe has a lover it clings to, unlike the duke whose estate it resides upon." Macauley shoved off the oak and strolled over to Roan, bumping the toe of his Wellington against the duke's assembled greenery. "How did you get sacked from Cambridge again? You're almost an academic. It's revolting. Bad enough you're an aristocrat without being blooming brilliant too. Two things I hate. Brains and blue blood."

Roan grimaced, embarrassed and cross. "The earl I tossed in the river, remember?"

"Ah, mate, I recall your debacle now." Macauley grinned, his eyes sparkling. "Every time I get bored with your scientific fossil such-and-such talk, you do something stupid that makes me remember why I like you. The recent skirmish in Parliament was inspired. If not for your temper, you'd be a waste of a life."

"Ask him how many languages he speaks. Top of the class at Cambridge in German," Markham murmured, adjusting the holly he looped around his forearm and throwing swift glances back at the house. He'd left Georgie and his two young children napping, and Roan could see he wanted to be there when they awoke.

Roan groaned, rising to his feet, tucking his collected greenery under his arm. "Three, including the Queen's English. Not so many."

"Did you have to mention fossils, Macauley?" Tobias slipped a toothpick between his teeth, trying to contain his glee. He'd been chewing on the bamboo sticks for two years in his mostly successful effort to quit smoking cheroots. "Next, he'll start telling you where he wants to go, that modest inventory of locales he keeps in his head. Premier stops in England for relics, I think it's called."

Roan shifted his bundle and frowned, wondering why everyone thought fossils were a tedious topic of conversation. The daughter of an impoverished baron walk away from him last week at Almack's while discussing his hope of finding a Dapedium specimen. Which definitely meant she was not the chit for him. "The Charmouth Mudstone geological formations are said to be the—"

"Enough!" Macauley cursed beneath his breath and started marching toward the imposing Jacobean dwelling, sitting atop a verdant Hertfordshire knoll that was known quite unoriginally as Leighton House. "There's a whiskey bottle with my name on it in that castle of yours, Leighton. Because I make the whiskey, I mean, it's *really* got my name on it. Nearly nightfall, so I'm going in search of simple pleasures. I've had it with talk of relics, love, and wicks. Give me a moment, and I may sneak away to my bedchamber and polish my own."

The men laughed at Macauley's joke that was likely not a joke, gathered their decorations, and fell in line behind him.

Tobias exhaled a misty puff and gestured into the distance. "Do you think Mrs. Meekins sent us on this excursion to get us out of the house? Surely, she has all the trimmings she needs. The house is done up grandly already."

"Yes," the other three men replied at the same time.

The foursome paused on the edge of the lawn, the forest surrounding the estate at their backs, the regal country home glittering like a crown atop one's head. The sun was setting, throwing an indigo and gold wash across the medieval brickwork of the Palace, the oldest wing of the house. In fact, this section was one of the foremost examples of surviving feudal architecture in England. Roan had students and professors stopping round all the time to have a look at it. He'd considered organizing tours to help pay expenses, but this was not regarded as proper form. Although his business mind thought it a rather brilliant idea.

He took a breath, the enormity of his responsibilities erasing the splendor of the place. He loved Leighton House as much as he feared it. Hundreds of domestics and tenants under his employ, a thriving but underprivileged village attached to the duchy five miles down the way. The main house constructed in the 1600s, the medieval portion in the 1400s. According to legend, Elizabeth had sat under an oak tree a hundred yards to his left when she learned of her succession to the throne in 1558. His legacy, his children's legacy, those of his ancestors, stacked like bricks upon his shoulders until he felt lightheaded from the weight of carrying them. Something he'd never told anyone, not even Pippa, was that he wanted children. More than simply the heir he was expected to produce. He could almost see them racing along beside him down the cedar-lined main drive when he traveled it.

This was a home that needed a family.

He was a man who needed a family. Pippa needed a family. Throughout time, they'd only had each other.

His problem was that he'd never quite figured out how to secure this want.

His step slowed until he came to a dead halt at the perimeter of the kitchen garden. Markham wasn't looking where he was going and ran into him, sending him stumbling into a rosemary thicket. The scent rose in overpowering upsurges, stinging his nose. This estate smelled like home and wholesomeness, unlike anything he'd ever experienced in the city. A row of barren fruit trees edged the brick wall surrounding the space, awaiting sunlight, warm weather, and spring showers. Herb and vegetable gardens that would feed not only his staff but some of his tenants. He gazed at the dwelling again, seeing it as Helena would when she arrived, his stomach sinking to his toes.

It wasn't a mere house. It couldn't even properly be labeled a mansion.

It was a castle, as Macauley had so unabashedly stated. What his manservant, Hubert, who'd been with him since well before the dukedom and was as honest as they came, dubbed a proud, pretentious heap. An immense country home built to showcase wealth no longer solidly around to sustain it. A rambling stone and walnut bastion Roan frankly adored. Even as he despaired over the staggering blunt needed to maintain it. It was majestic and dignified, nothing like he was, only what he pretended to be. Certainly set to make Helena Astley, wealthier than he by far, feel leagues beneath him, miles away in caste and circumstance.

But his effort to get Helena here was only an apology, wasn't it? A chance for her sister to obtain Town polish, take it back to London, and let herself shine. He was doing the Astley sisters a favor. And at the same time assuaging his guilt. Rectifying a nonsensical situation he'd created *twice* for a woman who seemed to have little interest in furthering their association.

Not that he'd ever officially asked to further it. He'd only flirted with her in the way a thirteen-year-old boy would, throwing out casual insults while yanking on the sleeve of her gown to gain her attention.

Although the situation with Helena felt like more.

It always had.

His brain buzzed the same way when thinking about her as it did when solving an algebraic equation. Their relationship was a question of chemistry and chance. Fate and inevitability. As phenomenally puzzling as the remnants of a long-dead turtle's skeleton embedded in metamorphic rock.

Tobias gave him a jarring knock to the ribs as he passed. "What are you standing here whispering to yourself about?"

Macauley glanced over his shoulder, derision twisting his features. He made no gentleman's move to conceal it. Sunlight shimmered brilliantly across the flat line of his frown. "He's chattering away like a girl because he's nervous. First woman he's invited to the medieval fortress if I'm golden on my wager. And when he does, it's the most confounding chit in London, innit? Don't make it easy on yourself by choosing one of the thousand simple ones who'd like you to invite them here, mate. Go with a demon in skirts."

"Leave him alone," Markham said in a rare tone of anger. "There's a biological wonder between certain people. You can't fight it. You'll drive yourself mad if you do. As if we all haven't suffered under its effects. I have been drunk with it. *Am* drunk on Georgie every time I look at her."

"I haven't," Macauley returned like a shot and continued his trek, winding through the overgrown shrubs, around the dry fountain, and down the stone path leading to the scullery entrance.

Confounding. The word rolled around Roan's mind like a marble set loose upon smooth stone. Helena *was* a bundle of paradoxes wrapped in gossamer that he found intriguing. Kind, at times ruthless, hot-tempered. Intelligent. Patient. At the horse race, just before he'd moved away from the table to let that boor Reginald Norcross occupy his still-warm seat, her gaze had met his. Her irises had colored the deep purple of the verbena that grew wild in the forest behind him. A tiny, almost unseen pulse tapped out a rhythm on the gentle curve between her neck and her shoulder. Her hair lit from the sun, not quite red, not quite *not*. Her lips were pink and plump, parting slightly as if she were set to call him back.

He'd never wanted another woman with such intensity, never felt so taken down a peg without being taken down a peg at all. The images that had flashed through his mind had been obscene and erotic. He wasn't proud of the many ways it had occurred to him to take her at that moment. His cock had been discreetly rigid the entire ride home from Epsom.

Had he done an appallingly foolish thing inviting Helena to the country for Christmas?

His head starting to ache, Roan decided to take the long way around the manor and turned the corner blindly.

And there she was. In the distance, a hundred yards away, standing on his pebbled drive alongside her dour companion, unaware he'd entered her universe. He watched her remove a small portmanteau from his coach and four—the least ostentatious equipage he owned, and it was beautiful—as elegantly as a debutante. Except no lady of the *ton* would have thought to carry her own luggage. He'd felt it his duty to send a conveyance for their journey, although Astley Shipping surely owned a rig just as sumptuous. She likely hadn't appreciated the offer, but he'd done it just the same. She halted to gaze at Leighton House, her step hesitant where moments before it had been daring. He recalled the first time he'd seen the dwelling as a twenty-year-old who'd just inherited a titled bundle beyond his wildest imaginings. The breathtaking shock was a remembrance he could summon. And often did when he needed a reminder of his responsibilities.

Or when he drove down the long drive after a few weeks away and thought gloriously upon seeing the house, this is *mine*.

Similar to what he felt now looking at her, emotions stinging his skin like sleet during a winter squall. Wonder, panic, certitude.

Dying rays of sunlight rolled over her like mist, turning her hair a dozen shades of auburn and ginger, as magnificent an assortment as he remembered. Her pale indigo gown, modest but lovely, as was her style, fluttering around her legs as she raised her hand to her eyes to get a better look.

Mrs. Meekins and his majordomo, Ridgley, poured down the stone staircase, circling her. And the half-sister Theodosia hopped from the coach with a girl's carefree wonder. Her animated voice rose above the wind that whispered past Roan's ear as she flitted around Helena and her companion like a butterfly while her older sister looked on with amusement and chagrin. He would have loved to tell her that no sound pleased him more than the laughter of children. Let the girl enjoy her adventure.

But Helena didn't glance his way—and he hadn't the heart to alert her to his presence. Watch formality enter her bearing or her mind. The sensation that swept him as he stood there staring was fiercer than lust, stronger than doubt and uncertainty.

It wasn't a foolish thing he'd done, inviting her. As Mrs. Meekins ushered the Astley sisters inside Leighton House and closed the massive oak door behind them, his conviction was absolute. Even if he wasn't completely clear regarding his motives. He'd never dallied with a woman outside his set—or an innocent, which he suspected Helena was. In experience if not knowledge. The docks she roamed didn't offer much in the way of protection from witnessing the baser side of life. The situation here wasn't much better—rife with risk as she had no one to protect her. No father, brother, uncle.

Roan would have to step in as her protector, then. From himself, which was ironic.

"She's fetching. But smashing good looks don't compensate equally for trouble."

Roan flinched, yanked abruptly from his musings to find Macauley had followed him, taking the long way around for no reason aside from a nagging paternal inclination. Xander Macauley kept watch over them, two dukes and Tobias Streeter, rogue king of the docks, like an older brother would. Roan loathed the attention even as it warmed his slightly glacial heart. He'd never had anyone care about him aside from his sister. And no one had ever done anything *close* to protecting him.

Macauley pointed at Roan's sister, Pippa, with the glowing tip of a cheroot he'd lit somewhere between the garden and this spot. She was waltzing up the drive, her maroon and black spencer trailing out behind her bracing stride like a wisp of smoke. "Trouble there, too, innit? Loads. Blondes always are. I sense these things miles away. Bothersome chits, that is. Even prettier than the one you have your eye on, which is unfortunate for you. Both women, I mean, are going to give you mental fits. That's my diagnosis."

Roan turned with a snarl. "Keep your eyes in your head, Macauley. Pippa is off-limits."

Macauley stepped back, arm raised, lips curling around his cheroot and sending it dipping low. "I'm merely stating the obvious, mate. You're loopy if you think I'd *ever* get tangled up with a duke's sister." He shuddered and blew a foggy breath into the air. "Did you forget my pledge to never marry? I have my reasons for staying clear of your aristocratic horde. Trust me, I do. Right bloody good ones."

When Roan tried to walk away, Macauley stopped him, his grasp commanding through layers of thick wool and cotton. "You're about the most intelligent bloke I know aside from Streeter. And the most impulsive. Let your shipping hellion be for a bit. I know what it's like to be thrust into a world foreign from the one you've always inhabited. Give her a moment to ground herself."

Roan stepped back, relieving himself of his friend's hold but retaining his advice. "There's more to you than anyone in England knows, isn't there?"

Macauley flicked his cheroot at his feet and ground it out with a glossy Wellington. "Stories for another time, mate. What fun would it be if we knew everything about each other? I'm a mystery wrapped inside a conundrum, according to the dowager countess I left in my bed yesterday eve."

Roan nodded. *Indeed.*

Well, he also had his secrets.

One being that his heart was telling him he hadn't asked Helena Astley to Leighton House to offer a mere apology.

Chapter Five

Where an Heiress Feels Intimidated

"The south gallery runs the entire length of this wing," stated the housekeeper who'd introduced herself as Mrs. Meekins. She paraded Helena and her sister through Leighton House a little more than a month after the duke made the startling offer to spend the holiday at his country estate. The hallway they currently traversed was the most majestic Helena had seen outside the British Museum. "The ceiling was originally white," she continued, "but covered with gold leaf by the second duke after he noted a similar one in Venice. The walls are wainscoted in cherry, not oak, the typical wood used."

Mrs. Meekins flicked her hand toward a cabinet sitting against the lushly paneled wall they passed with nary a glance, her chin rising to a daunting angle as if to say, *What I'm about to impart is significant.* "The hat, gloves, and stockings in that case are believed to have belonged to Queen Elizabeth, who visited the home often before and during her reign. She was known to have extremely slender fingers."

Helena smothered a laugh and looked back to see Theo covering her mouth and doing the same. It brought a joyful pang to her heart to see Theo's vivid sapphire eyes light with glee. Since her mother's death, Helena's half-sister had not laughed nearly enough. Or smiled. To a girl of fifteen, a trip to the country *was* an adventure, and it was the first time Helena had seen her excited about anything. If she'd thought to back out of her agreement to spend Christmas with the Duke of Leighton and his cluster, Theo's enthusiasm would have changed Helena's mind in an instant.

In the end, Theo giggled, unable to help herself. "What is the current one's number?"

Mrs. Meekins' lips collapsed into a dull grimace. "His Grace is the *seventh* Duke of Leighton."

"How grand," Helena whispered as she gingerly stepped in and out of strips of dying sunlight thrown across their path from the floor-to-ceiling windows running the length of the gallery. They passed a row of dour ancestral portraits, the aroma of dust heavy in the air, each subject she studied grimmer than the last. The aristocracy thought so highly of themselves for making it another century, without pocketing a pound they'd actually *earned*. Most of them were dangling by a silken thread from insolvency. Conceivably that was the reason for their glowers. This group knew that, at some point, their portraits would end up being auctioned to the highest bidder.

Mrs. Meekins folded her hands across her midriff and stiffened her spine until it nearly snapped. "The Duke of Leighton has an impressive collection of titles. Marquess of Rothesay and Earl of Holton, though they're rarely mentioned. I don't know why he doesn't refer to them more often. If one title helps push things along, think of what three will do."

Wearying of the conversation, Helena fell in beside the housekeeper, who was half a head shorter but making impressive time down the concourse. She walked like Helena imagined a general would if he had troops on the front line awaiting his arrival.

"Excuse me, but is there a space where I might work while I'm here? A study of some sort. A sitting room would be more than adequate. I simply need a desk, somewhere to spread my ledgers." From the looks of this palace of Leighton's, there had to be a vacant chamber she could use to review her correspondence. She'd agreed to this journey, but her responsibilities had traveled with her in her scuffed portmanteau. Leighton had taken the next fortnight hostage, but part of her time was all she was willing to give him.

Already, they'd passed a formal dining room, breakfast room, set of drawing rooms—each assigned a color to distinguish them—a parlor with French windows overlooking an herb garden, and a charming space Mrs. Meekins had simply referred to as the "morning room." How this differed from the parlors, Helena had no clue. The scents emanating from each differed as well. Cinnamon and lemon, ink and hearth fires, tea and biscuits.

Mrs. Meekins halted in place so quickly that Helena danced two steps beyond her, stopping herself with a graceless stumble over a wrinkle in a runner that looked like an Aubusson. "*Work?*" Her ring of keys jangling from deep within her apron pocket and the tick of a grandfather clock elongated the strained silence into painful seconds.

The slow burn traveled from Helena's head to her belly and churned there, a blaze she'd felt a thousand times. But her smile remained unaffected and as sturdy as the underbelly of one of her ships. "I own a company. You may have heard of it, Astley Shipping."

Mrs. Meekins sniffed and resumed her trek down the corridor. "Everyone knows about your shipping company, miss. The rags are quite fond of detailing your escapades in trade. But owning shouldn't necessarily mean *working*. We have menfolk for that." Her gaze cast back to Helena and down, a sweeping judgment.

Helena rummaged about for an answer that wouldn't set her on a path of destruction during her first quarter-hour in residence. She knew what she'd *like* to say. Arrogant cow. Maddening prig. Pompous windbag. "I would be so very appreciative if you might direct me to a suitable location where I won't intrude upon any planned activities. And an inkwell, I'll need that too. Foolscap, if there is any the duke can spare."

"She works all the time. Loves it more than, well, almost anything. Some posh country holiday isn't going to change that. Redheads are notoriously stubborn, you know," Theo chimed in, dancing between them and doing a lilting spin as they turned the corner and headed up a curving stone staircase. "I find shipping to be very tiresome myself.

But the surprises that arrive on each and every ship are a wondrous thing to behold. Scented soaps, crystal vases, orange candies from France just last week. Ribbon! Hairpins! Perfume!"

Mrs. Meekins showed the first crack in her armor, her lips turning up in a half-smile, and Helena amazingly thought it meant she liked Theo. Just a little. The girl was the more charismatic of the sisters. Sadly, Helena didn't have a bewitching bone in her body. "Miss Theodosia, your lessons with the Duchess Society start tomorrow in the azure salon, ten sharp. Do you remember which room that is?"

Theo hiccuped, which she did when she was nervous, then she laughed riotously to cover it.

Mrs. Meekins tutted softly and stopped before an oaken door the color of oolong tea, her hand finding a doorknob shaped like a lion's head and giving it a hard twist. "This is your room, miss. I'll have a maid, Delilah, sent up to assist during your stay since it appears you didn't arrive with your own. We can have a bath drawn if you'd like. Also, she'll make sure you arrive promptly for every appointment scheduled during your time at Leighton House."

Helena went to squeeze in behind Theo, but Mrs. Meekins halted her with a firm hand. "You're in the bedchamber next door. Delilah will help the young miss, don't you worry."

Helena blinked. Of course. This was a castle with a thousand and one bedchambers and servants too. Theo would be fine until they had to form a search party to find the dining room.

"Patience?" Helena inquired of the companion she'd not seen since they'd arrived. A footman had scurried off with their luggage, their lone domestic trailing along behind him.

Mrs. Meekins nodded down the hall. "In the rose bedchamber next to yours."

Helena fluttered her hand to her chest, unsure of protocol when she merely wanted to yank off the new slippers that were pinching her feet, remove the stays digging into her ribs, and collapse on the nearest bed.

Mrs. Meekins led her to the door next to Theo's, her gaze keen when it traveled back to Helena. This knob was shaped like a leaping tiger, which Helena thought might be significant. "His Grace requested the lilac bedchamber be assigned to you. It has the finest view on the entire estate."

Helena sent Mrs. Meekins away before she could give a pointless tour of the room, trying to ascertain why His Grace had given an unsuitable woman such a choice room. Helena sighed and tipped her head back against the door. It was spacious to the extreme, a bedchamber and sitting area combined into a vast suite. The walls were covered in lavender silk, the bed hangings a plush mix of purple and gold. Her gowns had been shaken out and hung in the mahogany wardrobe, one large enough to house every garment she owned. Her attire was new, possibly not fine enough for Mrs. Meekins, even if Helena had paid one of the best modistes in London double to prepare the items for her trip. Trudging to the bed, she swung her portmanteau high and plopped it on the thick mattress. It sank like a body into the bunched feathers.

She unfastened the brass clasp, tunneling her hand along the pressed velvet lining until she touched it. Then, drawing a breath scented with charred wood from the fire blazing in the hearth, she pulled the drawstring bag free. Turned it upside down and let the fossil spill into her hand. The rock was smoother than it had been ten years ago. The edges buffed from repeated handling.

Repeated silent accusations resounded through her mind for letting it mean anything to her.

The sound of masculine laughter drew Helena to the window like a strong tide was drawn to the moon. She nudged aside the brocade drape and glanced into a dazzling sunset tinting the Hertfordshire sky shades of crimson and pink. Turning the fossil over in her hand, she watched the Duke of Leighton cross the gravel drive to meet a young woman Helena guessed was his sister. He looped his arm around her shoulders and pulled her in close, pressing a kiss to the top of her head.

Helena flattened her gloved hand to the pane, her heart tripping in her chest.

She could admit the truth in the quiet of this room.

She wanted to turn over every stone in the Duke of Leighton's mind, uncover the pieces that lay scattered about for her inspection. Much as she'd done with every fossil on the shore when they'd first met. He'd given her clues during their sporadic association—as if he wanted her to know more. As if he wanted to *know* more. She wished she understood why when she was wholly inappropriate as anything *but* a plaything for a man like him.

Marquess of Rothesay. Earl of Holton. Seventh Duke of Leighton. The titles struck her as solidly as Mrs. Meekins's scathing glare.

Helena turned away in a huff, dropping the drape and shoving the fossil into her spencer's pocket. If Leighton was intrigued by her, it was for the wrong reasons. They did not, could not, ever suit. Instead, he would marry to procure the eighth in his line, to gain assistance with managing this sprawling, incredible estate and the others under his domain. A woman who would understand the intricacies of navigating society was his only alternative. A proper duchess, not a suspect heiress the *ton* called Lady Hell. Helena understood navigating shipping routes, negotiating trade agreements, and which ship was best for a path and product, and that was about it.

In the end, it was a simple conclusion.

She'd presented a challenge to a man who liked to solve them.

So she must, therefore, present no further tests for a duke.

Roan tilted his head, the sound of a creaking chair drifting down the darkened corridor. He kept his offices in the medieval wing, the oldest and least used, because he preferred the ancient granite and metal fittings, the hint of mystery about the place. The halls reeked of history and, admittedly, damp stone and abandonment. This section of the estate, less grand but more fascinating, fit his mood most nights when his obligations kept him awake into the wee hours. He'd been unable to sleep and had decided to slip into his study and review the list of items he was delivering to his tenants the next day. Firewood, foodstuff, clothing, blankets, medicine. This year, he'd also purchased toys. Dolls and miniature carriages, stuffed rabbits and bears. And sweets, mounds of sweets.

For once, his nerves were anticipatory versus anxious.

When he got closer, he could see flickers of candlelight straying into the corridor from an open door like ivy run amok. He frowned, puzzled. This parlor was seldom used. This *wing* was seldom used. Tight and airless, the aroma of mold lingered despite every effort to remove the stench. Halting in the entrance, he was surprised and not to see the object of his fascination curved over a desk that rocked when one placed so much as a quill pen atop it. He'd not yet allocated funds to begin work on this wing.

"Why did Mrs. Meekins situate you in this dismal space?" he asked and stepped inside the parlor.

The pen Helena held went wide across her folio, but she only took a deep breath and seemed to count to five before she looked up. Light from the candelabra mingled with a dash of moonlight that had managed to wiggle through a dirty windowpane and frayed drapes, adding attraction the moment didn't require. He almost smiled but caught it in time. Helena wore another cheerless gown that did as much for her as a gunny sack. She looked lovely, anyway. There was no way to make her look bad. He'd seen her in every manner of dress and element of nature and could attest to this fact.

She tapped the quill against her bottom lip, and his body quivered like a bow. "Why have I been relegated to a closet in the forgotten wing of your castle? Because your housekeeper disapproves of women who *work*. I'm being hidden, Your Grace. Much like the uncle you invite to the gathering who drinks all the brandy in the house then tries to place his hand on a maid's bottom."

He crossed to the hearth, moved aside the screen, and wedged another log on the fire, hoping his heartbeat would settle before he faced her. "That's ridiculous. We'll locate a better spot in the morning. Truthfully, I love this wing, a dirty, dismal little spot, but I don't expect anyone else to."

"I don't know why you suggest Mrs. Meekins's opinion is ridiculous. Yours exactly matched hers ten years ago."

Roan clenched his teeth, grabbed the poker, and gave the blaze a vicious jab. "So, we're back to Lyme Regis."

She sighed, tapping her quill on the desk this time while he pretended to be entranced with the task of enriching an already robust fire. "No, we're not. I've accepted your apology, which absolves you of the slight in every way, Leighton."

He calmed his temper, always a challenge, and turned to her. She'd moved from "Your Grace" to Leighton. This was sure progress. Glancing about the room, he searched for what to say. He hadn't planned on holding any late-night assignations. At least not until his return to Town when he was far away from Helena Astley. And he didn't know how to talk to a woman he was blindly attracted to. It seemed every time he tried, he mucked it up.

So, he stared at her like a foolish boy. The sight of her in his home, even if he'd prepared himself the past month, bathed in moonlight and the golden wash of a candle's glow, stealing his breath. Battling his desire to close in *and* back away, he moved in haltingly. Gestured to the sheet she held. "What's this you're working on?"

She murmured something unintelligible, her gaze going to her correspondence. Her chair squeaked in protest, making him fear the wobbly piece would dump her to the carpet. It was then he noted the spectacles perched on her slim nose. *Oh, hell.* As if he needed more to find enchanting. His body reacted swiftly as he imagined slipping the silver frames from her face and tossing them aside as his lips seized hers.

"A letter from a prospective business partner. It's in German. Hans, one of my dockworkers, usually translates for me. I'd hoped to review it before returning to London, but I forgot to ask for his assistance. It's fine. I have excise forms to sign, receipts to file. A document on increased landing charges to review."

Roan sent a silent prayer of thanks to the gods. *This* he could handle. A white knight swooping in to save the day. He loved doing that. When he'd never been allowed to with Miss Astley before. Crossing the room, he dropped into the threadbare armchair sitting before the desk, held out his hand, and wagged his fingers. "Hand it over."

Helena stilled, the expression crossing her face priceless.

Sitting up, his boots hitting the floor, he snatched the letter from her hand. "It should make me furious how little you think of me when instead, due to my extreme self-confidence, I'm charmed." He tilted the missive into the candlelight and read a few lines. "Your associate is interested in securing the shipment of his products on one of your clippers starting in May of next year. After that, every month, perhaps increasing the shipments to bi-monthly the following year."

Roan glanced up to find her gorgeous lavender eyes enlarged by her lenses, veritable moons breaking through the clouds of the night. "Would you like me to respond? Never fear, I'm an accurate translator of German, French, and Italian." He smoothed the letter on the desk. When the silence hit a lingering note, he looked up. Shrugged, grinned. "What can I say? I'm cracking good with languages. Head of the class at Cambridge until my temper got the better of me. The vice-chancellor didn't appreciate a prank gone a tad wrong even from his best pupil."

Helena reached to wiggle the sheet away from him. Without comment, she folded it twice, then slid it underneath her folio.

He settled back, relaxing in the comfort of her *dis*comfort. "I can't help that I became a duke, Miss Astley. You don't trust me because of it, which I understand, I think, but it wasn't my choice. I have few in society *I* trust. If I weren't aware of the incredible suffering that goes on in this life, I'd say it was my greatest misfortune to have assumed the title. So far, it's yet to do anything wonderful for me. Or for Pippa. We were fine before the ascension. Impoverished but happy enough. Muddling along. I would have figured out investing at some point. And I was a fairly respectable gambler. I had the means to gain the capital."

Helena rolled the pen back and forth on the desk, candlelight sparking off her lenses when she finally looked directly at him. Picking him apart, piece by piece, behind smudged glass. "The gossip rags have mentioned us, this. My trip to Hertfordshire. Your"—she swallowed hard, her moist lips parting, sending his cock to press painfully against his trouser close—"sham courtship. They're shocked, to put it mildly."

"They're envious, the virulent mamas and grasping daughters. Questioning, unsure, just where I like them. Like a pack of wolves, they stay back when they're uncertain. Confidence doesn't become this group." Roan folded his hands over his belly and stretched out his legs, hoping he seemed unaffected while wondering what Helena, shipping heiress and all-around independent miss, would do if he kissed her.

Framed her adorable face in his hands and made them regret his finding her in a vacant parlor on a lonesome winter night.

"I know about the rumors," he said, eventually finding the course of thought to answer. "I had the note sent round to the *Gazette,* telling them about it. Anonymously, of course."

Her gaze assessed, traveling his face, the length of his body while he held still as stone. He would have paid a thousand pounds to know what she was thinking. Roan had never met a more composed woman in his life. While he let his feelings dangle like loose threads from his cuff.

"I've interrupted..." She paused, struggling. "Whatever it is you were doing at this hour." She leaned in when he made a move to rise from the chair. He didn't think he could do this much longer and keep his hands off her. "Thank you. For the translation. And the offer to craft a response. I'll make a few notes and get back to you, so I don't take up any more of your time than necessary."

Take up my time, he mused. *Just take it.* "I'm happy to do it. I need practice, so I don't lose the language. What friends do for each other now, isn't it? Translations over tea and crumpets."

"Friends," she mouthed, rolling the word around as if it were an olive she was sucking the pit from. Beneath the rounded edge of her spectacles, her cheeks lit, a haunting rose that turned him inside out where he sat.

His decision made to further the association even if the lady was standoffish, Roan rose to his feet, backed up a step. It was either that or circle his rickety desk, loop his arm around her waist, scatter her folios and ledgers with a vicious sweep of his hand, then proceed to do delicious things to her body.

Step between her legs, tilt her head back and kiss the bloody life from her. That would be a fine start.

"Tomorrow," he murmured, thinking of Mrs. Meekins in the buff to calm what would be a noticeable erection if he didn't talk himself down from it. "Meet me on the front veranda after breakfast. Eleven will do."

She blinked and gave her spectacles an adorable nudge. "Pardon me?"

He laughed, mostly at himself. His raging infatuation was amusing, it really was. "No need for pardons. I translated your letter, now you do me a favor. I need an assistant for a task concerning my tenants."

"Your tenants?"

He walked backward until he was able to send his hand out and locate the doorframe. *Go, Ro, before you follow through on the impulse to touch her.* "I hear an echo resounding around this dismal little room," he muttered through the pain and pleasure of arousal.

"Theodosia has lessons with the Duchess Society tomorrow morning. I'd hoped to attend."

"You need lessons?"

Her lips folded in. "No. Yes." She lifted her thumb to her mouth and chewed delightfully on her nail. *Lud,* was he charmed. "Maybe."

"My undertaking will be much more amusing than classes in comportment and watercolors. Trust me." She had a spot of ink on her cheek he was having trouble looking away from. How many kisses would it take to buff *that* away, he wondered?

Her index finger skimmed a scuff in the desk as she hummed thoughtfully. He could almost feel the touch. "If I agree, no funny business. As in, it's just business."

Roan flattened his hand to his chest, a shaft of anticipation sweeping him. *Hell's teeth,* but he was in trouble with this girl. "Funny business? *Me?*"

"Am I going to be sorry I said yes? You like to win."

Roan grinned, knowing it was wolfish but unable to soften the blow. "As if you don't, sweetheart. As if you don't."

Chapter Six

Where an Heiress Begins to See the Man

Gingerbread and cinnamon. Roasted goose and burning pine. Linseed oil and crisp lavender. Frankincense and holly. From her spot by the parlor window, Helena decided that the scents dominating Leighton House were as enticing and addictive as its owner. Every square inch of Roan's castle encouraged one to sink down upon the nearest cushioned settee and while away the hours, daydreaming about biscuits and hot cocoa. From the ivy-entwined banisters to the evergreen-decorated window ledges, the presentation was delightful.

And disarming.

She didn't even want to *think* about the mistletoe stationed beneath each doorway.

Her stately Mayfair townhome was the opposite of cozy. Echoing and lonely were words that came to mind when she thought of it.

Behind Helena, Georgiana Mungo, the Duchess of Markham, and Lady Hildegard Streeter, the rogue queen to Tobias Streeter's rogue king, circled their two charges, Theodosia and Lady Philippa, while straightening postures and tugging on hems, reviewing proper topics to discuss over dinner and ones to avoid. Helena listened with half an ear to the boisterous conversation, realizing she'd made gross errors in nearly every conversation she'd ever had. Especially as she was more intelligent than most of the men she'd conversed with.

Which presented a problem unless she ignored the insufficiency.

Except for the Duke of Leighton. A fact that made Helena's head spin. She didn't like being caught unprepared. He spoke *three* foreign languages well, which meant he spoke three *very* well and two better than most. Amazingly, he'd been ejected from Cambridge over temperamental absurdity, not poor marks.

She liked intelligent men.

Secretly liked men who called her *sweetheart* in low, sensual tones when it was utterly inappropriate to do so.

Helena started as Theo sidled up beside her, restless, delightful, irascible Theo. Her sister's eyes were so wide with excitement, the azure orbs captivated her entire face. She was already the sister of Helena's heart even in the short time they'd known each other.

"The duchess rules are spoony, Hellie, but I'm having fun, anyway. Our house is so *quiet*. There are children and animals here! Like my village back home a bit, except this is far grander than anything I could've imagined. Did you see that Mr. Streeter brought his cats? One is named after a Shakespearean character. The cat, not his son. I shall put *A Midsummer Night's Dream* next on my reading list. Too, are you sure I need these lessons? Whoever thought to tell a girl to discuss needlepoint for hours must be headed for Bedlam, but I shall endeavor to make a lady of myself," she whispered, her smile bright, her hair tangled, her cheeks flushed. Helena didn't remember ever being this young. "Imagine, Theodosia Jane Astley, shipping co-heiress. And her sister, a duchess in training!"

Helena turned with a gasp. "This is subterfuge and nothing more. For our reputational protection, we must have a valid reason to be in attendance. Darling, we're not even gentry. I spent the first five years of my life in the slums until Papa made a success of his business. A little town polish is all we're seeking. Connections that may help you in the future. *Duchess*." Helena's heart quivered in her chest as the word passed her lips. "I'm pretending nothing of the sort. I thought it good to get your nose out of a book for a week or two."

Theo clutched her stomach and curled into her amusement, her wrinkled buttercup-yellow gown dancing around her ankles. "Oh, silly! I know what the scandal sheets wrote about you and the duke isn't true. Filthy rags. As for me, I'll be ever so happy with someone in the clergy. A baronet might be nice or an industrialist from America. Don't you import tobacco from the southern regions? I could meet someone in the warehouse one day and fall in love instantly across a sea of crates and posh merchandise. As long as they agree to my hopes for an education."

Helena smiled, her heart giving a protective, fiercely maternal thump. "I will support whatever makes you happiest. Unless he's an utter nob."

"I shall shy away from utter nobs." Theo grinned, the crooked tooth on top making her smile perfect. She tapped her fingernail to the windowpane. "Gads, whatever are they doing out there?"

The female portion of the Leighton Cluster—Georgie, Hildy, and Pippa—stepped in, crowding Helena and Theo as they sought to look out the frosted glass to the lawn. Helpless, Helena looked too, knowing well what she would find.

Roan Darlington, seventh Duke of Leighton, earl and marquess of what she couldn't recall, tall and lean and...

Gorgeous.

She chewed on her thumbnail, stopping herself from wilting like a rose cut from the bush at the sight. Broad shoulders testing the limits of an overcoat that had unquestionably come from the best tailor in London. Long legs encased in buff breeches that molded to every muscle. An ax held menacingly in his hand. She squinted, trying but failing to see that charming scar on his lip.

Unaware of the ladies' regard, Leighton gestured impatiently to Xander Macauley, who held a shovel and a bewildered expression. Dexter Munro, the Duke of Markham, was standing to the side mired in pensive thought. A bit like a conductor orchestrating the proceedings. Rounding out the foursome, Tobias Streeter had a bounty of evergreens tucked beneath his arm and was turning in slow circles as if trying to decide where to unload them.

"Looks like they're arguing." Pippa elbowed her way into the middle of the throng, nearly pressing her nose to the glass to get a better look. Slender and restless, she reminded Helena of a puppy. Reckless energy unfortunately wrapped in a prettier-than-her-brother-was-going-to-wish-to-deal-with package. "Roan loves to debate a subject to death. If you wait a moment, they'll be rolling around on the ground, throwing punches. Then they'll come inside with torn clothing, bruised faces, and huge grins, expecting us to admire their virility and good sense. As they comment upon how grandly they're able to *communicate*."

"Perverse creatures. Their friendship strengthens every time they toss each other into the dirt. But doesn't my Dex look stunning when he's thinking about a problem?" Georgie wedged in between them, bumping Helena's shoulder and sending her stumbling. "Mrs. Meekins ordered them to get ivy for the south gallery when the south gallery needs more ivy like Leighton needs another fossil. They've been underfoot all morning. It's like having four overgrown children running wild without any toys to play with. They're without their usual entertainments, be that work, women, and whiskey, and it shows. At sixes and sevens, the lot of them. A few knocks to the head might be just what the doctor ordered. Or the housekeeper as it were."

Helena shrugged before remembering that Georgie, the Duchess of Markham, had told Theo that ladies shouldn't shrug unless it was absolutely necessary. "But why an argument over ivy?"

"Why not? Roan is known for his temper," Hildy said in her breathy, unerring voice. She was one of the most beautiful people Helena had ever seen with her husband, Tobias, coming in a close second. They were a blindingly intimidating couple. Like something out of a painting hanging in Leighton House's equally intimidating gallery.

With a ragged sigh, Pippa gave a strand of her flaxen hair a twist. "The big one is striking, isn't he? His rig is quite fine for such a colossal frame. I'd like to see my brother try to take him down. Although he *did* once pitch Roan in the Thames, or so they say."

Georgie's gaze snapped to her young charge. She gave the window a rub as if she could wipe away the admittedly handsome image. "Oh, no, *not* him. Get any thought of Xander Macauley out of your mind, Lady Philippa. He's never going to marry. He's beyond the Duchess Society's ability to transform. I'll be forced to retire if we ever take him on as a client." She gave the windowpane another punishing buff. "Hildy, that's a warning."

"In other words," Hildy immediately returned, her words crimped with glee, "forget it, darling girl. You're a duke's sister while Macauley owns a shipping company, half of a malt brewing venture, and has talked about purchasing a deteriorating gaming hell for his amusement. He smuggles when he no longer needs to, chases light-skirts when he could do better, gambles excessively, and refuses to give up those filthy cheroots. Besides, he's ten years older than you, at least. The possibilities are unattractive even if the man isn't."

"I would never dream of it," Pippa murmured. "I was simply stating that he's the most handsome of the blockheads on the lawn arguing over pine twigs. But tastes are subjective, aren't they, in life and art? May I be allowed to say, however, that your claim seems hypocritical? After all, you're an earl's daughter married to a man who owns a shipping company. The by-blow of a viscount and part Romani too. And the *Gazette* just this morning said she"—Pippa jacked her thumb inelegantly in Helena's direction—"is being courted by a duke. My brother, that is. And she *also* owns a shipping company. So, there's a common theme here. And blue blood isn't it."

"Ivy. They're in search of ivy." Hildy frowned, unused to being challenged. Or being wrong. The exuberant puppy they were trying to train had a sharp mind. "The situations don't equate. I'm older than you. Tobias is tamer, more malleable than Xander Macauley could ever be. At least, in the end, he was."

"After you broke him," Georgie piped in with a sly wink. "Like one of those beasts you ride through Hyde Park. One outing and they're done."

Hildy sputtered a laugh, casting a rushed glance at the young women listening closely to this exchange. "I did no such thing! Hush up. In any case, a duke trumps an earl every day of the week. You're in a far more exacting position, Lady Philippa. I was forgotten and on the shelf by the time my darling husband came tripping into my life. Society had rejected me, and I them. Our marriage caused few ripples. Less than a penny being tossed in a pond. Although, Tobias worried greatly about it."

Pippa grimaced, clearly discarding anyone's opinion but her own. Unwilling to admit that her position was broadly publicized and thorny. More so than any woman standing in the room. "Then maybe I should become a wallflower too. Make the *ton* forget about me, so I'm able to make my own choices. I shall endeavor to prop up each ballroom wall I inhabit. Blend like mist into the environs."

Hildy linked her arm with Pippa's and drew her close. "It isn't that easy, but we'll help you navigate the precarious waters. That's the Duchess Society's role. We've gotten quite good at it, actually. Just this week, we negotiated a contract between the Earl of Trembley and Lady Myra Von Deetle. She wanted her dogs, all five of them, to move into his home upon her marriage. The earl is allergic or says he is, and at first, he refused, but after thoughtful discussion, he's agreed to visit an herbalist and let his intended keep her babies. And her fortune in her control, to a modest point. With his dire financial situation and her impressive dowry, there really wasn't much of a push. What's a few rowdy canines and a mild rash when one is stepping in to save you from insolvency?"

"I'll never put myself in such a horrid situation," Pippa whispered. "I'd much rather be alone."

Helena felt a pang of sorrow for Leighton. His sister would be difficult to manage through the *ton's* infamous marriage mart and then some. He seemed to adore her, which tugged at Helena's heartstrings more than it should. Theo wasn't going to be much better, perhaps, but a duchy wasn't riding on her shoulders. Only a dowry that could choke a horse. And an overprotective older sister who wasn't sure she believed in love. The man Helena sanctioned for Theo was going to have to be *perfect*. God help him.

Georgie leaned her slim shoulder against the window ledge with a dreamy sigh. "*Oh*, I think Leighton is going to use that ax."

The women paused for a breathless moment. A show of masculine beauty was honest entertainment on a frigid winter day.

"His Grace the seventh is stopping to look at his watch," Theo murmured around the end of the braid she was gnawing rather diligently on. "We only got to see one dashed ax swing."

Helena tugged her sister's braid loose and flipped it behind Theo's shoulder. "I'm meeting the seventh in thirty minutes. An errand he wants me to run with him."

Pippa stilled, then turned to Helena with tea-saucer eyes. A gaze that glittered with comprehension. "The gift-giving. He invited you to the gift-giving. He loves that part most. I went last year, but it took hours, so I begged off this time." She tucked her top lip between her teeth and hummed a tune. "This *is* interesting when nothing else about this day has been."

Helena ran her hand down her bodice, unnerved to be the focus of Pippa's shrewd consideration. What in the world was the gift-giving? "Um, yes? I suppose he did then."

Pippa's face took on a canny look, the light of discovery from a young woman who knew her brother better than anyone.

The moment left Helena with the sinking feeling that she'd once again misjudged a duke.

———

Roan relaxed against the carriage sitting in the drive, watching as Helena Astley took the stone staircase leading to the lawn with the stride of a soldier going into battle. A spencer in the typical sedate style rattled about her with the movement. The color suited her. A pale lilac that he guessed her modiste had selected because it matched her eyes. Her ever-suffering companion, Prudence, shadowed her like a hound, her glower sharp enough to pierce ice.

Helena undoubtedly noticed his regard, but she ignored it. And him. While the sensation of her closing in on him warmed him to his *toes*. She always came out with her fists swinging, which intrigued him to no good end. Since the day he met her, she'd never backed down from a challenge. Even the silly ones he'd inadvertently tossed in her path.

It must have been the rookery girl in her.

The problem was, in his experience, he'd found that independent women were hard to conquer.

Lucky for Roan, he'd hadn't decided to conquer Helena yet.

Her smile when she reached him was the rehearsed one he didn't particularly like, but there was enough legitimacy to smooth the jagged edges of his temper. She didn't comment if she noticed that he was casually dressed—buckskins, his oldest coat, and scuffed boots that weren't Hoby. He'd left the clothing made by Weston behind for this journey.

"Ready?" he asked and gestured to the waiting carriage. He'd made sure heated bricks and abundant lap throws were inside. Snow was in their future if he didn't miss his guess.

Helena tilted her head, and the morning sun tunneled through the soft lavender of her eyes. *Hot in Hades,* she was pretty. "Ready for what, Your Grace?"

"Leighton, please. Or make me the happiest of men and go with Roan." He waved away the coachman who'd started to climb down and opened the door for her with a flourish. "The fun is in the voyage, so let's see what that entails."

"The Leighton Cluster isn't coming, I see," Helena murmured, taking his hand and stepping inside the carriage's murky, lamp-lit interior.

"They couldn't be bothered, frankly. Activities planned with the children. Or in Macauley's case, he rode out early to find his adventure in the village. A willing widow is usually the solution to his angst." He released her immediately, although the impact of her touch remained, a gentle thrum through his body. Unfortunately, assisting Helena's cantankerous maid up next erased any pleasant feelings on contact. "Miss Prudence. Up you go."

The companion halted on the carriage step, gazing at him with what looked like pity. "It's Patience, Your Grace. Although I may well look like a Prudence."

Helena's laughter floated like the enchanting scent of summer past him. It was, Roan thought, the first time he'd heard her laugh. *Really* laugh. His heart gave a resounding tremor that must have communicated itself to his face—because *Patience's* look of pity turned to sympathy.

I can win her over if I decide to, he wanted to tell the grumpy frump. *I'm a bloody duke. And an earl. And a marquess. I'm skilled with women when I need to be.*

However, as he settled on the velvet squab across from his fixation and her glowering duenna, the flattering light from the carriage's lone sconce spilling over her, he wasn't confident he could enchant a woman who seemed to like him not at all and respected him even less.

Chapter Seven

Where an Heiress Becomes Mildly Infatuated

The seventh wasn't a bored aristocrat.

He wasn't foolish, insipid, or stupid.

After visiting the third cottage on his estate, Helena began to sketch a clearer picture of the enigmatic Duke of Leighton. Although, it was a struggle to gain a sound foothold on her reasoning between sidestepping those careless grins he threw out like rose petals. She'd been dancing around them all morning and into the afternoon. Suppressing the glittering heat that exploded in her chest and rippled to her nether regions with each tilt of his admittedly fetching lips.

She wondered how many women he'd gotten to drop their drawers with that smile.

At each stop on what had turned into a charitable grand tour of his estate, his footmen unloaded foodstuff, firewood, toys, blankets, clothing, candles, and stray bits of holly she imagined he and his band of misfit rogues had gathered while arguing this morning. Then, items tucked proudly under his arms or loaded atop them, he'd knocked on doors, peeked in windows, genuinely delighted by his tenants' delight.

His eyes absolute innocence and flirtation when he turned to find her watching.

Then, he'd detonate another of those smiles and send her back into a bewildered emotional swirl.

The condition of his tenant's cottages was a testament to his able management. Each dwelling was painted proudly in snowy white, the green trim adorning the windows and doors only a touch lighter than his eyes. New thatch roofs on some, repaired fencing around others. The land surrounding the residences looked ripe for planting, the buildings free of the disrepair that would invite winter where it wasn't welcome.

The years before her father had made a success of his shipping endeavor would never leave her. Frigid nights and bellyaching mornings with little food in the cupboards to quell the rumblings. Scant firewood to warm the flat. Her mother had died of cholera on one of those solemn winter days. Helena had been three, so her memories were ghost-like. She'd had one absent parent who had done the best he could—and that was that. There wasn't time to mourn what could not be changed. She could only hope to make things better for Theo.

Since her time with a duke was limited, Helena recorded details as if she planned to write a novelette about the experience. The snow that began to fall in feathery wisps as he gave out the last of his bounty. The scent of hearth fires and gingerbread riding the wind. The rare picture he was giving her into himself. How much he seemed to like children, and how much they seemed to like *him*. How incredibly different he was from the man written about in the broadsheets. Or perhaps she'd made an erroneous judgment on the cliffs of Lyme Regis and let it color every interaction she'd ever had with him.

He was, like most intriguing people, a confounding mix.

His temper was swift, but so was his wit. Helena found herself laughing, a sizzle in her bloodstream when he turned to her with startled eyes. With the attention he received in every ballroom he stepped into, how could her brand of awkward consideration be pleasing?

While she tried to figure him out, she documented the pieces.

He was left-handed. Had a small smattering of freckles across the bridge of his nose and a scar beneath his ear to match the enchanting one edging his lip. His eyelashes were burnished at the tip, amber almost, something she'd never noticed on another person. Maddening to all women, those eyelashes were long enough to cast shadows on his skin. He patted his chest often and gave a faint asthmatic cough she guessed was due to habit, not poor health. His nose was the lone feature on his face she would deem patrician. When he wasn't sure what to talk about, he spoke of fossils. His shaving soap was scented with bergamot. He squinted enough that she wondered if, like her, he needed spectacles.

So far, the duke bit was the only bit she didn't like.

She shouldn't have experienced such wonder in the discovery of him. When that wonder was a trap.

He was out of reach, and it would be heartache to think otherwise. She'd told herself this every time he crossed her path. With a look, the hardest one she could muster. Street, shop, wharf, market, all the places it wasn't out of the norm to see him. She'd taken hold of her attraction and brought it to heel like she would a mongrel.

Why couldn't she be attracted to a clerk or a stevedore? But of course, no clerk or stevedore weakened her knees or had her chewing on her lip with a wistful pang she hoped wasn't reflected on her face. No one but the Duke of Leighton had ever made her feel... feminine. Soft, like the buttery insides of one of her treasured lemon scones.

She didn't particularly *like* that sensation.

Nevertheless, she liked men. Or appreciated them rather. Enjoyed watching them throw crates of considerable weight upon their shoulders and tramp down the wharf, sometimes whistling a jaunty tune while they did so. She preferred stubborn jaws with a hint of stubble and legs a mile long. Husky voices, and before the Duke of Leighton, blue eyes. She favored men who could laugh at themselves—who didn't gain pleasure from laughing at others.

Her little secret: she had experience.

One time, one night. Truthfully, fifteen minutes of fumbling atop a chaise lounge in a debauched baron's parlor. It hadn't ruined her because she was her own guardian. Her own chaperone, which might be the problem. She made her own *choices*, even awful ones on occasion. But wasn't that life? She'd been disheartened, impossibly young, flustered, slightly foxed and fooled—and determined after the fact to never let it happen again. "It" being letting someone get the best of her. Get close to her.

Touch her, kiss her, *see* her.

The experience hadn't devastated her. It had merely confirmed the perfidy of men. She was almost glad she'd made the mistake. For Theo's sake. Helena was armed with information and knew better how to protect her little sister.

But her curiosity about lovemaking and passion remained. Dormant for the most part until the Defiant Duke. The most persistent person she'd ever encountered. Year after year, there he was, on street corners and bookshops, tipping his hat and winking, making her burn with daring glances he should have snapped a cover on like he did his timepiece and hidden it away in his pocket.

Now, she was interested. And at the same time denied, excluded. A river of *something* racing beneath her skin. Dangerous attraction, dangerous awareness. He was crafty, shrewd. He'd gotten her to the country by using a perfectly acceptable rationale. Where she was now captive and falling deeper under his spell with each blasted moment she spent with him. As her grandmother would have stated, his was a handsome trick.

Years ago, she'd witnessed a kiss in a public house that could have lit a thousand candles with its intensity. She'd written a love story in her mind in seconds. Then, as if they'd heard it, the couple linked hands, smiled knowingly at each other and disappeared through the doorway to find the closest bed, twisting silken sheets into a frenzied tangle with their enthusiasm. She'd read of such things in scandalous novels. It was a fantasy, however, because she'd gotten to see during her lone encounter with the baron how sexual relations really worked when they didn't work well. The act had been as sensual as organizing the unloading of one of her ships. A transaction that left her feeling soulless and confused. A rough transaction. Painful, which she didn't think was right, but there was certainly no one to ask. She had no close friends, no mother. Patience would faint dead away if she broached the topic.

Since Helena wasn't to have a proper husband, was it too much to want uncontrollable passion? With someone? Someday?

"What are you dreaming about over there?"

Helena gave herself a mental shake, turning from her investigation of the charming country lane the carriage rumbled down, to discover Leighton's astute gaze centered on her. Her cheeks lit. For a scandalous second, long enough to leave a lasting impression on her senses, like a still scene imprinted on your lids when you closed your eyes, she'd seen him crawling atop her on that chaise lounge, not that horrid baron. She wondered if it might bring pleasure, not pain if *he* placed his hands on her.

Patience's delicate snore journeyed from the murky coach corner, reminding Helena she was thankfully not alone with the duke she desired. "Your discussion of Cretaceous rock formations did her in."

A groove appeared between his brows as he stretched his buckskin-clad legs—miles long as she liked them—before him. The toe of his boot almost, *almost*, brushed the hem of her gown. Her body lit beneath her woolen spencer, giving her an idea of what would happen if he *actually* touched her.

"Women don't seem to enjoy talk of rocks, that's true. I sometimes use the topic to spirit them off truthfully, like a foul odor or a stray spark shooting from a hearth. Once I start on fossils, they drift away. A vapor I can't recall the scent or sight of three seconds later, it's so irrelevant. The ravenous mothers, however, remain through hours of igneous, sedimentary, *and* metamorphic. I've tried reviewing every stone in the book. This damn title keeps them attentive no matter how dull the conversation." He did that asthmatic chest rub, a gesture she found sweet and solidly unique to the man. "Dreams of their daughters being a duchess, I suppose."

Helena picked at a seam in the velvet squab, her gaze going to Patience to ensure she still slept. *Just ask him, Hellie.* "Why did you let me think you were a wastrel? You brought toys and sweets. Food. Fabric for clothing. Firewood. Blankets. These homes you've taken me to are well maintained. Your tenants *like* you. One even told me you have an orphaned boy working in your stable and sleeping in the main house as you prep him to be a groom."

Roan stilled, looking as shocked as if he'd taken a knock to the head. He had a streak of ash on his cheek she'd been eyeing since cottage number four. "I never..." His frown intensified, the groove between his brows deep enough for her to sink her pinkie in. "Why in the world would you think I was a wastrel? Bombastic, granted, moody certainly, but not a wastrel. My amusements are controlled, and I like a healthy return on my investments. I would never let my cravings control me." He shot a quick, perplexed glance at her. "Or I never have before."

"Why would I think this?" A laugh sputtered free. *Really?* She held out her hand, ticking points off on her fingers. "Tossing your shipping partner in the Thames. Brawls in Parliament. Dismissal from Cambridge. Opera singers. Actresses. A countess and a two-story fall from a balcony last year, wasn't it? A duel on Putney Heath where your shoulder was grazed by a poorly aimed bullet, a baronet too in his cups to see which of the three of you was the man he intended to injure. The tales are legendary. Or soon will be. Give them time, like wine, to age."

"Those are, were, I should say—" With a curse, he straightened his spine, his eyes starting to smolder, flaring from emerald to onyx. The infamous Leighton temper on display. She knew she was in trouble when this masculine demonstration sent a tingle rippling through her.

"I sent you an apology hours, *hours*, after my *faux pas* in Lyme Regis. Furthermore, quite a few messages after that. I recall four over the period of one year. I was an immature boy playing at being a man. Forgive me. Now I'm a man playing at being a duke." He tugged his hand through his hair, then, with an impatient move, yanked his gloves from his hands with his teeth. Her heart dropped clear to her feet with her whispered sigh of longing.

"I was saddled with this mess at the tender age of *nineteen*, Miss Astley. Finances in disarray, estates in penury. Domestics were terrified about being sacked. The funds needed to sustain the duchy less than I'd been given to do the job. Far less. Up-all-night-worrying less. Retching-into-rubbish-bins less. Villages attached to each estate part of the blissful obligation, churches and schools and roads to maintain.

"I wasn't trained or qualified for this position, not even so much as you were to inherit your father's company. You spent your childhood roaming the docks. You knew the *business*. I was a lowly son to a baron who *was* a wastrel. I knew almost nothing. The dukedom was a remote possibility, true. So remote I never considered it because two men, one nearly as young as me, had to pass without direct heirs to make it happen. But pass without direct heirs they did."

She felt the regretful twinge, a needle pricking her skin. Twisting her hands together in her lap, she denied the urge to rip her glove off and press her chilled palm to her cheek to abate the fever rolling through her. "Your funds are adequate now?"

He slapped his gloves to his thigh and flexed his fingers with a weary grimace, his gaze leaving her to search the countryside, the smears of snow sticking to the windowpane capturing his attention. Or so he let her think. "With keen management, enough. Once your kingdom grows, honestly, it's a hungry beast to feed. I feel the wolves nipping at my heels every so often still, but I've proven to be a marginally wise investor. And remarkably, though the *ton* disdains me for it, a skilled entrepreneur. Trade is in my blood, which appalls them. It's a reminder of where I came from, not where they want me to go. My father burned through blunt like coal, so I had to use my wits to keep us afloat."

"You could marry for money. It's what your drove does every day." The words felt like sand rolling off her tongue. "A healthy dowry for the title of duchess isn't the faultiest business agreement."

He rapped the windowpane, a brutal tap. "Thank you for the advice, Miss Astley. I'll consider it."

Her own temper flared. Why was he angry with her for proposing a logical solution? "You need an heir. And money never hurts. That's all I'm stating."

"I know," he said, sounding tired. He wrote on an invisible list hanging in the air between them. "Check, check."

His reaction was perplexing. What else was there for an aristocrat with his immense responsibilities? *Oh.* Her gasp was spontaneous, the word leaving her mouth hushed. Like a secret she'd never uttered to another soul. A *term* she'd never uttered to another soul. "*Love.*"

He snorted and gave the window another hard pop. "That one. The emotion Shakespeare described so eloquently in quite a few instances. And Jane Austen, poor, tragic chit. Pippa had never witnessed true love, a solid marriage, before Markham and Georgie. Streeter and Hildy. *My parent's marriage was a dreadful model. She doesn't trust the institution. I'm not sure I do. But I'd like to give her an example to examine before she makes her own choice. Provide it for her inspection, like my fossils.*

His shoulders dropped on an exhalation, his gaze catching hers, then moving away before she could record the shade of green his eyes had turned. "This is another clue to my common leanings, but I want a family. It's been Pippa and me for too long. I'm sure that sounds like a rudimentary wish. Very unrefined, I realize."

Goodness, he was straightforward. She'd never met someone who stated what they were thinking. *All. The. Time.*

He shifted his legs, perhaps uneasy with his honesty, his boot definitely brushing her hem this time. His gaze met hers. His eyes had gone the crystalline of moss on rock, leaves in summer, grass in spring. "Let's turn this game a bit and place you on the rack. What say you to love, Miss Astley?"

She shook her head, cornered. When she didn't like being cornered. She made pathetic mistakes when cornered—like that night with the baron years ago. "I don't want to get attached, lose my freedom. But sometimes"—she threw a glance at Patience—"I want to *feel.*"

His exhale ricocheted off the carriage's paneled walls. "*Feel.*" He murmured the word like he was tasting wine and berries on his tongue —and liked the taste.

"Once," she blurted, unable to stop herself. That corner she found herself wedged in making her say it. "I saw a kiss. In a public house." She closed her eyes and tried to remember. The hero and heroine of her romantic fantasy. The man's hands on the woman's waist, pulling her against his body. Helena had seen him flick her bottom lip with his tongue, and instead of disgust, warmth had radiated through her. Wonder. Curiosity. *Yearning.*

"You've never been kissed," he whispered, his voice hoarse.

She opened her eyes. Blinked twice to ground herself. Laughed. She didn't want to challenge the Duke of Leighton, who tossed people in raging rivers when challenged. What an arrogant cur he was at the bones of it.

"I've been kissed." And more, but she wasn't about to tell him such a shocking truth. When the shocking truth was pathetic. A little frightening even. "But not like *this*. This was obscurity and candlelight and desire. Nothing you would ever see in one of your swank ballrooms, Almack's, or the opera even. This was *real*. Maybe that only happens in the back alleys of my world." She went to chew on her lip, then caught herself. "Perhaps it was a mirage, and it doesn't happen at all."

Oh, Hellie, you issued the dare, you fool.

He straightened, leaning across the distance separating them until his face was inches from hers. *Freckles* are *a thing of beauty*, she thought. "What if I could make you feel? What if it's not a mirage, which I can assure you, it's not."

She held out a hand and pushed him back. Middle of the chest, sending her fingertips sizzling through kid leather. *No.* Not him. Not someone she might *like*. Could like. Was starting to admire. Not someone who was turning out to be a better man than he'd let on. Confidence games and enigmatic motives were not her style.

Brainy, partially lovable aristocrats were not her style.

Leighton went willingly back to his corner of the ring. "Meet me tonight. After dinner. The music room. Let's see if I can. You can leave the door open the entire time but don't bring Prudence."

"Patience. And why would I do that, Your Grace?" she asked, hoping she sounded appalled as opposed to insanely intrigued. She couldn't do that, could she?

"Don't add that bit of noble nonsense to create distance between us. If that's your strategy, let me climb out and ride with the coachman this very minute. Why wouldn't you do it, may I ask? A simple kiss. Between unencumbered adults? Consider it an experiment." He buffed his nails on his trousers in a show of indifference. "I love experiments myself."

Helena held her breath, then let it out in a rush. He had a rip in his sleeve from today's adventure that she longed to poke her finger inside.

"Is that all it is? Because I don't want a husband. I don't *need* a husband. A man would only muddle my well-regulated life. I'm happy. More than. Theo and I are just fine. We have the house in Mayfair and the business and, well, a lot." Her desperate speech trailed away. When she listed what they had, an image of the somber halls of her town-home presented itself forlornly before her. Tripping along behind that was the memory of the fumbling encounter in a darkened parlor with a man who'd not cared how much he hurt her.

Even after living on London's mean streets, she'd been innocent before that, at least a little.

His eyes smoldered, something in her sermon sparking his displeasure. "What else could it be when I told you I want to marry for love? When you don't even believe in the concept? We're at cross purposes in everything *except* conducting an experiment. This chemistry we seem to have, and sweetheart, we have it."

She traced a snowy smear on the windowpane, considering when she knew she shouldn't.

Roan anchored his elbow on the carriage wall and dropped his head to his fist, his expression caught somewhere between devious and angelic. "If I dared you, would you be more compelled?" His voice skimmed her like a caress. She could imagine him whispering wicked things in that silken tone. Could imagine blooming like a rose before him in reply.

"I don't respond to dares." When she did. Every blasted day. She'd responded to dares her entire life. Even her own. But the Duke of Leighton was a threat to her. His magnetism was a ripping tide that could carry her out to sea with its force. She was wise to stay on shore. The distance he spoke of. Avoiding that arcane chemistry, which she knew, in her *soul*, there'd be a wealth of.

His smile was like one of his river tosses. Submerged in sunlight and sensation. Then plucked free to gasp for air.

She shook her head, panicked. "I can't."

He nodded, convinced. "You *can*."

"I won't."

He shrugged, regal and unconcerned when she could see the pulse beating double-time above his thick woolen scarf. A place she'd love to press her lips, forget his world, hers, forget everything. Draw him into her soul and never let him go.

"I'll be there until midnight if you choose to accept."

She was coming to understand him well enough to know he wanted an answer.

So she gave him none.

Chapter Eight

Where a Duke Proves a Point

S he wasn't going to show.

Which was fine.

Roan was content with the peace of a subdued evening after a lively dinner with his guests. An entertaining night, the house consumed with the intoxicating aromas of nutmeg and cinnamon, vanilla and pine, of Christmastide. Although Helena had been seated at the far end of the table, and they'd not had a chance to converse, he'd found his attention circling back to her time and time again. In return, she'd craftily dodged his gaze over lamb in mint sauce, curried peas, scalloped potatoes, cheese, and fruit, whispering with her sister, and surprisingly, Markham's duchess. Perhaps not surprising for two of the most mischievous women he knew, they seemed to be developing a friendship.

He had a suspicion he could certainly not confirm that Helena didn't have many people she counted as friends.

While he pondered the pinch that depressing thought brought to the region around his heart, he studied the room with a shuttered gaze. It was his favorite place in the house. Tufted leather armchairs spacious enough for a broad body surrounded a threadbare damask sofa he could stretch out upon and nap the day away. Which he rarely did, though he frequently considered it. If he ever found the time amid this damned ducal nightmare to nap, it would be in this room. He liked that he could drop his boots on any table without a tremor of guilt. A speck of mud on the faded carpets, not heirlooms by any sense of the imagination, suited just fine.

He was plain Roan here, nothing grand or special. The man he wanted to be.

The man he was trying to present to the woman he was besotted with. At least if Helena rebuffed him again, if that was what he was angling for, acceptance, shouldn't she know the true man? Not the myth or the legend.

Anyway, so what if she didn't accept the dare?

He wasn't used to women rejecting him, but he would recover. The whiskey on his tongue was top-notch because he, Streeter, and Macauley created it in their profitable, recently opened second distillery. A paleontology book had arrived in the morning post and was open on his lap to a chapter detailing the discovery of prehistoric footprints of unknown origin in Algeria.

The music room was warm but not too. Lit perfectly, a cross between bright enough to sew by and dark enough for trouble. He'd even played an instructional chess game with his groom-in-training, Kieran, the orphaned lad Helena had mentioned earlier. Kieran had captured Roan's heart and given it a twist, like the woman he sat here stupidly waiting for. The boy was too thin but pretended to be full when anyone asked if he'd eaten. He watched the world through haunted brown eyes. Acted confident when he was anything but. Roan recognized this last move as he did the same thing himself. To this day, pretending, which got exhausting after a while.

Mrs. Meekins had complained about Kieran stealing items and storing them in a tattered satchel he clung to like a lifeline. So far, a fork, two leather-bound digests from the library, and a horrid copper vase from one of the parlors. Roan had taken a peek in the boy's bag while he slept the night before.

He'd instructed his stiff-upper-lip housekeeper to let Kieran be while the boy figured out his place at Leighton House. Roan remembered being scared like that even if he'd not been hungry. He'd had parents through most of his adolescence, though his father had been heartless, his mother removed. He felt certain Kieran would return the pilfered objects when he realized he wasn't going anywhere with them. That he didn't have to run. Or hide.

He was home if he chose to accept Roan's offer.

Because it looked like Helena wasn't.

Brooding and restless, Roan read the same paragraph twice before cursing beneath his breath and letting the book sprawl open on his lap. There was an immense spider web on the ceiling that he should have someone remove.

Her scent hit him first. Delicate, drifting across his skin. Jasmine? No, *no*, peony.

Closing the book gently, Roan turned to find Helena standing in the doorway, a much-desired apparition. She'd changed out of her evening gown—a bottomless crimson that had ignited a wealth of auburn strands in her hair and brought a delightful rosiness to her cheeks—into a lavender day dress of more modest presentation. One clearly selected, but not by her he'd bet, to match her eyes. She was chewing on her knuckle, an appealing bit of indecision before she realized the tell and dropped her hand to her side.

Her skin glowed, luminous as a pearl in the candlelight. The curve of her breast, the gentle bend of her hip. Her throat pulled as she swallowed, his desire feeding hers. Or the reverse. Blast and damnation, did he want to put his hands on her. Press his lips to the pulse point at her jaw and drink her very essence like wine. The gears of time halted, and he was again on that cliff watching a young woman take pleasure in her find on a barren seashore.

Don't get attached, he thought madly and without motive. *Don't go too far, Ro. It's just a kiss.*

"No one would ever believe, truly." She hitched a shoulder, a half shrug, looking young and incredibly vulnerable. "Us."

Her reticence, when Helena Astley was a force to be reckoned with, the only female shipping magnate in England, the only female *anything* just about, struck him like a blow. *Ruined* him. Dazzled *and* ruined. Laid him low and made him suddenly, very stridently, want to protect her. He'd only had this feeling for Pippa, never for anyone else.

To date, he'd only been given one person in this life to love.

Setting the book aside, he rose and crossed to the pianoforte, gave his superfine breeches a modest tug, and sank to the bench. *Slowly*, Roan, *slowly*. He let his fingers settle on ivory, toyed with the keys. Played a snatch of a song—Beethoven—as an ache landed in his gut. And lower as he crudely imagined what he'd like to do to her. Close the maple lid, lay her delectable body across the top of the elegant musical instrument he'd inherited along with everything else, tuck his head between her legs, and *feast*.

He brought focused attention to detail to any task he set before himself—and maybe a degree of temper. It was a potent mix, he'd found. Helena had no idea the amount of pleasure he could give her. He wasn't sure but speculated she could meet him. Pleasure for pleasure, move for move. He'd never clashed with a woman who'd been his match.

He would start with a kiss.

A negotiation on her terms.

He played a chord, two, three. "I'll wait for you to come to me. The decision is yours. Leave or stay." He tried but couldn't help but glance at her in time to see her eyes flash. *Ah, he had her.* She liked to be in control. He would keep this in mind. It could prove useful information in multiple ways.

Turning back, he let his fingers dance over the keys. He'd listened along during some of Pippa's lessons years ago and found he had a knack. When Pippa most assuredly did not. Uninspiring talents for an uninspiring man. Paleontology and pianoforte.

He felt the heat of her body, although her step was silent. She slid on the bench beside him as a flame erupted in his chest, his heart hammering. His fingers slipped on the keys and played a bitter note.

"I'll do this for curiosity's sake, but I won't change my mind." She brought her finger down on middle C. "About anything."

He stilled, letting his gaze wash over her. The doors to the terrace were closed to the chill, but the curtains were open. Moonlight played over them, over the pianoforte, along the shabby carpet beneath their feet. A river of silver and dark, mysterious indigo. Wrapping the moment in twilight, desire, impatience, fevered fondness. And that whiff of inevitability he always suffered when near her. "Shall I make it quick, then? To satisfy your curiosity. And mine, I'll admit."

Her cheeks lit, but her gaze remained steady. Her eyes were a *wonder*. He'd never encountered such a fascinating shade of lilac. They were like something in a painting you believed could only be fiction, not fact. "Quick, yes. I shouldn't like to lose myself. Either of us. Experiments are regulated, are they not?"

He laughed, his hand coming down hard on the keys. *Hell's teeth,* she was a vexing chit. "You don't believe we could generate the amount of heat you witnessed in that public house, is that it? Or you're afraid that we could?"

Her lips compressed as she huffed out a sigh. As sensual a pout as he'd ever seen—and he'd seen many. "I only want to understand. What it's like. I don't want to *change*. That kiss looked like... *transformation*. The kiss to end all kisses. A kiss that said everything. I'm not expecting a kiss to say everything."

The decision was like a flash of sulfur sparking in his mind. Swiveling, he swung his leg over the bench, facing her in a loose-limbed straddle. He held up his hands, then lowered them to grip the bench's beveled edge. "Kiss me, then. Satisfy your curiosity. I won't touch. In matters such as this, it's often simple chemistry. We may have none to speak of. If we do, we'll know."

Her brow rose in a display of suspicion.

He made a slashing cross over his heart. *Promise.*

She snorted softly in reply.

He smiled, a tad slighted but able to ignore it. "Word of a duke's honor."

She tucked her bottom lip between her teeth, her consideration worthy of a shipping agreement that would bring in thousands of pounds in profit.

Christ, he wanted to kiss this troublesome, perplexing woman. Show her. Teach her. Be *taught*. Be *shown*. Pleasure her until her fingertips went numb, her vision blurry. Until they were gasping and spent.

Until he'd answered every question he'd ever posed about her. Ten years of questions.

"Close your eyes," she murmured. Still sitting sidesaddle on the bench, only halfway turned to him. A safer pose than his, surely. While he was as open as his paleontology book. Her scent, peony and an exotic spice he couldn't define, filtered past, and he snatched a fast breath trying to identify it. "Go on, do it. Close them. It's the basic science of a kiss now, isn't it?"

As promised, he followed her command, his lids drifting low, wondering why this felt like the most risqué thing he'd ever done. When the story the scandal rags had written about his descending a second-story balcony at record speed to escape an enraged fiancé—of a woman he hadn't known was affianced—was utterly true. The duels, the fisticuffs, the wagers. Abandoned gallops down Bond at midnight atop a mare trained for an open field not pockmarked streets. Women bouncing in and out of his life, and he theirs, like they were taking part in a reel. Regrettably, he *was* that scoundrel they wrote about.

The scoundrel matched the title.

But there were other aspects of this duchy business. Of *him*. The care he undertook for his tenants. The villages attached to each. Repair of schoolrooms, roofs, fences. Parts he enjoyed, or better to say, aspects that fulfilled him. Discussions about salaries and pensions and healthcare, which was inadequate in this country at best. New babies to welcome, dying friends to mourn. He and Pippa hadn't had a family to speak of before this. Now they were a part of something bigger, but somehow, still struggling to come inside from the cold.

He'd had his face pressed to the pane forever now, it seemed.

Without sight, the sounds of the night trickled in. The tick of a clock. Helena's light breaths. The squeak of the bench as she shifted, placing her hand on his shoulder, another at his elbow. Her grip was loose, then firm, anchoring him to her shore. Where he longed to swim through the waves of her.

Roan wore only a linen shirt and silk waistcoat, his coat draped over an armchair across the way, and her touch burned through the thin layers, awakening his senses. Igniting his imagination. The vision of pushing her back atop the pianoforte again filled his mind, making him restless and achingly desperate for things he shouldn't want or couldn't have. His cock defied him, thickening and pressing against his trouser buttons.

He and Helena had chemistry.

A fortune in chemistry there for mining. And, blazes, did he love science.

He recognized this without the test of a kiss, reestablished the basic fact every time she waltzed into his view on a dockside street or across a market aisle. The hair on the back of his neck routinely stood up in her presence, a happenstance that hadn't occurred with anyone else. Ever. Goosebumps, awkward erections, stammering. He was an adolescent around her. Hell, he'd probably blushed a time or two.

Along with those apologies, he'd tried to tell her in more ways than one over the years that he found her remarkable.

Nevertheless, some battles could only be won after engagement. With proof thrown at the feet of the disbelievers. He mustn't forget he was waging a campaign. Although, he'd no idea what he'd gone to war over. Or what he hoped, exactly, to receive as compensation at the end of the fight.

The air around them quivered, pulsed. He felt trapped and liberated in turn by the containment. *Please*, he silently begged, *please touch me*.

She eased in, a strand of her hair falling forward to caress his cheek. Lifting it away, her finger drifted along his jaw, his ear, his eyebrow, as if she sought to memorize his features. Flickers of light exploded behind his eyelids, sensation in his chest.

Finally, her mouth brushed his.

Magic.

Tentative, curious, seeking magic.

Her bottom lip was plump, the top slender. Both as smooth as the inside of a daisy's petal. Her nose bumped his as she shifted for purchase, tilting her head to seek a fit he wasn't helping her find. Not yet. Her lips opened, her breath a scalding rush that had him giving up hope that he could supervise his arousal. Her fingers clenched around his shoulder as her tongue slicked once across his sealed lips, testing him. Begging admittance.

He gripped the bench hard enough to rend wood and prayed, hoping to wait her out. Just this once. Another minute, two tops. The things he would do when he finally got his hands on her raced through his mind like his horse at Epsom. Wild, impassioned. Chaos of the most pleasurable kind filled his being.

She explored the corners of his mouth, her hand skimming the curve of his shoulder to cup his cheek. Slanting his head at her direction. Discovering him as he longed to discover her while he kept himself still as stone. This was a demanding lesson in seduction when he was unsure who was seducing whom. A spiral of need pierced every defense he'd ever built against her, a trail of *want* shadowing her touch.

She drew her fingertips across his jaw, her tongue again seeking to engage his in play. He swayed slightly in desperate yearning. *Ah*, the agony. The ecstasy.

He could die from this, and he hadn't even kissed her yet.

After another valiant effort to engage, she pulled away, taking her heat and the wonder of her caresses with her. "Is this a jest to you? You're not participating. It's like I'm kissing a statue." Although her breaths weren't spilling free in fast little puffs because she was kissing stone.

He maintained a straight face with painstaking effort. Lifted his lids to find her warily studying him. His vision was spotting at the edges from the exhilaration claiming him. Maybe the gentlemanly thing to do would be to tell her how she was affecting him. "Then you do, in fact, admit you need me for something."

Her cheeks fired, her teeth coming together in a snap. "You *cad*!" She went to rise. Her elbow hit his shoulder when she yanked her skirt from beneath his hip, where it had conveniently wedged. "You smug bounder! Preening coxcomb! I knew I shouldn't have trusted a blue-blooded, misfit duke!"

With a grin, he looped his arm around her waist to keep her from storming away. Pulling her so close, he could see himself reflected in her pupils. He could envision chasing her down the many hallways in this fortress. And for her kisses, he would chase. "Oh no, Miss Astley, not yet." When her incensed gaze met his, he let loose the laugh he could no longer contain. "It's no jest. But I have rules. You were forthright about yours, and I agreed. Hear me out."

"Bother your rules!" She wrenched back, almost tumbling off the bench. "Your Grace, quit smiling this minute, or I don't know what I might do. The *ton* thinks you have a fearsome temper, well, wait until they see mine! We fight dirty in the stews."

Blimey, this was fun. When had he had this much fun without so much as a stitch of clothing hitting the floor? He spread his palm across her lower back to steady her, taking subtle possession. "You see, my darling heiress, I seek a kiss that says everything. The kiss to end all kisses. The kiss of the century. Why run the race if you're not trying to win? That's my rule. Or rather, my quest. That we don't limit ourselves."

With his free hand, Roan cradled her jaw, tilting her head until her gaze pierced his. She stilled with the effort, like a feather coming to rest on a feather coverlet. "I want to show you that the heat we generate is enough to make anyone, even you, believe in the power of desire. What we do with it is up to us, I suppose."

Because he knew more than he was telling her. In his gut, certain, clear-cut. Her pleasure would be his. And his hers. If they ever made love, it wouldn't be separate worlds barely joining as it often was. Detached intimacy, he'd come to think of it. The most desolate feeling was the seconds after, staring at an unfamiliar ceiling while the scent of someone you didn't love clung to your skin. Those moments brought satiation but also a wealth of loneliness.

With Helena, he wanted the experience to be different.

"Yes?" he asked, needing her agreement on the *one* thing she couldn't do on her bloody own.

She pursed her lips, considering. Then reached to trace the scar on his, from a punch he'd not ducked at the Rose and Thorn years ago. He'd tell her if she asked. "If I say I'll try for a kiss that says everything, you'll kiss me back then? Since I suppose I do"—she sighed, stubborn to the studs—"need you for this piece."

His breath ceased, dizzying, yearning, *want* coursing through his veins. "I will." Those two words meant more than they should, suggestive of a much more serious union.

From the clever turn of those lips, he noted that she was set on adding rules to the agenda. More abject steadfastness when he wanted her warm and willing, layered over him like a velvet cloak. More flirting, waiting, wondering, while his cock felt ready to rip through his trouser close. He was so affected by her with only a single kiss he'd nonchalantly participated in passing between them.

Taking advantage of her breathless pause and his violent craving, he captured her lips, his demand conveyed in his touch. A kiss that at the start reminded him of his first behind a hedge in Regent's Park with the daughter of his riding instructor. Awkward and fucking *necessary*. A fleeting touch meant to entice, not intimidate. But one with power behind it.

Although now, he had leagues of experience. His intent was fully manageable. Cool, calm, collected purpose. Practiced prowess. The ability to *seduce*.

Until the kiss ignited like a fresh wick dipped into a flame and raced away from him.

Just before Helena closed her eyes, Roan caught arousal spilling into them like cream into oolong tea. A feeling rose in him, one unfamiliar but welcome. An emotion strong enough to cause his heart to flutter, his breath to snag. The sensation was sharper than humble yearning, more potent than mere lust.

It scared him to death even as he embraced it.

Denying his helplessness, a skill he excelled at, he slid his hand up her jaw, skimmed her ear, the nape of her neck. Then turned around and demanded things he shouldn't. "I want the girl on the shore," he whispered against her lips. "Show me."

Her head dropped back as a silken breath snuck between them. "Why?"

He took her plump bottom lip between his teeth and sucked gently, the whimper rising from her throat, unleashing his hunger. "Because I've never been able to forget her."

Helena trembled and, after a charged silence, acquiesced. Easing her lips apart, her stunned sigh filled his mouth and traveled in a dead drop to his toes. Then her tongue, shyly, met his. Teased, tormented, battled. His groan was raw, exposing how little control he held. Sensation and awareness circling, shutting out light, sound, thought. She moved in readily after her initial reluctance, melting into the kiss. Into his body. Locking in the fit she'd sought before.

He gave. Challenged. Dared.

As he could in the boxing ring. He asked of her what he would of anyone he admired.

To show him the *truth*.

He knew some truths without her telling. She'd been kissed. And something in her eyes said it had been more. He didn't own her, but he wanted to. The thought of anyone touching her made Roan wish to put his fist through a wall. His momentary fit of masculine pique transferred into the kiss, into his need. His fingertips pressed into her scalp as he slanted her head. No more playing, no more tempting. Done, done, *done*.

The honeyed taste of her flowed through him, his skin sparking everywhere they touched until he was restless with yearning, his hands roaming her body. He sought to gain control but only lost himself further. She followed when he wasn't sure she should, mimicking his moves until, suddenly, they created their own harmony. She liked his tongue engaged in play. Hard play. His hand on her hip, the side of her breast. The kiss deep, urgent, then soft again. She whimpered in frustration and bumped him back on the bench, seeking to mold herself to him but unable to.

"This," he panted against her lips.

Yanking her skirt high, he lifted her leg over the bench, over his thigh, and pressed their bodies together, traveling into a carnal kingdom, no simple kiss, this one. Her sex was hot against his, liquid, he imagined. The thought of it, of plunging into her, her sheath tightening around him as she whispered her release into his ear erased any design he'd had to control this. This was a primal merging, passionate, sensual, animalistic, as the act often was.

He'd never experienced such heat in the moments before, never envisioned the opening act of a sexual play as the most pleasurable. Enough to live on, *love* by.

There, he thought raggedly when they began to move as they would when he lay atop her, thrusting, surging, creating a faltering union around wadded muslin and silk, *this is what I meant. This is real.*

Chemistry. Passion. *Desire.*

Their exchange grew into a mad pleasure grab, the walls between them disintegrating until their objections lay like forgotten rubble of the past at their feet. Roan lost all manner of imagined skill while giving everything he had to offer. At his most vulnerable, but he dove in headfirst, anyway. Impulsive fool. He felt sucked into her vortex, the moment filled with astoundingly basic perceptions that overwhelmed in sum. The weight of her head in his hand, her luscious hair tangling around his fingers as they spasmed with ecstasy. Her thigh looped over his, a gentle, deadly weight. Moist lips. Questing tongue. Inquiring fingers.

She twisted her hand in his hair and tugged lightly, sending a river of fire down his spine. Tenderly rough play that he returned. Reason slipped away sooner than he'd anticipated. Sooner than it ever had over a straightforward kiss that was turning out to be the least straightforward thing he'd ever experienced.

Moving faster than he should have, wanting more and deciding that was the correct wish, he slid his hand to the curve of her lower back, bringing her solidly against his chest, where she melted, boneless. No fight left in her. No teasing left in him. Her breasts were a plump intrusion, a carnal charm. She was a luminous surprise, soft and eager when the woman he knew from the docks was not. In perfect agreement with the exacting planes of his mind and his body. Because they were clothed—praise the heavens for small favors lest he forfeit all control—perhaps she didn't quite understand how she was affecting him. But he was achingly hard, his heartbeat drumming in time with the blood flow to his cock.

Too much, too soon, Ro, he thought frantically as he felt her stiffen.

She broke free, pressed her forehead to his, her ragged pant drawing him in as if she were the lone puddle of water in the Sahara. Then, dragging her cheek down his, she released another sleek purr that nearly unraveled him. Her hands danced over him, chest, stomach, back. Shoulders, neck, cheeks. Everywhere she touched, she left heat and a quivering privation.

His fingers crawled into her silken strands, sending hairpins to scatter about them like pebbles. Her chignon, sad to begin with, hit her shoulder with a thump and rolled over her breast. He tilted her head to look into her eyes. He didn't mind lying to closed ones but preferred to tell the truth to open.

"I'm a scamp like you, Hellie. A loosely bred man of noble blood and the streets. Until my rise, I was living not that far from those precious docks of yours. The only home my father could afford by that time because drink and *vingt-et-un* took the rest." He coasted his hand up her back, memorizing each bump in her spine. Memorizing the image of her sitting there in the twilight of his beloved music room, open to him for the first time.

"Here"—he glanced down at where their bodies met—"we *are* no different. Soft and hard, light and darkness. A natural balance. That chemistry I told you about. There are no dukedoms, no fleets of ships sailing the high seas. No sisters in need of guidance, no flock of chirping society mavens hawking our every move. There is merely this moment. Heat, wonder, desire. Years of curiosity resolved organically. Nature rules this space. You and I rule this space."

She bounced on the toes of the slipper still grounded on the floor and pressed her body to his from chest to hip, looping her arms around his neck.

Accepting his dare. Agreeing to his offer.

Consenting to science. Blossoming like a flower before him.

Complying, he framed her face with his hands and seized her lips hungrily, offering himself in a way he wished she knew he never had before. She made a sound, an anguished sigh of pleasure, one he wanted to hear next when he slid inside her. If she ever granted him that privilege.

She blurred the lines, doing the unexpected. Saying yes when he thought it would be no. Pulling him in, nudging his cock with her warm core, again and again, until they were gasping, drinking each other like wine. Lost. Miming acts best achieved horizontally. The challenge of that close-but-not-quite contact only drove his need higher.

A kiss to end all kisses. A kiss that said everything.

A kiss that was *more* than a kiss.

He touched her like he would a courtesan while holding her as gently as the rarest fossil. There was nothing playful about it. Nothing introductory, a chance to discover what the other liked. This was war —and it was *fantastic*. They bypassed overtures, moving from A to Q on the way to Z. The kind of embrace one dreamed of experiencing at least once.

Tongues meeting, dueling. Mouths shifting, slanting. Bodies bumping, grinding. Hands on a quest for pleasure. Her waist, her ribs, the plump curve of her breast. The nape of her neck, her jaw, her cheek. The effort merely to follow along, gone. He wondered what she desired him to do; he wanted to *ask*, but his thirst was too extreme. His demand was too colossal. Hunger. Possession. He heard himself groan and wondered at his unleashing—wondered at her awakening.

Roan knew he was in deep when he went to pick her up and carry her to the sofa—fully intent on ruining them both in a room with an open door. He would bolt it shut, *nail* it shut if the lock was broken. He realized he was destroyed when he imagined how her nipples were going to taste when he sucked the hardened peaks between his lips. When he realized her heartbeat had somehow transferred itself to him. Mad thumps reverberated through him, ending in a pulse between his thighs.

She was in his lap *fully* before he made a move to bring her there. Before he'd had a chance to toss her over his shoulder and carry her away. Ingenious chit, she yanked up the other side of her skirt and climbed right there like a cat, curling her legs around his waist. Bumping his hip into the pianoforte in her enthusiasm. He wanted to say no, push her back, deny what felt like a gift. Should say no, certainly. Protect her reputation and his heart. But he was unable to when a window had opened, and she'd stepped into his soul.

When she'd let him in, after leaving him standing outside her world for ten years.

Going with her approach, he took her firm, round bottom in his hands, working them against each other until there was nothing left to do except tear her clothes off and sink inside her. When her sex was separated from his by only a few paltry layers. When she seemed to desire him—*finally!*—as much as he desired her.

When they seemed, from this supremely successful experiment, to have been made for each other. Science winning the day. His favorite kind of victory.

This reasoning screamed *yes* to him and, frankly, his cock. Which had moments ago begun to take over. And he hadn't made a move to stop it. Because he'd never, never in his *life*, had a kiss compare. If he lost his mind to the process, who on earth wouldn't?

After all, he'd been obsessed with this woman for years. Luckily had come to find out, atop the sturdiest pianoforte bench in England, that it was for a good reason.

Obviously, fate intervened in its merciless way.

When a recently hired footman and a giggling maid who'd been looking for a place to share a quick tumble stumbled in and found the Duke of Leighton's hands full of Lady Hell.

And Lady Hell's hands equally full of him.

Chapter Nine

The Duke of Leighton was a trickster. Cannier than he looked with those dazzling smiles he passed out like sweets. The teasing words and handsome façade added up to a big bundle of trouble. Trouble she did not wish to be in.

Aristocrats could not, she'd always known, be trusted. He'd dared her while acting like she could *possibly* win.

It had been a kiss that said everything. A kiss to end all kisses.

And he'd bloody well known it would be, the swindler.

Transformative. Changing her even as she'd begged her body not to betray her. Turning her inside-out. Into a wanton, gasping, clinging, hungry woman she didn't recognize.

Regrettably, her faithless body knew what it had been after. Him. Always, always *him*.

Helena knocked aside the drape and gazed upon a Hertfordshire morning that properly exhibited the contradictions of the past twelve hours. A sky layered with blustery storm clouds, rays of sunlight piercing them to leak like wine across the frosty lawn. Dismal and gorgeous all at once. Ponderous and frothy. Light and dark, as a starving man had recently told her. Her thoughts were the same, careening between elation and disaster.

Elation at finally feeling. Knowing. *Wanting*.

Disaster because the source of her want was a blasted, damned duke. The most aggravating one in England.

"If it's the tedious discussion of fossils that is making you hesitate, which we understand, we can place a note in the marriage contract that Roan limit this to once a week. At dinner. One half-hour maximum."

Helena released a pent sigh and turned. Because she had to face this. And soon. No Astley had ever quit during a battle. Not one, and she would not be the start.

She perched her bottom on the window ledge, one wide enough to invite both Georgie, the Duchess of Markham, and Hildy Streeter to sit with her, and gazed at the women who'd been her constant, or near, companions since waking this morning. The gracious partners of the Duchess Society were helping her determine the best path to take in light of carnal catastrophe—and possibly making sure she didn't leap from the highest turret she could locate in despair. She hadn't yet *seen* a turret, but there had to be one somewhere. They'd shown up with tea and pastries, assisted with her gown, then ushered her down the domestic's staircase to the ramshackle salon Mrs. Meekins had situated her in but a day ago with the efficiency of a military patrol.

Guards with a mission.

Dazed, she let them commandeer her. When she'd never been dazed in twenty-eight years, not truly, not even after the disastrous night with the baron.

They'd had another desk brought in by two footmen who tried, but failed, to avoid glancing Helena's way. Georgie was sitting at one, Hildy the other. Facing each other like knights set to joust at any moment. Every effort was made—aside from strategic placement of desks, heated whispers, a flask that was passed around once—to have this appear a typical December morning in the country instead of the solution to a catastrophe. Roaring fire. Jam tartlets. Slices of rum cake filling the air with the tangy scent of nutmeg and cinnamon.

But across the room, a skirmish was being prepared for. From two battered satchels, the Duchess Society duo unpacked folios, foolscap, and various documents they'd scattered across every available surface while talking in a secret language Helena didn't have the capacity to try to comprehend.

They were talking about her future. Theo's future. The seventh Duke of Leighton, Marquess of Rothesay, Earl of Holton's future.

Helena simply could not grasp, although of course, she could grasp, she just didn't want to, that her life was shifting in a... pressing... *instant*.

"It's the fossils," Georgie whispered to Hildy. "I don't blame her."

Helena dragged the toe of her slipper mulishly through a cache of prisms thrown from a chandelier that had at some time in the past made its way to this room. The one spot of elegance amongst the neglect. It was a room fit for her in every way.

She couldn't express it, not yet, perhaps not ever, but she liked when His Grace—Leighton—*Roan*—talked about fossils. His deep, dreamy voice could lull her into a coma. Then, too, the spark in his eyes when he spoke of his passion for antiquities tilted her tummy and weakened her knees.

So, it wasn't paleontology she was objecting to.

Maybe it was his kisses. They were as subtle as a battering ram.

The kisses had certainly lulled her—into making the gravest error in judgment in her life. But ah, *heaven*, could the man kiss. She'd climbed him like an oak, settled effortlessly on his lap, and proceeded to caress every part of his body within reach. The parts she couldn't reach, she'd merely buffed like one would a silver teapot. He'd tasted amazing and kissed like someone born to the venture. His body was hard, and she did mean *hard*, whereas hers was soft. He'd groaned and quivered like he was a bow she'd plucked.

It had, his undoing, *undone*.

She'd stepped outside herself in his music room. Been seduced while *seducing*.

Who *was* that woman?

"With the, um, situation being what it is, the compromising way you were found, we assumed this part of your relationship could be counted as a positive. An enticement for the marriage, as it were.

Attraction cannot be denied." A delicate cough, a teacup being placed gently in a saucer. "When it cannot be denied. I've been there, I know."

This scant morsel of wisdom came from Georgie, who Helena had to remember preferred *not* to be called Your Grace. A woman who gazed at her husband like she wanted to lead him by his pristine cravat into the nearest available chamber at any hour of the day.

Her word on attraction was, therefore, good.

Helena squirmed on the ledge. Kicked her feet together. Reached to adjust spectacles that were sitting in her bedchamber. Should she tell them she could still smell the Duke of Leighton on her fingertips? On the hands she'd plunged into his hair and tugged as she rode him like she rode her mare, Aldous, along Rotten Row? Glancing at their concerned faces, she thought not.

The memory of touching him, being *touched* by him, stung her senses and her skin, blowing dust from corners long abandoned. Pebbling her nipples and making her thighs quiver, right there in a room where he wasn't. So, he didn't even have to be present to do this to her.

That's what his damned kiss had gotten her.

For a moment in that music room, it was as if he'd opened a curtain and let light pour in. Ardor and a vital, verifying sense of *rightness* she was clinging to in this sea of uncertainty.

Her body knew even if her mind did not.

"He wants what's best for you. And Theodosia," Hildy added in the event Helena didn't understand that being caught in a duke's lap by an aroused footman and a giggling scullery maid, neither of whom had particularly tenured allegiances with their employer, wasn't merely an issue for her but one for her sister. News traveled from below stairs faster than it did by coach. Should Helena not make the proper decision and agree to marry the duke straightaway, the reputations of multiple people would be at stake.

His whisper as she'd rushed from the room the night before fluttered like a heartbeat through her.

Marry me, Hellie.

"He wants too much," she said, appalled to find herself admitting what she'd known since Lyme Regis. Even if she'd lied to herself about it. His gaze had always been full of possession when she wasn't a woman to be possessed. The Duke of Leighton wanted to mine her secrets. Pick her apart like pieces of his pocket watch. Study her like he did his dreary, dried-up fossils.

She, in turn, wanted to make love to him until they were breathless. Until he begged. Which he'd been on the cusp of last night, she guessed.

She wanted his body and the pleasure he could bring her and was afraid that after that, she'd want his heart. Need him in some small measure that would be out of step with her life.

She'd never needed anyone, without suffering anything but disappointment.

Helena glanced up from her study of her slippers. She admired what she knew of Hildy and Georgie. Of the Duchess Society. She mostly admired that men in society were terrified of them. Surprisingly, they were married but independent. Scandalously, especially for a duchess, they *worked*. They expressed opinions that differed from their husbands. She'd seen it at dinner. Multiple times. And their husbands still loved them. They could be friends, perhaps. Someday. When she didn't have many, almost any, friends. But Helena didn't like being pressed into a corner. Even ones she'd directed herself to.

"I want it in writing that Astley Shipping remains in my name, under my control. I won't negotiate this point. I'm not giving up my business. My work." She picked at a thread on her sleeve and fidgeted on the ledge, a chill from the blustery weather outside snaking through a crack in the casing and dancing along her skin. "I'd like you to continue, the Duchess Society that is, to work with Theo. And me."

She yanked on the thread, dismayed to discover that the damage grew with each pull. "I cannot manage a household of this size. Domestics of the number Leighton employs. My father was a sailor, my mother equally baseborn. I'm unqualified for this position. I don't know how to be a duchess, how to—"

Georgie dropped to her knees before Helena and grasped her hand, halting her anxious tirade. "I'm willing to train you in the proper comportment of duchesses, Miss Astley. It's really much easier than running a shipping company, this I promise. For what it's worth, I'm unfit for the position as well, but I love the duke that the position came with, so I endure."

I don't love Roan, she wanted to tell them. *I desire him.* Very different circumstances. Objectives, expectations. Everyone knew desire faded.

Georgie tilted her head, her smile radiant. As if she knew what Helena wanted to say but didn't quite believe her. "Trust me. Trust Hildy. And maybe you should, possibly, go with your gut and trust him."

Chapter Ten

Where an Heiress Seeks Out Her Future

Helena located Roan not a half-hour later in the music room —dear heaven, could he find another space to inhabit? His long body was stretched out on the sofa she'd considered dragging him to the night before, his arm thrown over his eyes, his chest rising and falling in a steady, bottomless rhythm.

Her life was crumbling, revolving like a top across glossy marble, and he was sleeping. Napping. Like a baby.

Men.

She made enough noise to wake him, settling herself into the scuffed armchair that didn't look like much but felt like sinking into a warm crumpet. Rejecting the notion to drop her head back and close her eyes, join his slumber, she instead let her gaze wander. His face was chiseled. And beautiful. His hair was overlong. And gorgeous. Clothing fit him well, highlighting a body she wanted atop her, beneath her, behind her. She knew the ways, at least some of them. She should sleep, not sit there salivating over a duke. She'd gotten little after arriving in her chamber last night, turned inside-out from being kissed to within an inch of her life. Kissed as she'd always wanted to be, damn him.

Taking the dare, then being forced to pay for it.

Didn't that just figure?

The door behind her opened with a creak. Helena turned to find a ginger-haired maid, duster in her hand, a distracted smile on her face, inching into the room. Helena gave her a fierce look and shooed her away, unsure if she made an effort to keep the prince from waking or preserve her moment of sanity.

"You realize you're already halfway to duchess in tone and confidence, don't you?" Roan asked sleepily from the sofa. He followed this inane question with a yawn. "You had the poor girl scampering from the room like a mongrel who'd been kicked." He reversed the position of his booted feet with a vigorous stretch she couldn't help but record with a ravenous gaze. *Oh*, the cad knew what he was doing to her. "Impressive."

Pleating her skirt between her fingers, she tried unsuccessfully to erase the erotic images roaring through her mind. His eyes had turned a jet shade last night, near to black, highlighting tiny amber specks swimming through the green. Helena wondered how many other women in London knew about that change—then hated herself for thinking it. What did she care what he'd done and with whom? A hundred, at least, if you believed the gossips rags.

"I don't know how you can be so cavalier after the mess we've created, Your Grace. We weren't supposed to break any rules. Remember your grand plan to not break any rules?" She exhaled raggedly. "You can't seem to help yourself, and sadly, in this instance, neither could I."

He lifted his arm, his cunning gaze meeting hers. Nothing warm about those eyes at the moment. "Don't you understand how I can be so cavalier? Truly? This conversation has been years in the making, sweetheart."

She swallowed down a dry throat. Blew out another breath. Pressed her feet flat to the rug, straightened her spine. The room smelled pleasantly of woodsmoke and man. *This* man. She wanted to bathe in his scent. Walk over to his beaten sofa and climb right on him. Prove if last night was an apparition. When she didn't think it was.

"I didn't plan this," he stated and let his arm float back atop his eyes. "In case you're wondering. I got carried away on those marvelous lips of yours."

"But you're not unhappy about it either," she said, the lips under discussion tingling like he'd stroked his tongue across them.

He laughed faintly, his chest rising with the gust. His body was a treasure. Hard and lean and long. Muscle and bone covered with skin two shades darker than hers. As if he'd sat in the sun too long, but instead of getting pasty and red like most people in this country, he'd toasted a lovely shade of caramel. It made her wonder who in his family he'd inherited such luster from. It was positively common, and she loved it.

"Why are you laughing?" she snapped.

"You're unhappy enough for both of us. So, I'm taking the other path."

Helena settled back, studying him because his eyes were closed, and she could. If he became her husband, she could look at him anytime she desired. Kiss him, touch him. *More.* It would be her right. See him naked, even. Take a bath with him. She'd read that was done. Eat breakfast in bed without a stitch of clothing on. Lick every part of his body if she wanted to. Make love in a carriage. In her warehouse. On one of her ships.

She could think of a hundred places, actually.

But they'd be forced to talk as well. Manage estates and businesses and a family while sidestepping stubborn tendencies and combative natures. They didn't call him the Defiant Duke for nothing. When Lady Hell wasn't much better. She grimaced. The moniker suited her, much to his rotten luck.

But so did his.

He routinely did reckless things to place himself in the scandal sheets, which she did not. He smiled often, laughed easily. Got angry as quickly as she did, if not quicker. Was a rake, although they were supposed to make the best husbands. Had a fierce intellect, although he hid it well. Was honorable but cut corners when it suited him.

There *were* advantages. He was compassionate. He liked children, wanted children.

However, when she'd imagined marriage, she'd pictured a man with broad shoulders and a tiny brain. A man who'd go to work on the docks and leave her be.

But mostly, she'd imagined herself alone.

"Are you finished detailing the long list of 'why not's' about me?"

Helena blinked to find she'd closed her eyes, and Roan had opened his. Even pulled himself to a lazy sit, his boots resting on a table that looked lousy enough to house them, his arms crossed in what could be termed a defensive pose. She didn't want to spark his temper but was willing to handle it if she did. "I'm not a virgin. So you know. If being untouched is required for the duchess bit."

His fingers clenched where they circled his biceps, his only tell. After a silence that shimmered like a rising sun, he dropped his hands to his knees and shoved to his feet. "Brandy or whiskey, Miss Astley?" He strode across the music room, dodging the pianoforte that had been the setting of her doom and a harp of some age, heading for a mahogany sideboard in the far corner.

"Whiskey. If it's good."

"It's mine. Streeter and Macauley's." He saluted her with the bottle, his mood uncertain. "So, it's good."

She'd heard through the liquor channels that it was excellent but kept this comment to herself. He was vain enough, without hearing how excellent his whiskey and his kisses were.

Roan came back with two tumblers, a generous pour in each, and it was upon this review that she noticed the lines of strain on his face. His jaw was whiskered, his eyes bloodshot. His cheeks were leeching a touch of their normal bronzed splendor. He extended her glass with a hand that trembled. His vulnerability plucked her heartstrings, made air press out of her lungs until they were flat—and *she* was dizzy and breathless. She didn't want to feel anything for the Duke of Leighton. Apart from lust. Lust she could handle. Perhaps. Anything else, anything more substantial, she had no clue how to manage.

But there it was. Fondness creeping like ivy across brick. Creating cracks in what had been a solid foundation of rebuke.

She took the tumbler and a polite taste. Hummed low in her throat when the whiskey hit her tongue. It *was* excellent—and she knew quality. After all, she shipped the best. "I'm sorry to blurt that out. About my past. How like a girl from the docks. I simply didn't want there to be any surprises. You buying what you think is a thoroughbred only to find it's a lame nag. If this for any reason makes you rethink our situation, I understand." Admission made, she shrugged and glanced down. *Bother.* This was a dreadful enough speech to show the man she'd never be duchess material.

The sofa cushions whooshed as he collapsed upon them. "Rethink the proposal I was offering when you ran out of here last night, you mean?" When she didn't reply, he sighed, his boots shifting in and out of view. "Helena, look at me."

His silky tone sent a flush chasing over her skin. She liked his voice. And the imperious way he spoke to her on occasion. No one else in her life dared.

What would that commanding tone be like in bed?

After a flustered moment where her thighs had gone quivery, buttery soft again, she looked up to find his smile rueful, tender. "You're far from a lame nag, sweetheart. We're both adults. Or half the time, I try to be. If you had a relationship—" Taking a drink, he searched about for something to cast his gaze upon. A dreadful painting of the English countryside. A gilt clock on the mantelpiece. The faded carpet beneath their feet. Finally, a profound examination of his whiskey.

"Without my permission, I'm drawn to you. I didn't ask for it, but it's been the case since the first time I saw you on the shore in Lyme Regis. We both know this. I haven't made a great effort at hiding it with my tomfoolery and sophomoric games. I want you. And I need a duchess. It's also true that I'm possessive and known for my temper, so maybe *you* should rethink our situation. But if you agree, if we marry, I'll take you in every way you'll have me. Including your past, this man you loved—"

Her un-duchess-like bark of laughter cut him off midstream. "*Love?* Oh, Leighton, no. It was only once. And it was horrid. I'd known him for years. He was safe. One of your kind. Calm, gentle. At least until then. I was curious, and I thought he was the answer."

Roan stilled, his glass suspended. "Until."

"*Until.* He was a business partner of my father's. A known entity." Helena's gaze tracked Roan as he sipped, tossed it back actually, his throat working as he swallowed. "He'd been hounding me, for lack of a gentler way to put it, since I was sixteen. My father had just died. I was lonely. There was wine. More than I was accustomed to. I said yes after a fashion. End of story." She rolled her glass between her palms, wondering what else there could be to say when he looked like he wanted more. When he looked angry. "I make my own decisions, unlike society chits, one of whom you *should* marry although it seems as if you've decided on me. The pianoforte bench proving to be a horrid chaperone."

"You were seduced, Hellie. Taken advantage of. Mistreated. I may be many things, but I've never exploited innocence. Except my own." He gestured to her with his glass, a wrinkle forming between his brows. "What did you mean by 'my kind'?"

"Drat," she whispered, realizing she'd added that to the account.

"*Who?*" he asked, the word dropping like a stone down a well. Deliberately, his gaze met hers over the rim of his glass. His half-lidded study brought back the feel of his hands on her body, his teeth nipping her bottom lip. He'd looked entranced then too.

Don't start this relationship with lies, Helena. "Baron Fribourg."

Roan swore against the fist he dragged over his mouth. "He's seventy if he's a day."

"He looks younger."

"A young woman without protection. Well, you have it now." He slapped his glass to the table, his frown feral. "I'll kill him. What's another duel? Consider it done. Brawling with Macauley, Streeter, and Markham has gotten tedious, anyway. This task is better suited to my temperament. Defending my duchess. Sounds terrifying, doesn't it? I'm going to hunt him down when I return."

Helena laughed, amused when she should have been mortified. *My duchess.* Although it didn't appear that he was joking about killing the baron. "You most certainly will not, Roan. I can fight my own battles. I always have. Trust me when I say that Fribourg has come to rue the day. I've rejected every contract he's proposed while putting the word on the street that he doesn't pay his debts. No one on the docks wants to touch him. No one will if they wish to work with Astley Shipping again."

He paused, struck. His smile when it surfaced was blinding. "That's the first time you've called me Roan. I like my name on your lips. And I love your ruthlessness." Rising, he rounded the table and was kneeling at her feet before she could take another breath. Placing her glass aside, he seized her face in his hands and pressed her back into the chair, his lips covering hers.

The kiss caught her off guard but only for a moment. Then she dove in like she would a pond on a summer day. Complete and utter immersion. Her hands scaled his body to plunge into his glossy, silken hair. She slanted his head, perfecting the fit. He groaned and hauled her closer, murmuring raggedly what sounded like *yes*.

If she'd suspected the kiss last night was an aberration, it was not.

The same ripping tide swept over her, pulling her under. She burned for him, burned for *more*. When he dragged his lips along her jaw, she gasped for breath, her vision spotting at the edges. She'd never imagined a man could possess her—mind, body, and soul—in less than thirty seconds. He enjoyed other talents aside from paleontology and pianoforte.

"Care to climb on my lap again, darling Hellie? One of the ultimate thrills of my life was you clambering atop me on that bloody bench. Like a conquering mountaineer." He glanced back with an expression of parts wonder and mischief. "I feared the thing wouldn't hold, but hold us, it did."

Then he sealed her doom by winking. Sly, his smile crooked, that adorable little scar paling against his skin. He could be very charming. So, well, almost *sweet*. Near to perfect except for the catastrophes he embroiled himself in when she liked to stay belowground herself. Routinely, like clockwork, he invited trouble. Then there was a dukedom she wanted no part of. Still, the benefits, she couldn't forget the benefits. He was witty, intelligent, physically beautiful, arrogant.

The characteristics she would want in a man if she were searching for one, which she wasn't.

Her panic was swift. As unforeseen as a bolt of lightning on a sunny day. Breathless, she shoved him back. His hands, his lips, were twisting her thoughts into a knot. "I don't know how to need someone." *Love* someone. Although this she couldn't admit. It sounded foolish and dramatic. Unsophisticated, which she was.

Even if Roan had stated his desire for love, only the lower classes concerned themselves with such things. Society marriages were business. Everyone knew that. Why she had to muddy already muddied waters, she had no clue.

"Sweetheart, we're aligned on this point." He rocked back on his heels, hung his head, and released a fatigued breath. "Because I don't either."

"This is *want*, not love. What's happening between us. Want fades like a glorious sunset. Like the taste of peppermint on your tongue. Potent, then gone."

He dug around in his waistcoat pocket and rolled what he found inside between his fingers like a magician before drawing it out, his mood pensive. When he removed it, a stray sunbeam piercing the window caught the gemstone and threw a prism of color at their feet. His eyes when they met hers were as solemn as she'd ever seen them. He may not love her—but he wasn't taking the situation lightly. He flipped his hand over, palm up, silently asking for hers. After less than a second's hesitation, she gave it.

The ring he slipped on her finger was simple. A narrow gold band, a round sapphire. Fleur-de-lis emblems etched on either side of the stone. Nothing ornate, ostentatious, or worthy of a duchess. It looked old, solid, an enduring piece of jewelry.

She loved it. It suited her.

"It was my grandmother's. She left it to me when she passed. She was a very spirited woman. Wise, loud, cantankerous. You would have liked her." He touched the sapphire once, a quick tap, then got to his feet. Paced two steps away, muttered something too low for her to hear, then returned to her. "Her marriage was a love match, unlike my parent's. She married outside the *ton*, the best decision of her life, or she claimed. Her father was an earl of some repute, known for his irritability and his wisdom. She said I reminded her of him. I wanted you to have this because it means something. Or it did to someone long ago."

"Considering our unpredictable natures, we need all the luck we can get. This ring bound two souls who had significant life circumstances between them and bound them happily. The trinkets attached to the duchy, and there are some in a vault in the city, mean nothing. At least to me. If this is too plain, we can visit a jeweler in London. Streeter has one he recommends. Used to give his mistresses these overpriced tiaras as a parting gift. I've always gone the route of flowers and chocolates myself. Anyway, I simply thought—"

"I prefer this, Roan." Closing her fingers into a fist to hold the slightly too-large ring in place, she titled her hand, the sapphire sparking in the candlelight. "But a marriage of convenience doesn't require romance." She hated to tell him that mentioning former mistresses during the asking wasn't very romantic.

His jaw hardened, a muscle ticking off seconds like the clock on the hearth mantel. "I don't like that term. And frankly, I haven't found my need for you to be convenient."

She'd not found her hunger for him convenient, either. "When?"

"Soon. This week. The servants won't keep our indiscretion to themselves for long. A simple kiss, perhaps we could have contained, faux coitus on a pianoforte bench, now *that's* a losing premise. Rumors are likely already blazing a path through every drawing room in London. Luckily, this estate has the most charming medieval chapel in England. The stained-glass windows were created in the early 1600s if you have any care. All scenes from the Old Testament. Too, I've just given an eye-bleeding amount to the village vicar for an addition to his church. He'll come running the moment I call, I guarantee. I've already sent word about obtaining a special license. The issue could be concluded in a matter of days. We may forgo the banns."

"Wait, slow down. There are matters to discuss. The marital contracts, for one. Where we plan to live in London, two. Three, my sister. Four, the dowry amount being transferred to you."

He made an unnecessary trip to the hearth and back. Yanked his hand through his hair, leaving it jutting in adorable tufts about his head. "No."

She shoved to her feet, unable to quarrel while sitting. Or refusing to. "What do you mean 'no'?" *To having Theo live with them?* Her heart thumped once, hard.

He halted before her, suddenly, almost as if he'd thought to move past. Tipped her chin and captured her lips, giving her another of those miraculous kisses. It was as if he could not keep his hands from her. He tasted of berries and tea, sin and temptation, the past and the future swirling like mist to wrap around her and *enclose*. He didn't stop until she'd melted against him, her argument forgotten. A dirty fighter, her duke. A combat style she silently admired.

"I'm marrying you because I want you, not because you're wealthy as Croesus. And truthfully, because we've given ourselves no clear choice lest we ruin your reputation and slice a significant chunk out of mine. Pippa is going on the marriage mart again next season, and a scandal will do her no favors. Theo, the same. The *ton* won't forget simply because a few years have passed if that was your strategy.

"Never fear, we'll draw up contracts so woefully partial to you that the Duchess Society *and* my solicitors will weep. You have your business. I have mine. You have your money. I have a quarter of that if I'm lucky. The two never really need to meet. To mix." He licked her bottom lip, persuading in his cunning way. She knew she was being manipulated, but the manipulation was so adept she let it happen. "I don't want to own you, darling Hellie. And I'd rather not *be* owned."

"You make it sound easy when we're not easy people," she whispered, going up on her toes to better reach his mouth. *Lud*, he had muscular shoulders. No padding like most in the *ton*. As well sculpted as any bloke working the docks. "Our marriage will be a scandal. Your dukedom won't recover. They'll cut you on the street."

He moved to her earlobe, a part of her body he'd discovered made her knees tremble and rolled it between his teeth. "A scandal they'll forget as soon as another more enticing comes along. Give it a week. A month. No one cuts a duke. Or a duchess. Not for long."

"I'm obstinate. And you're... you're conceited."

"I prefer smug."

"You're impulsive, and I'm cautious. I'm used to doing things my way. But of course, you're used to the same. We're going to brawl more than you do at Gentleman Jackson's. Take verbal swings daily. Polish our swords on each other's skin."

He laughed softly, his breath dusting her neck. His lips covered the sensitive spot beneath her ear as his tongue danced out to taste. "My advice? Let's make love so often that we'll be too exhausted to fight. I'll be on my best behavior if I know you're going to reward me each night."

She choked on a breath. Did people make love this often? She could imagine wanting to touch Roan every day, but she was undoubtedly a depraved sort.

He tilted his head into a split of golden candlelight. His grin was devilish and only heightened her desire to have him. "Twice a week?"

A troubling thought sprang into her mind. "What about your other women?"

His grin fell away, and he took an abrupt step back, dropping his hands from her. "You think I would marry with the plan to compromise you?"

Uh-oh. He had a cross look on his face she'd unfortunately seen before. "Well, I, that is, no." She shrugged one shoulder. "Perhaps."

He retrieved the glass of whiskey he'd abandoned, lifted the beveled crystal to his lips, and drained it in one punch. "You know, Miss Astley, I've long recognized how little regard you hold for me. I should be unsurprised that you think I'm a double-dealer in every aspect of my life. It's not the best way to start a marriage, but at least you're honest."

"I don't think that." When she did, just a bit. Always had.

And they both knew it.

He snorted, popping his glass on the sideboard. "I'll let you know when I receive the license and secure the vicar's participation. Anyone can direct you to the chapel."

With this ducal decree delivered, His Grace, the Duke of Leighton, strolled nonchalantly from the room. Leaving his future duchess with the clear impression that she'd hurt his feelings.

Philippa Darlington wasn't afraid of anyone or anything.

She was a duke's *sister*. A lady. Or she would be when she learned how to tame her rebellious tendencies. Ladies were made, not born, according to the Duchess of Markham. There was still time to bake the cake, as their cook, Helga, liked to say.

I am refined. I am elegant. I will someday be a fully baked cake.

She repeated the mantras as she marched along the west wing corridor at a stroke after midnight, peeking into every vacant parlor without success. Shadows from the wall sconces leaped across her path, her rustling crimson skirt, the toes of her slippers. The hallway smelled of linseed oil and the blasted evergreens Mrs. Meekins had scattered everywhere. If anyone doubted what month it was, it was *December*.

Not afraid, Pippa.

Certainly not of that stunning male specimen she'd been told by a footman was hunkered down in this desolate section of the house. The stunning male specimen she needed to ask for help. She'd probably find him engaged in a midnight rendezvous much like her brother's, a bottle in one hand, a tittering maid in the other. Which made her want to find him more, not less. Which spelled trouble for all involved. Mostly her.

Her brother's reputation wasn't first-rate—but Xander Macauley's was utter rubbish.

Light-skirts, frays, dunks in the Thames. Complete disregard for the stock rules of society, rules she didn't want to live by *either*, but as a woman, she had absolutely no choice.

Of course, the bounder was in the last room she checked. A secreted game room she visited more often than anyone on the estate. She stumbled to a halt in the doorway, fascinated and cursing herself for it. The muted light, what little of it there was, painted a romantic portrait. Very Henry Raeburn-esque. Hearth fire and candlelight, the taunting scents of winter and man. He was alone, no chit in his lap. Bottle by his side, though he seemed immersed in a chess set, not drink. She slumped against the door ledge, her fingers curling into tight fists.

Oh, oh, oh, he was pleasing to look at. Why not enjoy the show? She was surely going to have to marry some hideous society fop, marquess this or viscount that, not a chap with broad shoulders and rugged features, eyes the color of stormy gray skies, hair the ripe hue of a chestnut, too long, too shaggy, well past the need for a proper cut, but perfect with that face. She even liked his lips, though they tilted toward hell every time he gazed at her.

Frowning, grimacing killjoy.

He didn't respect her any more than she respected him. He thought her a child, a nuisance, an annoyance. Which she mostly *was*, although she wanted to be more. She'd recently turned twenty-one, and the Duchess of Markham said the next year would be the year she blossomed, the year she left childhood behind. Left being an annoying nuisance behind.

Who cared what Xander Macauley thought, anyway? He was rude. Arrogant. Uncouth. A scoundrel. A rake even, should a commoner be able to be deemed a rake. Possibly that was reserved for the upper reaches, and this man wasn't upper *anything*. Raised in the stews to become a titan of industry, he was infamous. Mysterious, intriguing. Women tracked him down on the street like hungry hounds. Inviting him in the servant's entrance even as they barred him from their pointless balls, their silly musicales, their tedious poetry readings. She'd heard and read all about his escapades.

Captivated despite her misgivings, she chewed on her thumbnail, weighing her options. Everyone in the *ton* knew infamy was a curse. The supreme goal in life was to fit in, blend in, and become invisible, part of the paneling or the weave of an overpriced rug.

The elements of self that made a person matchless, an individual, were to be hidden. Ladies weren't built on the shoulders of scandal. No one wanted to know what made Philippa Darlington unique, except possibly her brother, and he didn't count.

"Are you going to skulk in the doorway all night, Blondie, or will you bother to tell me why you've run me to ground?"

Pippa smoothed her hand over her hair, as shimmering as a stalk of wheat the Earl of Dunford had told her before he tried to steal a kiss. Leading her to dump a fresh glass of ratafia on his head, further distancing herself from her objective of merging into paneling and posh carpets. "I'm coming in. I wasn't taking a stroll for my health."

He didn't glance up *or* stand when she entered, merely nudged his knight two squares to the right and dumped his chiseled chin in his fist to study the board. Not a wise move, she could tell him. Should have gone rook to QB5. She frowned, dusting her hand down her bodice. She'd changed into her most flattering day dress, subtle but horribly becoming, and he wasn't even going to lift his leaden gaze from his darned marble chess pieces to praise her effort?

"I'm waiting," he murmured and went to make another disastrous move. This bishop to KN5.

"Stop," she whispered in pain from his abysmal play. Going against the Duchess Society's teachings, she stepped closer. "You're botching your game completely. Try this. And this." She shifted pieces at lightning speed, the game playing out in her mind. "Moving pawns has weakened your defense. It's an elementary blunder. You can't retract those moves once you've made them. You must constantly attack. Like in life." She went through the steps again, so he could see the strategy, playing both sides of the board, pawn, rook, knight, king, king, queen. "Checkmate."

His hesitation was so slight that another person, one who wasn't assessing the situation closely, might have missed it. Her problem was, she assessed Xander Macauley much like she did a chessboard. *Every* time she got the opportunity. He definitely, *definitely*, recalibrated before he glanced at her. Reset his broad shoulders, his crossed legs. When he met her gaze, his eyes were lost to shadow and heavily hooded lids. His smile was flat, hiding the dimple that could flash at any moment in his left cheek and make a girl tremble right where she stood. "Your poor brother. That's all I can say."

"How insulting." She bumped the table with her hip and stumbled back. "As if I'm anyone's trouble but my own. I suppose I should pretend not to know how to play or pretend to play poorly to make some daft rotter feel confident about his cleverness. His wit. Beating a female at a rousing game of chess. Bravo! Another thing to hide about myself. I'll add it to the list. Build up every man in society on the bones of the more intelligent, more fearsome, women beneath them."

Her heart soared when his eyes expanded, his body coming out of its negligent slump. They were the color of the ash at the bottom of her bedchamber hearth this eve, light and luminous. A thousand shades of gray. She'd shocked him. For once! For once, he was actually *listening*.

"No one's asking you to hide. Not entirely."

When she went to argue, tell him exactly what being a duke's sister was like, that it meant hiding *everything*, he raised his hand, cutting her off. "If they're asking this of you, defy them. On your terms. Be true to yourself while quietly surviving this civilized muck you're embedded to your knees for life. Because at the end of the road, you're the only one you answer to. Fetching simple, innit? Fool them or, if you must, let them see you." He dropped his chin back to his fist. "Just know that being seen may not change a damned thing. Their acknowledgment isn't going to heal you, mark my words. Complete you. That's the quickest way to burn a hole in your belly, waiting for acceptance."

Fetching simple. My, she wished life was fetching simple. Maybe it was for *men*. And why did she have the sudden feeling Xander Macauley was talking about himself as much as he was talking about her.

He picked up his tumbler, gave it a leisurely twirl, then took a casual sip, eyeing her over the beveled rim. She would have exposed one of her secrets, and she did have one or two, to know what he was thinking. "Have a favor to ask of me by any chance, Little Darlington?"

Little Darlington. This she would press like a rose between the pages of her memory. "You're his friend, so I suppose I do."

Macauley's dusky brow winged high, the first hint of a smile tilting his lips. His dimple was going to pop at any second, she just knew it. She stilled in anticipation, as if she was waiting on a snowflake to tumble from the sky. "What's Leighton done this time?"

She sighed and reached to slide the rook two spaces to the right. They only had each other, she and Roan, and she wasn't going to let him circle the drain. Or go down it because of his perilous infatuation with an unsuitable but utterly charismatic heiress. A woman who watched her brother with equally sizzling but guarded glances. Pippa could protect him as well as he could protect her. *Better* than Helena Astley, who hadn't realized she was in love with him yet. "He's in the music room. Where almost no one goes. Except, from the gossip I've heard, Lady Hell."

Macauley balanced his glass on his belly, and Pippa tried very diligently to ignore how flat it was, his long body flowing from that chair like a lazy river. "Got caught mauling the chit on the pianoforte, am I right? Resourceful, the duke. I'm liking your brother more every day." His gaze drifted to the middle distance, a wistful expression twisting his features. A look of remembrance, the private smile following it, devastating.

The sting of jealousy caught her by surprise, constricting her chest until she was forced to rub her hand across her ribs to soothe it. Suddenly, she hated Xander Macauley, sprawled out there looking sated from a memory. Hated being a duke's sister, hated the *ton*, hated the stays digging into the underside of her breast. Hated the season she was going to be forced to endure. Already hated the man they'd try to attach her to.

"He's foxed, and the wedding is tomorrow morning. Someone who can manage him needs to get him to bed. His temper is smoldering like that fire you have going in the hearth, and the servants are hiding. I can't go knocking on the Duke of Markham or Tobias Streeter's doors after midnight. Do you see the way they look at their wives?" She bumped a pawn with her pinkie, a blush warming her cheeks. But she was going to say it, anyway. "Their children are asleep. God knows what the parents are up to."

His shout of laughter caught her like a rogue wave, nearly yanking her feet from beneath her. Looking up, she watched him curve into his amusement, arm snaking around that lean waist of his. She thanked the heavens her skirt covered her shaking knees. If he knew he affected her even one lick, he would never let it go.

"I'll double down on my sorrow wager for your brother. I can't wait until he unleashes you on these poor society sods next season. London will never be the same." He took a sluggish sip, his silvery gaze glowing. "I promise to line my birdcage with the broadsheets you splatter with ink. You're going to be passive entertainment for me, Little Darlington. When I'm always open to being entertained."

I was already unleashed, she wanted to tell him, *and the ratafia incident claimed the evening.* But she would not lower herself to his insolent level with an explanation that would sound ridiculous at best. Besides, he probably already knew about it.

"Are you going to help me or not? If not, I'll find someone else." Although she had no idea who else to ask. Her brother had three friends, one of them this acerbic rogue. And Macauley was the only friend *without* a besotted wife willing to snuggle at a moment's notice. Or more. She'd seen the hot glances between Tobias Streeter and Hildy, the Duke of Markham and Georgie, to prove it.

Hence, the lone man out's solitary chess game, a poignant portrait of country life.

She tapped her slippered toe on the carpet and gave him her most mature guise. "Well?"

Macauley blew out an indignant breath, his shoulders slumping. "Marriage is like an infection with you people. Everyone's contracting it. I'm afraid to touch Leighton, lest I catch it."

"Trust me," she murmured, "you'll never catch it."

He slid his glass to the table, his gaze going to his gleaming boots, which he smacked together once. Hard. "No, I won't catch it. Never, *ever.* That is why being in this room with a naïve but soon-to-be much sought-after chit is a risky thing indeed. Don't think because I break the rules, I don't know them."

Bother that, she thought. *As if you'd ever take advantage. As if you'd want to.* Pippa moved a pawn on the chessboard, mindless play now. A play of pique. "Roan wants this union. Wants Helena Astley, even if he doesn't realize it. Otherwise, I would have tried to talk him out of it. He does occasionally listen to me. And I love him to bits when he's not trying to control my life."

"Ah, *cor,* your brother's been after Lady Hell for years. Finally found the nerve to place himself firmly in her path." He rose with a stretch that unfolded divinely, a ripple down his long, lean frame. He was taller than she'd imagined up close like this. And smelled like a sliver of masculine heaven. Earthy and sweet all at once. "At least he went outside your horde to find her. A girl from the rookery, if you can factor it. If I wasn't so leery of him hooking himself to such a hellion, I'd be proud. I've heard she wears trousers in that warehouse."

Pippa slammed the knight to the board, her gaze going hot. "They're not *my* horde. They're not my anything." And she didn't want him thinking about her future sister-in-law in *britches*.

He circled her without so much as the edge of his sleeve grazing hers. "Blondie, you keep telling yourself that. Someday, you might begin to believe it."

"Arrogant rotter," she whispered, wondering if this were true, and they were her horde for life. Stuck with them like she was the speckle birthmark on her cheek.

"Reckless brat," he returned, his boot heels tapping out a jaunty rhythm as he strolled into the corridor. Away from her without a thought to remain. To him, she *was* a troublesome brat. He wasn't tempted, not at all. She had nothing with which to tempt a man like Xander Macauley.

Not yet. But someday...

Don't, her mind screamed. *Pippa, no.*

Despite good sense, she followed the impulse. Sealing her doom. His coat in hand, the plush velvet collar pressed to her nose, his incredible scent snaking through her before the clock on the mantel had registered another click. She stood like that for long enough to recall every word he'd spoken to her. His speech about her being herself. Advice that thawed her in places she'd not known were frozen. Horrifying if he suspected, which he didn't. Cocksure bounder. As if she'd ever tell him anything private.

One of her secrets? That she was attracted to him. A fierce, worrisome fascination that kept her up at night on any chosen day she happened to see him. Always at a distance, across a city street, in a shop, or bounding down the hallway after leaving her brother's study—but the experiences stuck like dung to her boot. Something that felt like *want* sending dull vibrations through her.

The wrong man. Too old. A commoner. A *rake*. Her brother's almost best friend.

No woman would be able to tame him—and she felt sorry for any woman who tried.

Unfortunately, his step was as hushed as a thief's. He *was* known as a smuggler, among his other diversions. His broad forearm extended into view without a word spoken. Without a whisper of her breath or his sounding in the silent chamber. "I believe that's mine."

Her world tilted, her shock such that her vision scrambled, presenting a watery, wretchedly romantic portrait. *Oh, oh, no.* She peeled her cheek from velvet to find Xander Macauley, with a frown worthy of utmost trepidation for the injured party, twisting his lips, his eyes gone the burnt color of turbulent emotions and recrimination.

She had no way to explain her actions. No way to describe her enchantment.

No way at all.

So she stared, unable to puncture the charged silence. Unable to think of one word to say. An excuse. An apology. An angry retort. Which was a first. Mesmerized by a muscle flexing along his jawline, his lips clenching until a pale ring formed around them. Something unknown to her but known to her body wrapped her in ethereal awareness. Recognition pranced along her skin, through her veins, and burst out into her chest.

It felt remarkably like *freedom*.

"Enough," he whispered breathlessly. *Breathlessly.* Took his coat in his slim-fingered fist and yanked it away from her. "Careful, Little Darlington, as you navigate these treacherous waters."

Without another word, he strode from the room, and this time, she knew he wasn't coming back.

Chapter Eleven

Where a Duchess Gets a Duke

The wedding ceremony was private and thankfully brief.

Roan's chapel was the most gorgeous religious dwelling Helena had ever seen. A massive marble altar surrounded by high pews in a glossy wood she guessed was oak. It befitted a duke, a king, a deity. The stained glass he'd casually mentioned taking up an entire wall and throwing a rain-streaked rainbow across the assembled participants. Hildy and Georgie had populated the chilled narrow space with a veritable floral hothouse that suitably masked the scent of molding pages and incense.

They'd gone with a wintry theme of ivory and ice blue, making for a lovelier ceremony than any Helena could have envisioned had she ever envisioned one. The vicar was gracious and enthusiastic, his heartfelt wishes for happiness and a long life with her beloved duke making her feel like a fraud. She'd pretended to have a megrim coming on when he started talking about children and rushed through the chapel's side entrance to gulp breaths of frigid air into her lungs.

Although, people committed this fraud every day of the week except Sundays. Marrying for reasons apart from love. She wasn't impractical. She knew a sound business decision when she saw one. Or rather, the corner she and Roan had painted themselves in offered few choices, as he'd unromantically acknowledged.

The only impediment this lovely, frosty December day one week before Christmas was the bridegroom.

Roan Darlington, seventh Duke of Leighton, Marquess of Rothesay, Earl of Holton, etcetera, had appeared at his wedding reeking faintly of whiskey and clearly unsteady on his feet. He and that hooligan Xander Macauley had stumbled in minutes before the nuptials, one holding the other up. She couldn't say who was in worse shape, straightening collars and cravats as if they'd come from the house at a dead run. Which she guessed they had.

The Duchess Society contingent had not been pleased, to say the least. She'd never seen such frightening expressions as the ones Hildy and Georgie had sent in his direction as he strolled down the aisle. If looks could kill, indeed.

It was unfair, a *curse*, that he appeared even more stunning partially undone.

Helena kept her temper in check only because she'd injured his feelings the evening prior. Turned his heartfelt, bumbling proposal into something it wasn't. For once, Roan hadn't been trying to manipulate her or charm her. Instead, he'd been honest about their situation, open about his attraction, the ring he'd presented beautiful and meaningful. A mistake, perhaps, but she'd been honest too, having no expectation that he would stay faithful.

A commitment that filled her with a multitude of emotions she was terrified to explore.

While she, of course, planned to be faithful. Truthfully, she'd never wanted another man. It wouldn't be hard to desire Roan with everything in her.

Which was *not* the treatment prescribed for a marriage of convenience.

Nerves and doubts aside, she'd stated her vows in a clear voice while gazing into those absurd green eyes of his, his hair damp from the snow, flakes clinging adorably to his lashes and curling the ends of his hair, realizing her life was changing in an instant.

The hot thrum in her veins told her she wanted him in the same famished way he wanted her.

This vow meant she could have him.

Duchess. The word tolled like the chapel's bell as she strolled arm in arm with her husband across the lawn, up the stairs, and into Leighton House, the oak door closing behind them a symbol of finality.

After a boisterous wedding breakfast in the formal dining hall, the layered white iced cake centering the banquet table marking the special day, the dazed bride and groom were allowed to depart. She and Roan had spoken little, and he'd dodged her examination, likely contrite about arriving at the ceremony in such a sad state.

While she found she wasn't vexed in the slightest—a pang of affection striking her every time she gazed at him. Coming to understand the man was having a startling effect on her.

Immediately upon entering the corridor outside the banquet hall, he took her hand in his, whispered, *hello duchess*, then paused. Flipped their linked fingers over and brought them close to his face. He did, in fact, she thought, need spectacles. "What's this?" he murmured and ran his thumb over the ring he'd given her.

Helena flushed, heat sweeping her face as she shifted from one confining formal slipper to the other. "It's a little large. The ring. So I used a length of muslin to hold it steady. My fingers are slender, like Elizabeth's were, you know, the gloves in your gallery."

He squinted and traced the strip of cloth. Even bloodshot eyes and slightly pallid cheeks couldn't ruin that smile. "What gloves?"

Dear heaven, she thought with a sputtered laugh. He really had inherited this pile and had no idea what was housed in it. "Never mind."

"We'll have a jeweler size it properly when we return to London. For now, come," he said and dragged her in the direction of the neglected west wing, superfine clinging to his broad shoulders, worsted gray wool to his long legs. Even without the best tailor in England outfitting him, when the best tailor *was*, he'd look glorious in any garment he chose to wear. Of this, she had no doubt.

Down the hallway and across the dimly lit gallery to the opposite wing, the wing a servant had told her was haunted, she followed the

Duke of Leighton, as she'd vowed to do for life not two hours earlier in his chapel. In *their* chapel.

Her breath scattered, sending a fierce exhalation from her lips that he glanced over his shoulder to catch the meaning of.

She shook her head. *No, nothing.* When her mind was full of everything.

She couldn't ignore the way his hand wrapped around hers was making her feel. Heart-hammering awareness. Inevitability. Urgency. Exultation.

He halted before the dingy parlor Mrs. Meekins had assigned to her and held his arm out, *entre.* Reluctantly letting go of his hand, she stepped into the room. Turned a leisurely, pleased circle. It was now a proper, very regal, very stately study. A masculine space, which she appreciated. Not a doily or watercolor in sight. "You've been busy."

He shuffled his feet, boyish and cavalier. Yanked on his sleeves, straightened his cravat, unnecessary tidying when his clothing was in ideal order.

Helena toured the parlor, stopping to trail her fingers across an escritoire that was at least two hundred years old. She was in the business of evaluating merchandise, and this was a valuable piece.

Roan scratched his chin with his shoulder, his gaze roaming the much-improved space. "The antiques in storage could fill another castle. The bookcases alone should have been sold years ago when I needed funds for the roof in the east wing. Anyway, they're lovely, and now they're here. It's horrendous how much furniture I found when I went digging. I need to contact an auctioneer immediately. Funnel those funds back into this monstrosity. The rest"—he shrugged charmingly—"was nothing more than an afternoon spent cleaning. The servants, not me that is. The new drapes I had to scramble to obtain. A rug switched from a vacant chamber on the floor above. Or two above that, I can't remember. This one's Savonnerie."

She dragged her slipper across it, bemused. She'd never received a present before. Except for the fossil Roan had given her at Lyme Regis. Her father had not seen the value in gift-giving, and everyone else in her life was paid to be there. "I see." She picked up an inkwell in the shape of a tortoise and held it into the candlelight. "Are you trying to tell me something?"

"I am. That I want you to have your own space where you can work. While giving Mrs. Meekins a warranted poke for selecting this dreadful room in the first place. I made sure she was in charge of the transformation. Consider it my wedding gift. And my grandmother's ring. I'm sure I'll think of something else wonderful if you give me time."

He dipped his head, his yawn coming out of nowhere. Covering his mouth with his fist, he smiled, then laughed behind it. "I'm sorry, I didn't get much sleep. I'm the rottenest bridegroom in the history of bridegrooms. You have my abject apologies. For the temper tantrum that precipitated it too. I don't like that you think badly of me, even when you *should*. When I've acted like an arse on multiple occasions and invited merciless condemnation by everyone in society. Macauley found me in a pitiful state last night and proceeded to make it worse. We plundered every liquor cabinet on the estate, each stop leveling out my ire. Mac is rattled by the marriages and accompanying children floating about in his life and is fleeing back to Town. Something about an urgent business issue when his angst has nothing to do with business. I couldn't get the truth out of him no matter how many drinks I poured."

Helena was suddenly incredibly grateful she had capable employees in London. Ones who raced to satisfy urgent requests. "I have something for you. It hasn't arrived, but it will. Shortly." She licked her lips, her heart starting to dance when his gaze focused on her mouth and held. "A wedding gift."

He moved farther into the room, halting to rest his bum on the high back of the settee, crossing his arms over his broad chest. For a split second, an expression of astonishment swept his face. With a tingle of recognition, she realized he'd never been given a gift either. "Do tell."

"You remember the piece I sold to William Thatcher Cole last year?"

Roan whistled softly and came off the settee. "The chondrichthyan from the Chalk of Sussex?"

She giggled behind the arm she brought up to hide it, understanding the depth of her dilemma. Goodness, Helena. *Giggling.* "I have no idea what it's called, Your Grace. I only acquired the antiquities because the Earl of Elderton had an imprudent night of gambling and had to sell off part of his collection to cover his debts. I donated everything to the British Museum if you care to visit. Second floor, near the back. Except for the one trinket. This unattractive hunk of granite with a fish of some sort embedded in it that I told you I sold to Cole."

Roan rocked back, dragging his hand across his jaw, his lips crooking endearingly. "You have a collection in the British Museum?"

Suddenly bashful, she trailed her pinkie across a scratch on the escritoire. "Someone has to, don't they? The other person trying to purchase them was a Russian count, a buyer known to break up collections and sell them willy-nilly to the museum paying the highest price. I didn't want the items to leave the country." With her fingertip, she wrote his name—*Roan*—on the desk's surface, then jerked her hand away and tucked it by her side. "I still have the one bit, the ugly fish bit."

He grinned, delighted. Helena felt her own smile blossom. She'd never pleased anyone without merchandise or money being part of the discussion. This gift business could get addictive. "You're giving me the chondrichthyan?"

"If you want it. My wedding gift to you. I've already sent to London for it."

"I want it," he whispered, his tone hot enough to melt butter. "Too, we must contact the museum straightaway. They need to change the collection's designation to 'made possible by the Duchess of Leighton'."

Helena let that statement sink in. She lifted her hand to her head and squeezed. "Dear heaven, I'm a duchess. You've made a sailor's daughter your duchess, you foolish, foolish man."

"Merely satisfying a duke's will, darling Hellie," Roan returned. Then he yawned again, his shoulders shaking with it.

"Go to bed, Roan. You're barely able to stand. But at least you made it through the ceremony."

His lids slid low. "Not without you."

"I'll find you. Every servant will leap at the opportunity to satisfy a duchess's will."

"No need to find me. I've had your possessions moved into the suite attached to mine. I'm not letting you out of my sight, sweetheart."

Speechless, she gripped the edge of the escritoire. This was *real*. He was her husband. He'd expect all manner of things from her. Potent, sensual images fluttered through her mind like the whisper of wintry wind.

"Helena, look at me."

She opened her eyes, unaware she'd closed them.

"Do you remember when we first met?"

Remember?

She remembered everything. His gray waistcoat, the sun glinting off the polished metal buttons. The rakish tilt of his hat. The sun-kissed hue of his skin. His laugh. How intelligent and *different* she'd found him before he'd proved himself to be just like all the others. How seeing him for the first time across a crowded parlor had been as exhilarating as champagne hitting her tongue, rosy effervescence, a giddy rush of pleasure through her veins.

"Somewhat," she lied, unable to give him her memories as easily as she'd given him the chondrichthyan.

"I recall even if you do not. The intrepid young woman on the shore, the curious young man on the cliff. I say we circle back to those people until the new year. Until we return to London. No dukes, no duchesses. No 'Your Graces.' No *ton*. No ballrooms, teas, dinner, theatre. No bogus society performances. I'll let you see me. You let me see you. I promise not to be guarded, my natural tendency, if you promise the same. Let's find out who *we* are. Since we didn't start with... *love*." He glanced away, his hand coming out to brush his chest, his asthmatic habit. "Because I've always wondered."

And now you're mine, she thought quite abruptly. Possessively. *Your body, if not your heart.* A piece of him she was fully willing to seize.

"That's a fearsome look," he murmured, dropping his chin to his hand. "Absolutely frightening."

"What if we don't get along?"

He blinked sleepily and gave the settee a yearning gaze. "I'll talk about quays and cutters, barges and navigational routes until I win you over. Translate every letter you have arriving in German, French, or Italian until you realize you can't live without me."

Giving up the battle, he rounded the settee and collapsed upon it, his legs so long they hung over the scrolled side. As was his way, he threw his arm over his eyes, shutting out the playful mix of candle and sunlight. "I'm moderately charming if you let me run with my talk of fossils. Get it out of my system. Then the interesting topics get rotation. But like a roulette wheel, it does often come back to rocks."

She enjoyed his talk of fossils. His rare smiles, his quick temper. His ferocious mind. She feared she liked him. If so, where would *that* place her?

She moved the inkwell behind a miniature statue of David that she thought was an odd adornment for her study. "Where will we live?"

"Wapping. Above that warehouse of yours if it pleases you. Mayfair, since we both have townhomes there. You choose. You and Theo." His voice had dropped to a drowsy lull. "Personally, I loathe Mayfair. I much prefer the docks."

"I have a cat named Rufus," she blurted, panicked.

He was being so agreeable. So endearing. Where was the man who made her mad as Hades with nothing but a sly look? Surely a cat would rouse his ire. Rufus could be a terror. He routinely dropped dead mice on her pillow. Did the seventh Duke of Leighton want *that*? And his owner *wasn't* duchess material. Wasn't anything close to what a duke needed. Roan had forced the issue. Her attraction to him, her weakness, had also forced the issue. There was no backing out, but she didn't want him to be disappointed when he recognized who she was.

Did he not understand when everyone else in London did?

She was not a suitable choice.

He murmured a low sound that curdled in her belly, warming her in places only he touched. Seconds ticked by until she thought he'd fallen asleep. "I like cats. Go round, feed Streeter's when he's off with Hildy. Nick Bottom, named after Shakespeare. And the other one, tiger-looking beast. I forget its name."

"But—"

His delicate snore echoed through the room. With a sigh, Helena tiptoed to him, wondering why she feared waking him when he'd showed up at their *wedding* feeble from drink the night before.

She stared down at him, inevitability rooting her to the spot. This man who could drop to sleep in seconds on any random piece of furniture was her husband. She was his duchess. He owned her, even if he thought he didn't.

But she owned him too.

She reached to touch his face, then pulled her hand back, pressing her arm to her side. His valet had missed a spot on his jaw, and she had the insane urge to press her fingertip to the stubbled spot. Watching his chest rise and fall, a keen sensation settled over her. A feeling she'd had once before. When she'd played rigging monkey and climbed a ship's mast, missed her step, and tumbled. Falling, her stomach lifting, air backing up in her lungs.

"I'll help you sell your unwanted antiques to obtain funds for the estate," she whispered, unsure why she felt she must tell him this now. When he couldn't hear her pledge. After all, they were going to be business partners, and she had so many merchant contacts, she could sell everything Roan had to offer in a single afternoon. She guessed many in the gentry, flush with funds but lacking refinement, would welcome owning a footstool a long-ago duke had placed his posh feet on.

Helena located a woolen throw folded neatly over the back of an armchair. It only covered Roan from knee to neck, but it was better than nothing. She tucked gently, letting her hand glide down his chest and along his ribs. Her husband was well constructed. Muscular but lanky, not a bit of excess. Lean in all the right places, broad in the rest.

Rocking back, she lifted her hand to her mouth and smiled wickedly behind it.

She couldn't wait to see what lay beneath his finely tailored clothing.

She would give him her body.

The challenge would be protecting her heart.

The mattress shifted, startling Helena out of a leaden, exhausted sleep.

Lifting the counterpane, Roan slid in behind her, pulled her against his hard body, then fell into one of his instantaneous slumbers. His warm breath skimmed her neck and cheek, his hand curled firmly around her hip, burning through her muslin nightdress. Sending shivers from head to toe, one after another, until they consumed her. Would he insist on sleeping in the same bedchamber?

Was this done?

Most husbands and wives of the aristocracy had separate quarters to her knowledge. Because they didn't like each other very much. Marriage was tolerated, not embraced.

Helena quieted, letting the night lap about her, bath water for her soul. Roan smelled pleasantly of whiskey and bergamot. Mint from a recent toothbrushing. He'd stripped off his clothing and wore only a pair of thin drawers that left little to the imagination. She could feel his sex pressing into her behind, thick and long, not as hard as it had been during their errant kiss, but undeniably fascinating just the same.

Soon she would touch him and *know*.

She wanted to know.

Listening to his hushed breaths, she marveled at her change in circumstance. Finally, she had the beginnings of a family. Roan, Theo, Pippa. Snuggling against him because she could, he let out a breathy little huff and tugged her closer. Remarkably, their bodies fit. He was leagues taller, but lying down masked the difference. Her valleys met his peaks, and so on. Like they had from the dawn of time. Gently, she removed his hand from her hip and brought it around, pressing their linked fingers between her breasts. His wrist was covered with crisp hair, a mottled ridge from a scar running the length of it. He was wiry muscle and sinew, smooth skin and heat.

Drifting off, she searched her feelings as dreams encroached.

Contentment.

For the first time in forever.

Chapter Twelve

Where a Duke Takes a Duchess

Roan awakened in a place he'd only dreamed of waking.

His face tucked in Helena's lemon-scented hair, his arms full of plump, lovely Astley female. He breathed deeply and drew her in.

His *wife*. His duchess.

The thought astounded. Simply astounded.

Stretching, his stiff shaft tucked between the pale moons of her bottom like it belonged there. There was no way to hide his condition upon rousing to find he'd made his way to her in the middle of the night. A memory that drifted to him in wispy fragments. A chilled corridor, dying firelight in the bedchamber hearth, strands of hair lit by moonlight spilling across his silken sheets. He'd stood a moment, staring down at her, wondering at the play of emotion in his chest. The shifting of his life's foundation.

Then he'd given in, as he secretly wanted to, and climbed into bed. *Their* bed.

Helplessly, his arms clenched around her. With a sleepy sigh, she nestled against him.

He found the invitation too tempting to reject. She was *his*. He no longer had to deny himself. Deny her. No more pretending. Helena was his wife, and he wanted her.

And he felt sure that she wanted him.

Skimming his hand down her stomach to her hip, he drew her nightdress in delicate fistfuls to her waist. Nosed her hair from her neck and laved her skin, rousing her gradually. Caressing until her breathing changed, her bottom bumping back against him in permission. Without a word but with permission. All he needed. His hand rounded her thigh and settled between her legs, his groan issuing from deep in his throat as he found her moist, ready. How long had he yearned to touch her like this? He couldn't remember a time when he'd not ached to.

He delved into the discovery of her as intensely as he would the study of a fossil.

He wanted this to be awe-inspiring after the unpleasantness of her prior encounter. He could go slowly. Give her everything she desired. This was about her more than it was about him. Stroking her sex, he circled the swollen pearl that held her pleasure until he got a signal that he'd hit upon a rhythm she liked. A deliberate caress, rougher than he would have expected she'd respond to. Her hand shot out across the mattress, palm flattening as she moaned and lifted her hips, releasing a choked muffle that took his breath and promised to never return it.

"I've dreamed of you," he whispered and worked the tip of his finger inside her tight channel, his mouth at the nape of her neck, her jaw, her earlobe. *Hell's teeth,* she was wet. Slick. The sweet taste of her skin overwhelmed him when he'd wanted her for nigh on forever. This was better, however, than anything he'd imagined. And he'd imagined considerably. A thousand nights spent touching himself while thinking of her.

"This, Hellie?" he asked and stroked until his palm met her mons.

She murmured an unintelligible response and tangled her leg around his, arching against him, urging him to continue.

Unable to help himself, he ground his cock against her. In tandem, his finger slid deep while he pretended *he* was sliding deep. It was the most pleasant torture imaginable.

"Show me what you like," he rasped against her shoulder, pumping into her, his thumb going high to tease the flesh centering her core. He'd learned long ago that this attention was what most women needed to climax. And Roan never forgot an important lesson.

With a gasp, she covered his hand with her own, curled her fingers atop his, her fervor threatening to break his restraint. *Not yet*, he silently advised them both. He wanted her to come this way first and was determined to have her shatter two, possibly three times, before he made love to her. He wanted her to beg. Plead. To understand she needed him.

At least for this.

Stunning him, she guided another of his fingers inside her, stretching. Showed him the rhythm she liked. Fast, hard, slow, then fast again. Her breath caught, urgent and frantic. "What would you say, Your Grace, if I told you I've touched myself like this? And pictured you? Your body folded over mine. Since Lyme Regis." She moaned, ragged and unrestrained. "One of my little secrets."

"The thought makes me crazier than I already am for you." He nipped her shoulder through her nightdress, his free hand rising to cup her plump breast, tease her distended nipple. He considered the actual possibility of coming without anything more than this. An occurrence that had not happened since he was an unskilled lad.

She turned her head toward him, her arm tunneling around his neck, seeking, and he swooped in, seizing her lips. A sideways kiss, not perfect. When it was *perfect*. A soulful joining, irresistible, as he finally had her literally in hand. Fondling her breast, easing his fingers inside her body, leisurely now to tease. The kiss drew out her sighs, her breath, into his lungs, his heart, a languid river of sensation through his body. They were sculpted, made for each other. What he'd sought his entire life. Completion on top of undeniable pleasure.

She gasped and broke the kiss, lowering her cheek to the mattress, closing in on her climax. "Don't stop," she whispered into silk, her appeal a murmur gliding across the sheets. "Never stop."

It was then he glanced up, a bit wildly, a stray moonbeam catching in the cheval mirror tilted at the precise angle to reveal the bed. And the bodies entangled upon it.

"Open your eyes, Hellie," he whispered, his finger buried inside her. Her hand atop his, guiding him. Her eagerness sent an arrow through his heart.

She blinked, dazed, his command drawing her from a sensual haze.

"Look. There."

Her gaze wandered, then focused on the mirror, her gasp shocked. Provoked. Aroused.

"Some people like to watch," he murmured in her ear.

Her lids lowered, her hips rising, sending his finger deeper. "You like to?"

"*Yes.*"

The air around them heated like a stone in the sun after that. The room compressed until there was only a duchess's bed—and her cheval mirror. The image of two bodies moving in time to their own erotic rhythm. Light skin against dark. The shift and play of muscle and sinew. The sight of his possession and her surrender. His surrender and her possession.

She was flawless. Should he have ever considered his infatuation with her unreliable? Creamy skin, a wealth of hair shot through with threads of ginger between her thighs. Her head tossed back, eyes the color of lilacs focused on their reflection. Her leg wrapped around his, propelling her hips high and into him. Her breast filling his hand, the nipple rosy and peaked, begging for his lips should he be able to reach it. A task he would gladly accomplish soon.

"I'm going to suck your nipple between my lips next time, swirl my tongue around it until the taste of you is imprinted upon my soul. Until you feel you can come from nothing but this simple, devastating act."

She came apart with a cry, her lids sliding low, the image in the mirror leaving her sight but not leaving his. Helpless abandonment, her body went rigid, pulling everything from the moment, from him. Like air drawn into hungry lungs. Deep thrusts, anguished moans. Seconds, minutes, while she pulsed, moistness coating his fingers, his wrist. Her skin heated, a light sheen of sweat covering them both.

His cock was painfully hard. His skin was sensitive to any touch. His heart was hammering in his chest.

He'd never experienced the like. Partially clothed, employing tactics he considered preemptive. Setting the stage. While this was anything but preemptive. It *was* the performance. Undiluted chemistry, without a beat of planning on his part or hers. He'd simply woken to find his arms full of her—when he'd envisaged his arms being full of her so many times.

She returned to him gradually, her breath churning, her frenzied heartbeat slipping into his skin like a needle as he grazed his finger over the pulse in her neck. Lifelessly, she let her hand drop from his as he rolled her to her back and kissed her. Needing a moment before she broke their hold. Before he let her go.

"You," she whispered against his lips. Gestured mutely to his extremely hard and unable-to-hide member.

He pulled back, his gaze locking on hers. Her pupils had expanded, black spilling into lavender. His breath caught, desire rushing through his veins.

Her smile was knowing, wicked, age-old feminine enchantment. Her hand worked between their bodies, grazing his ribs, hip, thigh. Over his drawers and inside them. Her touch when she reached him was indelicate. Artless. Her skin was chapped from working with her hands. This tiny detail about her lit him up like nothing had in his life.

Her lashes lowered, hiding her penetrating deliberation. She wanted to please him as he'd pleased her. This was obvious. "How, Roan?"

He brushed her lips with his, deliberating. He didn't want to move too fast, unleash his hunger when she wasn't ready. Then she squeezed him with a devilish laugh, and he gave up, collapsed to his back, letting her win. When he would be the winner.

Lifting his hips, he worked the drawers free and tossed them to the floor. "Anything." His voice was raw, a jagged split in the moonlight. It was enough. She was enough. More than when he'd almost come moments ago. Which he was *not* about to admit. When she sighed, he could see she wanted instruction, guidance.

God knows, he was willing to give it.

Taking her hand in his, he wrapped her fingers around his shaft and stroked. Touching himself as he preferred to be touched. Long, measured strokes. But the hook, the key to his awakening, was the expression on her face. Her lids fluttered as she explored, learning his shape, what made him moan, what made his hips lift as hers had, pushing him deeper into her curled fist.

She caught the rhythm quickly, an able student.

He groaned, losing sight of reason. His hand clenched the sheets, his head arching against the mattress in aroused agony. From her startled hesitation, he imagined his wanton abandon took her by surprise. When it shouldn't have. His hunger for her was fierce and always had been.

"Tell me when you're close."

"I'm close," he returned immediately, the tingle at the base of his spine a clear signal to his impending climax. He glanced at the mirror, then had to look away from the carnal image they presented if he wanted to last another *second*. "I was close twenty minutes ago."

"Then I shall slow down," she whispered cheekily, her grip easing, her thumb sweeping out to circle his swollen crown. Twice, before she began again. Teasing. Taunting. Extending his pleasure and shoving his arousal back a step.

He turned his head, his gaze finding hers. "Where did you learn this?"

She grinned, so damned beautiful he wanted to shout with joy that she was *his*. That he'd somehow in this mad world found her. "I'm not telling."

His jealousy was profound. Immediate. He raised up on his elbow. "Him?"

Helena took the skin on his shoulder between her teeth and sucked until his breath shot from his lips, sending him collapsing back to the bed. "No, never. This is what I imagined with you. Only you. Your Grace, I have a vast imagination. And, I admit, I've read some naughty texts."

Then she hushed him with her lips, her hand, her body. The crush of her breasts against his chest, her leg thrown across his thighs. His cock was hard and ready in her slim fingers. Bringing him to the edge, then backing off. Again. And again.

It was titillating and raw. The night theirs. This bedchamber their world.

He couldn't last. He needed to come. He couldn't hide his loss of control. Protect her from what happened when he released. When he wanted her to see him at his most vulnerable. The basic truth. Even as he feared, in some small way, *letting* her see him.

"Now, Hellie," he whispered. "*Now*."

Her ragged hum of encouragement was all he needed, his body taking over. Black edged his vision as he spilled, breath tangled, heart hammering, fingers clenching in the sheet.

He'd been close to pulling her atop him, going faster, *further*, than she was perhaps prepared to go.

Her touch was a marvel. Her skill was surprising and captivating. She brought him to a place he'd only traveled alone. A place where he didn't hide any part of himself. A place where he was simply Roan Darlington, a boy from the streets who'd been cast into another life. Brother, collector of fossils, tradesman, and finally, because it could not be denied, *duke*.

He closed his eyes for a moment as his body settled. As she shifted and burrowed into his side, where he pulled her close. Kissed the crown of her head with a sated murmur. Drew the fullest breath he'd taken in years and let it fill his chest with hope. And other feelings he wasn't ready to acknowledge.

Before he could tell his duchess he wanted more, that there *was* more, much more, he drifted into a satisfied sleep.

Chapter Thirteen

Where a Duchess Deliberates

L ovemaking was a marvel.

Not that she and Roan had made actual *love*, but the experience this eve had been profound, surprisingly erotic, changing her perception in ways outside her control. Making her a woman, a wife. Giving her a view into her husband's longings, his *preferences*.

The mirror, for instance. An experience she'd also found she liked *very* much. Watching his broad body curved around hers, his hand cupping her breast, finger tucked inside her, had been a sensual fantasy come to life. She'd not known she would like it or that he would share his secret desires with her.

He wasn't going to hold back. He was going to give all of himself, unlike most society marriages. In this arena, he had already proven to be honest about his passions.

The look on his face as pleasure seized him, the sound that had ripped from his throat, had nearly brought about another release on her part. His long body rising off the bed. *Oh*, these were images seared like a brand into wood, marking her, never to be forgotten. That she, rookery girl, sailor's daughter, scandalous tradeswoman in an era when working was a curse, had made a viral, vexing man like Roan feel such pleasure had been enthralling—and *powerful*.

Power in the hands she'd used on him.

Power in her touch. In her kiss.

When she'd only been powerful before in matters of business, of trade.

Helena took a swift glance around the bedchamber to ensure no one had noticed her divergence down a sensual, mental path she'd been unable to keep her mind from traveling since she'd left Roan sleeping soundly in their bed two hours prior. Although the cottage she currently occupied was overly warm, fueled by a raging hearth fire and desperation. A duchess's flushed cheeks could easily be attributed to the heat but were the least of her problems. She'd come down to the kitchens for a late-night snack and overheard Mrs. Meekins discussing a babe in the village, on the way without proper medical attention.

Unfortunately, the local physician had been called away to attend to a dire situation involving a case unrelated to birthing, which he'd flippantly told Helena was the "natural order of things" and not so much medicinal as religious in nature. An event the assembled group of women could handle. The village midwife was occupied with another family, and Helena had seen no choice but to go herself. A decision Mrs. Meekins had told her was an appalling one, and well outside what a "proper" duchess would do. A basket was the typical contribution from the noble family in town. But what good were supplies for a baby, or a mother, who died during the process?

Helena had wanted to punch the physician in the face, using her husband's tactics, and might if she ever chanced to meet him. As if the misfortunes that often accompanied birth were a natural occurrence.

Helena leaned over the woman twisting in agony on the bed, sheets tangled about her ankles, the faded cotton stained with sweat and blood the color of dahlia blossoms. "Mrs. Howell, your baby is on the way. You're going to be fine. Just stay with me, breathe through the pain if you're able. We have a plan."

She hoped she sounded more confident than she felt.

"Are you sure, Yer Grace?" came a muffled voice behind her. "Cause Doc Milliner, he won't agree with this plan."

Helena turned to Mrs. Howell's sister, Delilah, who stood shuffling in grubby slippers beside the bed, streaks of charcoal exhaustion rimming her eyes, crimson staining what was once a lime-green day dress. "No bloodletting, no purges. We keep clean sheets on the bed, and washed hands are the *only* hands to touch your sister and this babe. I don't care what that jackleg doctor said. I've attended many births in my district, a vile area, should you not know. The foulest in London, some say. Most midwives don't even think to venture inside the stews. So, we handle our own. There's no quicker way to have a mother succumb than to use those dreadful methods."

"Jackleg," Mrs. Howell whispered with a weak laugh. "Your Grace, you're like no duchess I ever imagined meetin'."

Helena turned back to her patient, realizing she had few choices in the matter. Hadn't that been her life in the past week, the reason she had the right to be called *Your Grace* at all? Hadn't it been her life since her father died? Sometimes one did what they *must*. Mrs. Howell was now, by marriage, Helena's responsibility.

Nevertheless, instead of regret, she felt pride shimmer through her like sunlight through the branches of a towering oak. Women such as these, without anything but love to their names, survived despite the odds. No fancy titles, no silk sheets, no silver cutlery. No fancy carriages or blood oranges at breakfast. She'd been surrounded by the like her entire life. It's who *she* was at heart. All the "Your Graces" in the world weren't going to help her with this situation. "Call me Helena, please, since we're going to get to know each other well."

Mrs. Howell smiled softly. She had lovely eyes almost as green as Roan's. "Then you must call me Myra."

Helena fished an herbal salve from her skirt pocket and smoothed it on Myra's chapped lips. "Done. Now, you remember what I said we'll have to do, don't you?"

"Shift the babe to allow for the wee one to arrive. Since I've been at this bout for near two days now," Myra whispered, sinking like a ghost into sheets they'd changed twice already, with Helena sending a footman scurrying to the estate for more. "You've done this turning trick before? I've heard it talked over but never seen it meself."

Helena smoothed her hand down her soiled bodice, battling to keep her expression calm when nerves were rippling through her like a pebble had been tossed in the pond of her heart. "I've participated, yes. And researched it after the fact. It's called the podalic method. Many midwives employ it. We simply turn the baby until we get a foot or both into sight, then bring him or her into the world through the proper channel. After that, you merely need assistance, which is what your sister and I shall provide."

"A gel," Delilah murmured from her position before the hearth, where she stirred a cauldron warming over the fire. "It must be. We have six boys betwixt us already. Can't have another. Running me ragged, the little devils are. Don't care if they're filthy, smelling like dung. Racing around like crazy hounds, a fresh scrape every day. We have a name ready for this sprite, we do. Maria. After Prinny's mistress, cause she's the one he secretly loved. Married her, too, with courage of soul, a bit like your duke taking you, but it wasn't legal like. Poor Caroline. She only got a rotten year to be a queen with a conflicted king who didn't treasure her. Can't name a babe after *that* heartache and calamity."

Helena smiled when tears were a relentless sting in her eyes. So, they thought Roan's choice to marry her was courageous. Perhaps it was. But she needed to keep her mind on her task and away from the tempting subject of her duke. Turning a babe was a dangerous endeavor. She wouldn't admit it, but she'd seen the method employed on only two occasions. With one, the babe had lived, and he was now a young man of ten who worked in her warehouse. The other time, they'd lost both mother and child.

Helena glanced back to the bed, took Myra's hand in hers and gently squeezed. "Are you ready?"

Myra nodded, though her chin quivered, a tear trailing down her cheek. "As ready as you are, Yer Grace."

Roan paced a path in the fresh snow in front of Giles Howell's tidy cottage, a dwelling where they'd just last month replaced the thatch roof, his mind awhirl. He'd woken with the sun piercing a split in the drapes to find himself alone in Helena's bed, naked and satiated but with no duchess in sight. After hastily dressing, he'd gone in search of Helena, only to find she'd been raced to one of his tenant's homes to assist with a difficult birth. Against Mrs. Meekins's advice, which she'd been clear to tell him as he shrugged into his greatcoat and followed his wife into the winter night.

Roan and Helena hadn't discussed her responsibilities yet, and he hadn't wanted to alarm her with the enormity of her duties. But the essential truth was, she had responsibilities. To his tenants, to his staff. As he did. He prided himself on being accessible, unlike the previous duke. It appeared his duchess was similarly inclined. Even if it meant stepping outside the conventional boundaries of her new station. It tugged at his heart that she cared about people, no matter their class.

He'd spent the last—he slipped his timepiece from his fob and tilted it into the moonlight—eight hours biding his time. Helpless, as many a man felt on a day such as this.

He and Giles, the expectant father, had mucked out every stall in the small stable attached to the property, avoiding talk of what was happening in the cottage. A child being born under challenging circumstances. In the end, Giles had been unable to stay away, leaving Roan with his poignant thoughts about his future children and two stalls left to clean. Left him to think about what had happened between him and Helena the previous night. One of the most sweetly erotic encounters of his experience. If he'd not fallen asleep with his release, they might have moved a step in that direction. Children. Creating the family he wanted with his every breath.

His heart skipped, and he halted at the western edge of the property, a frosty breath shooting from his lips. A gust ripped out of the trees to send dark-brown leaves and wisps of snow swirling about his feet. He folded his woolen greatcoat about his body and shivered.

Was Helena going to walk out that cottage door and tell him this was more than she could handle? Not what she wanted. Him. Her piece of the duchy. A family. Any of it.

He didn't know her well enough, not yet, to say if this is how she'd respond to a crisis. And the uncertainty was killing him.

With a muttered curse, he set to clearing a fresh path in the snow. The pacing was at least keeping him moderately warm. His carriage was parked around back, and he'd so far denied the offer from his coachman to return to the estate or sit in the conveyance and brood with a now-chilled brick and woolen lap throw. Giles had invited him inside, and although it was not where he wanted to be...

If another ten minutes passed, he was going to assess the situation.

Thankfully, Helena stumbled out after he'd completed two circuits of the small yard. Her gown was stained, her hair tangled and hanging past her slumped shoulders. She didn't see him as she crossed the portico to lean weakly against the railing. Dropping her face to her hands, she released a plaintive sound into her palms.

Roan had her wrapped in his arms before he had time to evaluate the decision or ask if she wanted the comfort he'd vowed before the village vicar to provide for the rest of his life.

She didn't fight, his first signal to her exhaustion.

"Sweetheart, I'm sure you did everything you could." He pressed a kiss to hair that smelled faintly of lye soap and illness and buried beneath that, the always soothing scent of lemon. "You couldn't possibly know how to handle this. The physician better locate another village to service before *I* locate him. Leaving an expectant mother in need isn't going to happen ever again. I've already made a note to look into securing a proper midwife."

Helena's shoulders shook, and it was a moment before Roan realized they shook from laughter, not tears. She lifted her head, her smile silvery magnificence in the moonlight. "The baby is fine, Your Grace. Myra's sleeping. Her bleeding is light, nothing unusual. And it was a *gel*, as they'd prayed for. Maria, named after Prinny's mistress." She buried her brow in the middle of his chest and blew a breath through layers of clothing that curled along his skin like smoke. "I had to turn the baby, and it worked. I didn't kill anyone this night."

She sounded dazed and disbelieving, her voice trembling in a way he'd never heard it tremble before. He moved her back a step. Her cheeks were flushed, her eyes red-rimmed. She'd fought a battle in there. "Turn?"

Helena's lips tilted, that knowing smile. Although it wobbled at the edges. Why had he ever imagined there was anything she could not do? "I know quite a bit about midwifery. More than I wish to. This isn't my first time assisting with a birthing. *Proper* midwives, as you termed them, often avoid the slums. We make do."

He hummed beneath his breath, the notion coming to him that he didn't know his wife well. Respect her enough, either, apparently. Understand her deep connection to her grimy piece of London, the infamous stews and docks that bordered the Thames. Appreciate how bloody clever she was.

She grasped his jaw to bring a gaze that had wandered into the middle distance back to her. The tenderness in her eyes rocked him where he stood. "I'm not scared of life, Your Grace. And perhaps, unlike most, I don't expect perfection. I've never *seen* perfection."

She shivered in his arms, and he moved to assist her into the carriage. Get her *home*.

She shook her head wearily. "I can't go. Not for hours yet. Until they're both strong enough to make it without me."

Roan swallowed, the unfamiliar sensation catching him in the center of his chest and spreading to his knees, the tips of his fingers, the back of his neck. He'd hit the mat at Gentleman Jackson's with less force. Taken a blow to the head with less *damage*. Moonlight slithered over them to pool at his feet as he stood there realizing, their mixed exhalations a warm vapor in the air. Admiration, fondness, gratitude. He wasn't going to have to walk this damned road alone after all.

I'm in love with Helena Astley, the Duchess of Leighton.

Unlike almost everyone in the *ton*, Roan loved his wife.

An emotion he wasn't sure how to handle, contain, or share.

Chapter Fourteen

Where a Duchess Finds Friendship

Two nights later, at Christmas Eve dinner, Helena and Roan put on a performance as proficient as any on Drury Lane. Laughing and conversing with the Leighton Cluster while the duke and his new duchess played teasing games under the banquet table. Thighs bumping, fingers brushing. Secret caresses that punched a hot jolt between her thighs as if she'd pointed and said, *There, that's the spot.* Like an arrow embedded in a straw target.

A comparison that made her giggle and smile behind her hand, drawing Roan's regard. Someone at the end of the table shouted to him, and he seemed to have lost himself in her gaze. With a pat to his chest and an unbidden cough, he turned away as if embarrassed to be caught mooning over his wife.

With a bemused pinch in her belly, Helena watched Roan tell a madcap tale about a horse race that had ended with his spending the night in the dungeon of a haunted castle in Derbyshire. Amused fondness she hoped was not reflected on her face. He liked to embellish stories with his hands, his smile so many flavors of lovable she could do nothing but feel horribly possessive and think he was the wittiest man in the room. She didn't discount his appeal. She never had. Or his temper, which erupted quickly when one silly little numeral in life's equation didn't total as he thought it should.

His intelligence impressed her most of all, and he was clearly also the cleverest man she knew. Yet, he acted like this was the least of his charms. Put everything else forth before his mind. When she'd always put brains first because most men assumed women didn't have them.

He quite fascinated her. When no man had ever fascinated her.

He laughed at something the Duke of Markham said, a baritone chuckle that reminded her of the ragged sound he'd made when he discharged, to put it crudely, in her hand. After which he'd promptly fallen asleep, leaving her to stare at the ceiling, snuggled close to him thankfully, replaying the most sensual of encounters while her lover snored gently beside her, his body hot as a hearth.

There would be no sleep this night, however.

At least that's what he'd whispered when he arrived at her bedchamber to escort her to dinner.

Helena Leighton, later tonight, in my massive bed fit for a duke, I'm going to—

"Your Grace, would you care for flummery?"

Helena snapped out of a fantasy that she hoped was not a fantasy to find a maid with a gap-toothed grin and hair the color of pewter holding a tray of elaborately sculpted desserts against her plump bosom.

"These be shaped like swans because the last duke liked swans better than any other bird. We have molds of every kind known to England. Scrawny swans, fat swans, ugly swans. And some other fowl, too, maybe sparrows." The maid lowered her voice to a whisper, but Helena could tell Roan was leaning in to hear what she said. "The current duke don't seem to care what shapes his flummery is. Like a common man, that way."

Roan grinned, the tiny scar on his lip winking in the candlelight. There were untold secrets in that smile. Titillating expectations layered amidst bold claims. Ownership. Anticipation. His smile said, *I know you, but I'm going to know you better. I'll lay you across my three-hundred-year-old tester bed and have my way with you.*

At least that's what he'd *promised* to do.

She accepted the swan flummery and the camaraderie being directed her way down a banquet table filled with a king's assortment of foodstuff and friends. Holly, ivy, mistletoe, and rosemary lay in decorative swirls around each silver chafing dish. Bowls of oranges, apples, and candies were situated around the hearty cuisine in various mismatched tureens.

Georgie, the Duchess of Markham, reached to touch Helena's hand at random intervals, bump her shoulder, *include* her in intimate jests. Drawing her into the Leighton Cluster's fold. Hildy Streeter's smile was infectious, her welcome unmistakable. The ladies of the Duchess Society had not only taken Theodosia under their wing but also the new Duchess of Leighton. Helena wasn't insulted by their offer to help her transition into a role she wasn't prepared for. She was relieved and, deep in her heart, astounded by the petals that were softly opening around parts of her heart she'd long closed off. Inclusion into this odd family her husband had chosen to surround himself with—and her hesitant, yearning assent.

Theo looked happier than Helena had seen her look since her mother's passing. Feeding Tobias Streeter's cat, Nick Bottom, scraps of meat beneath the table and giggling at jokes she didn't understand. She needed a family. Needed music and lively banter, the more boisterous, the better. They could show her how to be a lady, so-called, but no one could teach her to be happy unless she was. Helena was the chit who'd grown up without, a lonely girl in a towering Mayfair mansion with only dockworkers and servants to talk to. It didn't have to be that way for Theo.

This unexpected marriage might be the chance to break the cycle of Astley isolation. Remove herself from the groove she'd unintentionally tumbled into.

Maybe it wasn't only about how much you loved someone, but how they made you feel when you were with them.

Helena gazed at Roan from the corner of her eye, twisting her linen napkin into a knot. Agreement in her heart would mean falling for him.

Which she wanted to do. Wanted to *let* herself do.

But the line of portraits marching across the wall behind her, a stern, aristocratic bunch, represented centuries of superiority that kept her backing up a step in dread. It was a spineless response from a formidable woman, and it shamed her, but there it was. Like she couldn't force Theo to be happy, no one could force her to *trust*.

The questions circled like a hawk, damning her.

When would her duke acknowledge that she didn't belong in his world?

When would he realize he'd made a mistake in marrying her?

———

Even with doubts swirling, lust conquered all.

But they had to wait.

Through dinner, port, and an impromptu musicale by a reluctant but proficient Lady Philippa. Through multiple toasts to the holiday, to marriage, to calm seas in the new year scattered amongst Roan's teasing touches, his daring suggestions whispered in her ear for her and her alone, she was a raging inferno. Knees quivering, nipples puckered and scratching lightly against her shift. Anticipation and blind lust made her glance at the mantel clock in the music room, *their* music room, a hundred times at least. Finally, Tobias Streeter had noticed the honeymoon couple's impatience and cheerfully called an end to the evening. Probably envisioning getting his hands on his wife, Helena guessed.

But they were free and took advantage.

They raced to their bedchamber. *Raced.*

"You're not fast enough." Roan panted and reached to toss her over his shoulder when they hit the first landing, taking the remaining stairs to the chamber two at a time. The hallway was thankfully deserted as he'd given his staff an early night, so no one saw his hand drift under her skirt to cup her bottom as he loped down the corridor.

"Your Grace, stop!" She swatted his back, marveling at his strength to pick her up as if she weighed little more than a child. His ownership should have made her furious; instead, it made her want to surrender. When she had no idea how to surrender. When she danced, she led.

When she negotiated, she won. As if her body was trying to convince her, flashes of his face when he'd found his release fluttered through her mind.

You have power over him, those images said. *Use it.*

He reached the ducal suites in a trice and burst into his bedchamber, kicking the door shut with his boot. Letting her slide to her feet, his hard body pressed her into the door. Cradling her cheeks, he tilted her head for a kiss that contained no subtlety or tenderness, only blatant hunger.

Finally able to unleash her passion, she knocked his hat from his head and wrestled his coat from his shoulders, showing him without words as well.

They were comic for a moment, gasping and laughing, hopping on one foot, then the other. Struggling to reach ties, tapes, and laces—breaking those that could not be released fast enough. Creating mad disorder and a mound of discarded clothing. Waistcoat, drawers, boots. Stockings, corset, petticoat, slippers. Her lovely gown in a puddle by the settee, his superfine trousers in a spill atop it.

"You have the most luscious underthings for a woman who dresses rather sedately. I'm surprised every bloody time. Very French, your lingerie, sweetheart. Today's were the pale orange of a peach. Remind me to send your modiste a note of thanks. She genuinely knows your character. Serene on the outside, a torrent of sentiment beneath." He streaked his finger over her collarbone, and she shivered. "You are well matched with Mulberry silk and bobbin lace."

Blushing, she ducked her head, but he caught her chin and brought her eyes back to his. "I must say"—he let his gaze roam her naked body—"I didn't imagine your beauty well enough."

Nor had she imagined his well enough.

He was magnificent. Much like the sculptures of Greek gods that were to be housed in the National Gallery when it opened next year. A divine mix of broad muscle and lean contours. Hard contours. His member brushed her thigh, making her shake with want. She caressed a mottled scar on his hip and watched in fascination as her touch rippled through him.

With a ragged exhalation, he stepped in, pushing her back against the door. Raked his hand through her hair, bringing her mouth to his. Before her world blurred, she saw that his eyes were filled with fire. Then, it was only him surrounding her. Everything else ceased to exist.

He tasted of mulled wine and chestnuts. Sin and certainty. The security she secretly longed for and the vulnerability she feared. Their tongues tangled, seeking, hands roaming. Desperation made for an astonishing kiss. Mindless ecstasy she was becoming used to. His groan reverberated through her, spilling down her throat like brandy. They'd learned what the other liked and dove in rapidly. In seconds, it was as if they'd known each other forever, been connected like this forever.

Breaking free, he dropped to his knees, his hot breath racing across her nipple before he captured the sensitive bud between his teeth, his arm going around her waist to draw her close. Held her up when her knees trembled and threatened to spill her at his feet.

"I've dreamed of this for ten years, Your Grace," he murmured, moving from one peaked point of pleasure to the other. "Ten agonizing years."

Helena tipped her head back against the walnut door, her lids fluttering. His tongue was doing wondrous things. Magical, transforming her. She was mutable, liquid, her desire pooling like honey around them. Weak abandon. Her thighs softened, her body melting like iced cake in the sun. She'd never imagined such a simple thing as his lips closing around her nipple and sucking, a baby's motion, could have the power to make her dissolve.

"Roan," she whispered and threaded her fingers through his hair. She wanted him to move lower, kiss her core, *touch* her but wasn't sure how to ask.

With a soft laugh that breezed across her nipple, his gaze lifted to hers. It was a sight unseen, a fantasy beyond her wildest fantasies. Roan Darlington, the Duke of Leighton, on his knees before her. Her breast in his hand, his other gripping her hip until she felt his sure possession. His emerald eyes feral, his dark hair mussed, her fingers tangled in the shaggy strands. Then reaching, he stroked his cock once, slowly. "You see what you do to me? Should I do the same to you? Make you so wet a river flows between your luscious thighs?"

Her sigh was tortured, echoing off the bedchamber walls.

Nodding his head, on a mission, he gave her nipples a final, thorough caress, his breath dancing across her body as he traveled south. Stomach, hip, thigh. She quivered, fearing she wouldn't be able to hold herself up much longer. Her tattered moan alerted him to this fact.

When he picked her up, she voiced no complaint. Instead, accepted his kiss in breathless, whimpering enchantment as he crossed the chamber.

The bed met her back, where she sprawled. Going against what she expected, and with a speed that proved he too was maddened, he tugged her bottom to the edge of the mattress and moved to kneel on the floor between her spread legs. Kissed his way up her right thigh, then her left, closing in on her core, which had heated until she suspected it would sizzle when he finally touched her there.

"Roan, *please*."

"Shhh," he murmured and lowered his head, exhaling resolutely across her skin. His fingers stroked through the triangle of curls at her apex. "I want you to feel more than you've ever imagined you could. Experience the many ways I can delight you." He licked her once, lightly, sending her heart into a furious rhythm. "This is only a start. I'll spend my life finding out how to please you if you let me."

Tunneling his arms beneath her, he lifted her to his mouth, covering her sex, drinking from her essence. In between the devastation, he told her how she tasted—*wonderful, like wine*—how satiny her skin was. How moist, how tight when he slid a finger inside her. Her body clenched, a reckless spasm, a shiver of reaction relaying what was to come. Her hands plunged into his hair, those wondrous, overlong strands, and pulled until he groaned in response. His tongue moved against the juncture that held her pleasure, held everything, and she bumped her hips high to capture the explosive sensation.

"That's it," he whispered and spread her wide, his fingers shadowing his lips at every turn, circling, pressing, twisting until she couldn't breathe, couldn't think, her body locking her mind in a trunk for later use. The play was devious and delicious, winding her tight like a clock. It wouldn't be long before she shattered.

Trying to capture this before it vaporized with her release, she glanced at him crouched before her, the glow from the hearth's fire dancing across his bronzed skin. It was the most erotic vision she'd ever witnessed, and she could not look and last another moment. In an elemental move, when a ripple of pleasure she couldn't contain shot through her, she wrapped her leg around his back, drawing him in. Tangled her fingers in the sheet and twisted until she feared it would rip. Hoped it would rip.

"Look at me, Hellie."

Opening her eyes, she found his open as well and fixed upon her. Black bleeding into the deepest, darkest green. "Let go, right now, *here*, in this moment. Then the next, when I make you mine, my promise if I'm unable to voice it is, if it doesn't last long, and it won't, I'll make it up to you. As soon as my body will let me." He reached out of her sight, but she understood he stroked himself as he'd done earlier, his groan ripping through the chamber. "You have me on the edge, Hellie darling, ready to lose myself when you've yet to touch me. I can't tell you how rare that is, how incredible this is. You've quenched a thirst I thought never to satisfy."

With a final look at his dark head dropping between her thighs, she closed her eyes to the decadence. Arched into him and followed his command. *Let go.*

Mind, body, soul.

Rapidly, the reaction whipped through her. Filling her ears with the sound of her heartbeat. The cry she emitted was unlike any she'd ever heard, her body clamping around his fingers and his tongue for long seconds as the orgasm split her in two. Bright lights burst behind her lids, her skin heating as if she'd gone to sit by the fire, a full-body flush. A moist, molten fury. She accepted the sensations until they became too much. Overpowering her. With a gasp, she shoved him away and tried to turn on her side, hiding from them both. Hiding from her sincere response to such wanton attention.

"As if," Roan whispered and crawled atop the bed, pinning her to the mattress with his weight. His mouth seized hers as they fell into another of the instantaneous kisses they'd begun to perfect. He angled his hips, his shaft digging into her thigh, the creases at her core. Boldly, she trailed her hand between their bodies, wrapped her fingers around him and stroked. She would tease him as long as he would let her.

He groaned low and dropped his brow to hers. His chest rose once on a staggered inhalation. "*Now.*"

She worked him into place, wanting this, yes, *now.*

He propped himself on his elbow, bracing his broad body over hers. His hand went to hers, and for one tantalizing moment, he stroked with her. Then he moved her hand away, positioning himself. "Easy," he instructed and thrust, sliding delicately into her. When she suspected he wanted to nail her to the bed. "We have all the time in the world."

Yes, no, yes, she thought fervently, experiencing an overwhelming sense of urgency to get to the *place.* Where he was entirely hers. Where they were joined. From his trembling shoulders and heaving chest, she imagined he felt this too. As he moved inside her, the expansion, the sheer hardness was nothing she remembered. The moistness between her thighs, the sense of being transported to another realm entirely was nothing she remembered.

Her pathetic encounter with the baron had meant nothing. *Been* nothing. She could leave it behind, forget. And forgive. Herself most of all.

Roan caught her lips in a possessive kiss as he moved within her. Stretching, filling. Pleasure darts of fire danced along the back of her legs, her bottom, her spine.

"I'm doomed to want you every day, Hellie. Every hour. Every second. Never experience another release without your taste on my lips, your scent in my nose. The feel of you imprinted on my fingertips."

Speechless, she bowed into him, lifting her hips, sending him deeper faster than he'd anticipated. The move seemed to snap his tenuous control. He pulled back, nearly slipping out of her, then thrust. Again. And again. Forceful, moving her up the bed, the sheet wadding around their entwined legs. His hand cupped her breast, his thumb circling her nipple.

The kiss, the touch, the assault fractured her mind and her control.

Their skin was damp, combustible, smoldering like the coals on the hearth fire. He pressed, going deeper, until their hips bumped. Skin slapped. "There," he whispered against her cheek, her jaw, the rasp of his stubble a sensual echo in her ear. "You're mine. *Mine.*"

"Yours," she returned in a raw murmur.

Stilling, surprised by her agreement, he slipped his hand under her bottom and hoisted her against him, grinding, his weight falling to the arm he braced by her head. Her nipples pebbled, the hair on his chest abrading them as blissfully as his tongue.

She caught the skin on his shoulder with her teeth. Nipped, sucked, marking him. Guided his movement with a shaking hand locked on his lean hip. Impassioned. Without deliberation. A cataclysm of sensation, *want, need, yearning*.

Pressure. Pleasure. Completion.

He caged the fingers of her left hand in his and linked them on the bed, trapping her. "Look at me, Duchess."

Helena opened her eyes to an incredible sight. Moonlight washed over her husband's muscular body. His eyes glowed, dazed, fiery. A bead of sweat at his temple, cheeks flushed, lips moist. A muscle in his jaw flickered with his struggle to remain in control. With a wicked smile, he positioned her leg high on his waist and settled into her, the angle drawing him deeper, which she'd not thought possible.

Her exhalation reverberated like a stone dropped into a dry well about the room.

"I want you to watch me come, Hellie. I want to watch you." His lips dropped to hers, a demanding caress. His fingers tensed around hers as he stroked, pressing her arm into the mattress. His confident domination sent her arousal surging. Long, languid strokes of his shaft from crown to base while his gaze tracked her every breath.

She'd at last found the courage to concede.

With sensual purpose, he trailed his hand over her hip, down her thighs, and between their bodies. He thumbed the engorged nub of flesh he'd earlier taken between his lips, thrusting harder as he circled, teasing her sex, eliciting a visceral response she couldn't inhibit.

She was his at that moment.

And he was *hers*.

She jerked against his hold, and he grinned, laughed, though it was tattered. He shouldered away the sweat at his temple, his movements slowing, teasing her. "I'll tie them next time. A cravat has many uses, sweetheart. I think you'd like it, and I know I would." Groaning, he shifted, bumping her hip with his. "I'm willing to let you do the same. I'll be your jubilant captive."

She licked her lips, her vision blackening at the edges. *Ties? Captive?* Dear heaven, that sounded Machiavellian. The thought of Roan tied to the bed made her throat go dry.

Lost to pleasure, she forgot to fight him, although he freed her as they peaked, bracketing her jaw in his broad palm and kissing her hungrily. Her hand gripped his shoulder as she curved into him with a cry, nails digging into his skin.

The next moments were animalistic.

The air in the bedchamber ignited to that of a summer day, coal fires, lightning flashes. Glimmers of moonlight and his shaken gaze drilled into hers. They were one in the best of ways. In the most sacred of ways. In a way she suspected she wanted for the rest of her life. Addiction, this man. His touch overwhelming and empowering at once.

The decadent swells crested, wave after wave until she was boneless. His muffled moan skimmed her neck as he dropped his head and shook over her, *in* her. On and on, it went. The ripples of sensation, the awakening, her body opening to him, taking him, depleting them both.

This was nothing like she'd dreamed, *nothing*. Succumbing, she collapsed to the bed, and he followed. Both gasping, snatching air into overworked lungs. Skin slick, the air redolent of passion, lavender sheets, moonlight.

He pressed his fevered brow to hers, releasing a blustery breath that glided like silk across her cheek. "Bloody hell if that wasn't the best Christmas present I've ever received."

She glanced at the mantel clock and noted it was just after midnight. Indeed, it was Christmas. And she was married to a duke whose body now rested atop hers in a sweaty, fragrant, delicious tangle.

She looked back to find his gaze on her, bright with intent. "What?" she whispered softly, her heart picking up speed. What if he—

His lips parted, but only a tender sigh escaped. "Merry Christmas,

Hellie," he finally said when she was sure this wasn't what he *wanted* to say.

I love you lingered in her mind, a distant echo. But the sentiment could not be forced past her uncertainty. A determined dismantling of the marital structure they'd put in place.

Where love wasn't a factor.

Chapter Fifteen

Where a Duchess Makes a Hasty Decision

Helena crept down the servant's staircase just before dawn in search of goodies to bring back to bed. The scent of freshly baked bread followed her along the dim corridor. Roan had woken her an hour earlier with a scandalous invitation she could not refuse.

Had not wanted to refuse.

Evidently, dukes liked to make love in the wee hours of the morning. Duchesses did as well, it seemed.

She pulled in a giggling breath and pressed her hand to her quivering heart. The last time had been different. Leisurely, beguiling. They'd been face to face on their sides on the bed, her leg thrown over his hip, kissing hungrily as he thrust inside her. She'd sought to memorize every moment. The way he captured his bottom lip between his teeth when he was getting close to release. The specks of gold in his eyes, the amber tips of his eyelashes. That devilish scar on his lip. His stubbled jaw. The dusting of dark hair on his chest. His lean, long, luscious body.

She imagined a hundred ways they could pleasure each other, his suggestion to employ cravats lingering like a haunting velvet mist in her mind. She didn't know why the thought of this made her glow like a candle, but it did. The compulsion to show him her true self, good and bad, naked and clothed, was powerful. This very day, as the sun rose on Christmas morning, she was going to tell her duke she loved him. She'd made the decision while watching him sleep after their final, devastating bout of lovemaking. It was time, and if she said it first, she suspected he would echo the sentiment.

After all, in his own cautious way, he'd been pursuing her for ten years. Surely it must be love.

She reached the kitchen with a dreamy smile and a stumbling step, half of her heart, more than half perhaps, in that tumble of a ducal bed upstairs. The voices were hushed, amused, clandestine talk amongst servants. Helena stepped into a shadowed alcove upon hearing her name, the sting of cinnamon and rosemary rolling out in a warm vapor to envelope her.

"Sent his solicitors to every broadsheet in England, threatening, he did. Tobias Streeter's heavies, too, as if more muscle was needed. A duke's seal bleedin' wax across Town, dark as blood. If them papers write one nasty thing about the new duchess, he'll knock 'em to the mat like he does his opponents at that fancy boxing parlor. He or that rookery crew of his, someone will pay. This lord has friends in low-slung places, not a lick like the last one. That puffed-up soul couldn't fairly fight a female even. Toppled from his horse, his extra bulk didn't think to save him. Snapped his neck clean in two, a fateful day that brought the current duke to our doorstep. A much better man, all told."

Helena peeked through a crack between the door casing and the wall to see two scullery maids, heads bent, mob caps bobbing. One whipping eggs in a ceramic bowl, the other slicing neat wedges from a wax-covered round of cheese.

"That's to be his life with her, Dorothea," the one slicing cheese drolly stated as if this deduction was so painfully obvious it shouldn't have been up for conversation. "Bringing him low like a bird with a nipped wing when he needs to rise high, fly out of the gutter himself.

No matter how genial she is, and she is quite fine in manner and form, *quite*, and very pleasant too, but she's not much higher on the step than you or me. Who in that arrogant bunch of swells is likely to forget that? They'll hold it against him, they will, the arrogant curs. Hold it against the children."

"No one will forget, Elda," Dorothea murmured in delicate approval.

"My da was a cobbler. Her Grace's a seafarer, wasn't it? Likely started as a deckhand. I had a cousin who went the naval route. He started out swabbing decks, no better than a groom shoveling dung." Elda popped a bite of cheese into her mouth and chewed thoughtfully. "He's doing very well, a tidy cottage in Portsmouth and a pension of some sort. I bet Her Grace's da was much the same. Hard work and brains to build an empire. One *she* now runs. Remarkable for a woman in a man's world. But society toffs don't care about hard work and brains. Especially when it's a baseborn chit telling them what's what. Her lack will bleed through generations like tea through cotton."

"She helped deliver Myra's baby. Caught on her way out. Assisted without complaint, according to those in attendance. Good as any sawbones. Better! She'd be right wonderful for this village and our lonely duke is my take. Even with her modest beginnings. Wonderful for Lady Pippa, who needs a firm hand like a horse needs a lead. When have you seen a duchess willing to get her hands dirty, bloody even? Deal with a stubborn sister that tilted the *ton* on its ear her first season out? Dumping ratafia on a blueblood's head is a very unwise move. Her Grace has her hands full there."

"Still cracked to make her his duchess is all I'm saying."

Dorothea banged her whisk against the bowl, knocking off excess batter. "Maybe it's love, Elda. That would explain his dizzy spin. Men in love get loopy and make all kinds of horrible decisions. Near the same as when they drink too much."

"Dorothea, really? I sometimes forget you're the impressionable kind. No one in their class marries for *love*. Caught on a pianoforte bench like two cats in a sack. Didn't you hear?"

Dorothea sighed with another whisk bang. "I heard. We all heard.

But I've seen the way he looks at her when he thinks she's not looking back. A hot bath that stare. Could melt silver."

"Bother. I'm not saying she's not capable. She can more than do the job. She's no fat wit. Just that society won't *accept* her. A bad marriage could bring the Leighton kingdom down about our heads. Best household I've ever worked in. The last was a baron with swift hands if you get my meaning. I had to quit before my time came as he liked to sample everyone in the manor. Men and women. Also, my sister Isabelle heard from a friend who heard it from her brother, footman for a viscount or earl or some such, that there are wagers in that silly betting book in Town. Soon, everyone will be talking, and the talk won't be gracious. Because the folk starting it aren't."

Dorothea cocked her hip and propped her fist on it, jabbing the whisk like a sword. "Wagers?"

"About her. About him. About this *marriage*." Elda threw up her hand in dismay, a hunk of Stilton hitting the floor. "I can't explain the workings of dandies and fripperies, the petty games the elite play to pass the time. But mark my words, His Grace will go mad when he finds out. Toss another bloke in the cut or something worse. Business deal or no, this union, she's his duchess. Another disgrace, then we're on that carousel of gossip rags and scandal, driving us into the dirt like the fifth duke. Remember the ghastly tales told about him? Drank himself into a shallow grave in that weed-choked cemetery down the lane."

Helena brought her fist to her lips to stop the sob that threatened to break free. Turning, she jammed her back against the chilled stone and tipped her head to stare blindly at the beamed ceiling. The tears came, against her will, tracking down her cheeks, bleeding into her collar in sticky trails. Everything impressionable Dorothea and practical Elda had said was true. She *was* baseborn, her father indeed starting his career mending rope and swabbing decks, rising through the ranks with a deliberate purpose he'd never applied to rearing his daughters.

Wagers filling the betting book at White's. Roan intimidating editors to keep her out of the scandal sheets. *Dear heaven*. She'd never felt ashamed about her background, truthfully, until that moment.

She bit her lip until she tasted blood, slammed her fist against the stone. She'd *known* this would happen. That he was crazed to marry her. Bloody demented to demand it. She'd been bloody demented to agree. She'd gone against her well-honed survival instincts in agreeing to any of this. Roan and his blasted kisses!

"What does getting caught like two cats in a sack *mean* exactly? I've always wondered. It doesn't sound pleasant. Not a proper descriptor for my encounters with, um, another cat."

Helena yanked her head up to find Xander Macauley lounging in the shadows, hands negligently fisted in his trouser pockets, riding cap askew, a caustic expression shaping his chiseled features. He moved silently for such a large man. Like a thief. Or a smuggler. Which he and her husband, she suspected, were on occasion.

Helena wiped a knuckle hastily beneath each eye. "I thought you were gone. You skipped dinner last night, only to scurry back to London now like a rat."

He shrugged, his gunmetal gaze darkening nearly to black, giving no quarter. "I'd hoped to leave yesterday, but there was an accommodating widow in the village. I'm down here, thinking to filch supplies for the journey. Running to what's comfortable from what's not. Sound familiar?" He tucked a cheroot in the corner of his mouth but thankfully didn't light it, his smile utterly savage. "You have a troubled look in your eyes, the effects of the verbal trouncing you just received from your scullery staff. Fleeing as soon as you can pack a valise, appropriate your dried-up companion and your sister, am I right?"

Helena's breath hitched. *London*. She needed the reassurance of her warehouse, the comforting stench of the Thames surrounding her like a cloak. The thump of longshoremen parading down the pier. The squeal of ships skirting into the harbor. A plate of lemon scones perched on the edge of her father's battered desk. Her cat, Rufus, sleeping atop a pile of frayed rope. Stevedores who followed orders and, yes, occasionally sneaked peeks at her bottom, but a group she trusted even if they'd never sought to befriend her.

And she needed reassurance now. The word fluttered through her consciousness. Roan had whispered it—*now*—into her ear as he claimed her.

Curiously, from the pulses vibrating through her, it felt like he still claimed her.

Macauley chewed on the cheroot, his lips tugging low. "Let me guess. You have urgent business to attend to."

She swallowed hard. "We've had another burglary that needs to be investigated. A minor but recurring issue I need to solve."

He inclined his head, regal as a king. "Of course."

Dashing away her tears, she turned and stalked in the opposite direction, hoping Xander Macauley would complete his filching and leave her alone. But he kept up, easily matching her stride with his long-legged one, escorting her down the darkened corridor, ducking when the medieval beams neared his hard head. *Incorrigible brats and reckless duchesses*, she thought he murmured under his breath.

"Go away," she ordered through gritted teeth. This wasn't the first time they'd battled, but always before it was business.

"Afraid I can't do that. Not after fate placed me in the exact spot I was supposed to be, poking my nose in Leighton's love affair." He sighed when she lifted her skirt well above her ankles and took the stairs with an unladylike scramble. "You can't go alone if running to the city is what you're planning to do in this desperate state. I've never met a woman who made a solid decision during or after tears. Many a champagne glass shattered at my feet to prove it."

"I certainly can go alone." Didn't he know? Helena Astley, Lady Hell, answered to no one. However, the Duchess of Leighton, answered to quite a few people. With a shiver, Helena pushed that dreadful thought aside.

"Ah, Duchess, I won't stop you. I'm not fighting for love I don't believe in. But I can't let you go alone." He growled as if the following statement pained him to admit. "Because I *do* believe in friendship."

Helena halted on the stair, turning to him in amazement. "Friendship. For Roan or me?"

Macauley glanced into the distance, gnawing on the cheroot anchored between his teeth. "Both, I suppose. More trouble I don't need, innit? Goddamn convoluted life. Family of misfits." He looked back in time to see a tear meander down her cheek before she scrubbed it away. Cursing, he yanked a handkerchief from his waistcoat pocket and shoved it at her, a shockingly elegant strip of linen, his initials neatly stitched in the corner.

The man surprised her. Ruffian and elegant swell wrapped in one bristly package.

"Where's the hardheaded chit who negotiated me right out of a contract with that American tobacco king? A deal that lost me ten thousand pounds with one stroke of the quill. The shipping heiress who owns a fleet no one in England can match for speed or invention? Where is she in all this? Doesn't seem to me the girl to run."

"I don't know." She felt bereft *without* Roan but weaker because of the love for him pressing hard on her heart. She was a capable woman of trade, but she was vulnerable in this, emotions and heartache.

Unsure. Terrified. Inexperienced.

Macauley snatched the cheroot from his mouth and tossed it to the stone step with another foul curse. Grinding it beneath his bootheel when it hadn't even been lit. "This love business ruins people. Absolutely ruins them. It's the plague, and I'm getting the hell out of here before I'm caught in the contagion."

"It's not love," she lied.

"Listen, Duchess, you're sick for each other. Leave that ring you're spinning round your finger like a roulette wheel if you don't love him back. Toss it in his face on your way out."

She dropped her arms to her side, the thought of taking her ring off bringing a peculiar ache to her belly.

"I didn't think so. You forget, I've seen this before. Streeter's been my best mate since we were lads racing through Limehouse's alleys and nooks. Growing up with too little food on the table, dressed in rags. Building our business from the ground up like nothing London has ever seen. I watched him tumble and tumble *hard*. Hildy's everything he always wanted, even if he didn't know he wanted her. Leighton's no different. Blimey, he's worse. Been in love with you for *years,* according to Markham."

With a scowl, he waved her off when she tried to argue, an exasperated dent appearing between his brows. "If you're not ready to let him protect you, be your white knight like all men must be at some point to feel essential on this earth, then run. It's the kind of love you *should* want, his, I think, but the duchess bit makes it unappetizing. Can't argue with you there. I'd run like the devil, too, if I were in your position."

She sniffed and dragged her wrist across her nose. "As if you know. About the love bit."

"You're right. I damned well don't know." He tunneled his fingers through his rumpled strands, leaving them standing in ferocious tufts on his head, clearly distressed to be giving advice about matters of the heart. Helena hoped she was around to see him tumble, against his wishes when it happened, to be sure. "Let's just say I understand your desire to refuse membership in the privileged brethren, Duchess. More than you know. Here's the plan. Leave your sister here to ease the confusion. We can't get out quickly with too many in tow. And if you want this, you'd better leave before Leighton wakes. We'll make sure Hildy and Georgie know to bring Miss Theodosia to London when they return after Twelfth Night. Give her a chance to complete her lessons with the Duchess League—"

"Society," Helena supplied and gave her ring another hard twist, her mind lingering on what he'd said so casually. Roan, in love with her for years? *My*, that would explain things. His scorching stares across crowded avenues, the repeated apologies, the boyish teasing every time he got within reach. Their largely inane disputes over antiquities. If he'd only told her sooner. But she wouldn't have been more suitable years ago, now would she? And she might have fought harder against loving him, back then. Age had brought *some* wisdom.

Macauley bent to pick up his smashed cheroot, slipping it in his coat pocket. "When he comes running after you, and he will, a gullible sister hanging around won't help the situation. Merely another witness to his debasement. Save the man a little dignity, will you?"

"I'm not staging this expecting a romantic balcony scene in Act II if that's what you're implying, Xander Macauley. Roan won't come running. His pride won't let him. I told him this marriage wasn't advisable. I wasn't the woman for him, a proper duchess. I'll taint this duchy right down to the planks. You know his temper. He'll be furious at my resistance. But I'm right to go back, go *home*. Get far away from him and his responsibilities. Maybe if society thinks this marriage is business and nothing but, they'll forgive his transgression. Appreciate his inventiveness in securing the largest dowry in history."

Macauley grunted. "Did he accept a shilling?"

She looked away, chewing on the inside of her cheek. They both knew the answer to *that* question.

"I'll be honest, Duchess, because like your duke and his temper, I'm known for it. Sounds crude, but you have a well-loved look about you that I suspect means you waited a bit too long to decide to back out. Although absconding on Christmas morning after you've mussed the royal bedsheets *is* rather extraordinary, even for you."

Her cheeks burned, but she didn't deny the accusation.

Macauley gave her a jaunty half-salute and a smirk she wanted to erase with her fist. "I admire your ingenuity *and* your courage. Maybe, just maybe, you have the spirit of a duchess even if your birthright is as blemished as a beggar's. The ability to inspire comes from within, to my way of thinking. I know about bloodlines and choosing not to accept them, but that's my story. This is *your* life. Your bum you're placing on the line. Waking alone is certain to light a fire under Leighton's. The man's a toff, but he's not a coward."

She frowned. "This isn't a ploy to get his attention."

"Sure, sure." Macauley grasped her arm and started up the stairs, tugging her alongside him. "If you're dead set on leaving, I'll make sure you get to Wapping safely. But my carriage departs at dawn and not a second later. Climb back in bed with your duke, my advice, or if you must, you and that pinch-faced duenna meet me on the front drive in thirty minutes. I'll drop you on those docks you love so much, then I wash my hands of this muddle. Wash my hands of every female on this estate, in fact. While I wait for my friend, the duke, to come and kick my arse for my involvement in his affairs."

Helena yanked her arm from his grasp. "What other woman on this estate could you possibly be concerned about?"

He growled a truly uncharitable response and hustled her up the stairs.

Chapter Sixteen

Where a Duke Wakes Without a Duchess

Roan kicked off the counterpane and lay for a moment in sated bliss, intoxicated on sex and the aftereffects of champagne he and Helena had shared in the middle of the night, sitting on a woolen throw he'd spread before the hearth. If he'd been able, which after three sessions, he had *not* been, he would have made love to her there as well.

He would add that to his running list.

The images flooding his mind were stark, raw, sensual. Helena atop him, her hair a ginger spill across ivory sheets. Her neck arching as she tilted her head to the sky, letting a cry of delight ring free. That anguished sound had snipped every rope securing his ship to port. Left him to voyage into areas he'd never before traveled into. Giving everything of himself and more.

He reached for her without intent, the mattress flattened from where she'd slept but the sheets cool. Leaning, he rummaged around for his drawers, slipped into them with a stretch that conveyed how he'd spent the night. Muscles pinging gloriously from overuse, a stinging bite mark on his shoulder, another just below his collarbone.

The tips of his fingers tingled with the desire to reclaim her, fold her over his desk, step behind her, and slide inside her velvet folds. Another item on the list.

Helena was everything he'd dreamed she would be.

Everything he desired. His duchess, his *love*.

Intelligent, kind, generous, fiery of nature. She would make a wonderful mother. This he knew in his soul. Make the best, most unique duchess that society had ever known. Aside from the issues, and weren't there always issues, they could well turn out to be the happiest couple in England. Next to Hildy and Streeter, it was hard to beat those two.

He only needed to tell her one thing. The love thing. He'd whispered the magical three words last night but at perhaps an inopportune time. She'd been sliding under, he on the cusp of blinding pleasure himself.

He wasn't sure she'd heard him. Then he'd fallen asleep before he could repeat the vow.

Roan crossed to the window, nudged the drape aside to stare into a misty morning when he heard the sound. Turning in alarm, he shivered as a slice of frosty air trickling in around the faulty window casing caught him at the base of his spine. From the brocade settee, Kieran beamed and waved the powdered biscuit Roan had heard him chewing, seemingly unphased to be greeted by a half-clothed duke in the duke's private bedchamber.

"She's wif the smuggler, Yer Grace," Kieran proclaimed, popping the last of the biscuit in his mouth and dusting his filthy hands on his britches. "Rode out before the sun come up. Right outta here on Christmas morning, pretty as you please. I ain't an official groom yet, but I helped prepare the carriage right well. Got the lap blankets and the warmed bricks, did everything but tuck them in. Gave me a wee present too. A bag of sweets and a half crown she said I should save for my future!"

Roan propped his elbow on the window ledge, a prickle of unease dancing up his spine. "*Who* is with the smuggler? And who is the smuggler, may I ask?"

Kieran dug another biscuit, this one chocolate and almond, from the battered satchel hanging from his shoulder. "Yer duchess is the who. The smuggler be the hulking fella. The frowning one with eyes silver as that half crown I got. Ghostly the way he stares right through you."

"Macauley," Roan whispered. The boy had inexplicably described him to a T. Yet, why would Helena be with Macauley? Striding across the room, Roan plucked his rumpled clothing from the various places each piece had landed when he and Helena combusted, suddenly realizing dressing was his best course of action. "Start at the beginning, if you please."

"The beginning is, I got hungry. Tummy growling hunger. So, I crept down to the kitchens, in the dark, no candle because only a baby needs a candle. Hid under the chopping block. Best place to hide to sneak treats."

Roan yanked his cravat into a less than serviceable knot. "Like you've been pilfering silverware and the like."

Kieran ran his stockinged toe over a weave in the Aubusson, his gaze meandering along with it. Roan made a mental note to buy the boy new clothing. For pity's sake, his tattered trousers were held around his waist with a length of twine. "I reckon I have a need for a fork every so often, sir."

"Of course." Roan jammed his foot in his boot, then hopped around to secure the other. Even if the end result was him appearing downstairs looking as disheveled as he felt, that was preferable as his valet, Graves, didn't need to hear this tale. The man already thought he was far beneath the title. "Continue."

"The maids were nasty, without knowing it. Just gossip and the like. Gets boring doing all work and nothing else. She was listening outside the door. Yer duchess. In the shadows. I saw her glittery slippers." Kieran took a bite and chewed, gestured airily, crumbs flying. "Heard them whispering about you getting caught like two cats in a bag in the music room. How she's like us, poor stock. Decent stock but humble. Unfit for such a regal thing as what she's been given. Ruining the dukedom and all. Bringing possible disaster down on our heads."

Roan stilled, an arm stuck in his coat sleeve. His mind was waking faster than his brain wished for, sending every ounce of happiness draining from him like he'd sliced a vein and bled on the carpet. "Unfit?"

Ruining the dukedom, bringing disaster down on their heads?

Kieran shrugged as if this wasn't a valid question. Bloodlines were straightforward, like those of the horses he was set to work with. Noble or extremely inconsequential. "Left as the sun was peeking out, the sky turning the color of apples. I like apples. Anyway, I watched the proceedings from the shrubs before announcing myself and offering to help. Mostly because I was getting scratched by branches for my trouble. The smuggler tried to slow down the show, make noise and such, right beneath this very bedchamber window. But you're a sound sleeper, Yer Grace. Finally, he had to pile her and that cranky friend of hers in his grand carriage and ride off down the drive. Headed for Town, I imagine. He looked fairly miserable about the whole thing when I would have reckoned it an adventure."

"Which maids?" Roan asked, teeth clenched, blood starting to rush in his ears. This was Lyme Regis all over again.

Kieran tilted his head, scratched his chin with his knuckle. "The scullery one with the crooked teeth. The other, I don't know, but she has hands as big as a butcher."

Roan wrestled his lapels into position, prepared to fight. "Why not tell me before she *left*, Kieran? That would have been most helpful. Now I've got to go haring off to London on Christmas morning chasing a runaway duchess and her cantankerous abigail."

"Except for dealing with the old crone, consider it an adventure, sir. Like I said." Kieran yawned and settled back on the settee. He'd had a busy morning. "Anyway, yer duchess told me not to. Remember the half crown I told you about? But here I am, doing it anyway, because we're close, you and me. I got the feeling you wouldn't like her leaving. But she's one of us, sorrowful state of it or not. We low folk tend to stick together."

One of us.

Roan would count on that being enough. Count on his staff, his village, everyone that mattered coming to love her as much as he did.

Giving his little body a hard stretch, Kieran closed his eyes. "She left something for you on the mantel."

Roan strode to the hearth and seized the velvet bag sitting atop it. Yanked on the drawstring, the fossil he'd given Helena in Lyme Regis tumbling into his hand. He could still remember foamy waves battering his ankles the morning he found it, the laughing girl on the shore the only person he'd ever had any intention of giving it to. The only person, aside from his sister, he'd ever considered *his*. Helena thought this was her way of saying goodbye—when it proved she'd never forgotten him.

Resolute, the Defiant Duke shoved the fossil deep in his pocket and closed his fingers around it. It warmed against his skin, sending a bolt from his heart to his toes. He wasn't going to let this duchy or society's displeasure steal the woman he loved.

Even if his runaway duchess didn't know it, his campaign to win her heart had just begun.

<hr />

The chattering maids Roan had regrettably come to find were named Dorothea and Elda stood red-faced and sniffling before his desk, dabbing their eyes with the hem of their stained aprons and murmuring about how they'd never expected the duchess to hear them gossiping. About how they held her in high esteem even if she'd been born low. How lovely she'd been to the staff. And so on. Her assistance with the delivery of the baby had traveled the village as quickly as a virulent infection.

Roan marveled that his wife was becoming something of a legend.

The maid's apparent fear of being dismissed fleeced his anger by the second.

Mrs. Meekins stood in the corner, wringing her hands, her expression flickering like a candle's flame, incredulity to exasperation and back again. She'd wanted to handle the situation, and likely, he should have let her.

Roan spun his signet ring on his pinkie and watched crimson facets dance over the desk's glossy surface, wondering why he'd delayed his journey to London for even ten minutes to impose punishment he no longer had the heart to impose. This damned duchy. He sighed as Mrs.

Meekins jingled her ring of keys, tapping her foot to an internal rhythm. She wanted to mete out harsh punishment it was plain to see.

As if he'd sack a domestic on Christmas.

"Is there anything else I need to understand that you mentioned, so I may make it up to Her Grace accordingly?"

Dorothea sucked a noisy breath through the gap in her front teeth. "We may have mentioned the bets in that fancy betting book in Town. Not even sure you know that tidbit."

"And you sending your henchmen to the broadsheets to hush the gossip, we mentioned that." This from Elda, the big-handed one.

Dropping his head, Roan scrubbed at the back of his neck. *Christ*, was there anything his staff didn't know?

"We didn't set to make this harder on you, Your Grace," Elda whispered, "what with this sudden marriage to someone you'd not planned to ask."

Roan tugged on his gloves with neat jerks, tucking the kid leather tight between each finger. "It wasn't sudden. I've been chasing Her Grace in some immature way for ten years," he found himself admitting because he thought he should. They would understand his feelings if they were going to chatter like mad about him. "Frankly, nothing hasty about it."

Dorothea spun on her heel, jabbing her finger indelicately in Elda's stunned face. "Told you his stares were hot enough to melt butter!"

"*Enough*," Mrs. Meekins said, but the command held a breathlessness that stated she too was stunned by the duke's admission. He had perhaps killed two birds of a sort with one adoring confession.

Elda whipped her apron free of flour that drifted like snow to the floor. "Boot is quite on the other foot, ain't it, then? Did you, by chance, share with Her Grace the chasing morsel? Impolite of a mere servant to ask, but maybe her fleeing ain't all to be placed on our shoulders. Can't blame a woman who don't know the facts, now can ya?"

Roan held up his hand when Mrs. Meekins made to step in and kill the conversation. He'd only gotten advice from Tobias Streeter and the Duke of Markham in the past, men who'd botched their romantic efforts the first time around and nearly lost the loves of their lives in the process. "And you propose what then?" he murmured, trying to recall the jeweler Streeter had used for the tiaras he'd been known for chucking at doxies like sweets.

"Actions, Your Grace," Dorothea said and stepped closer to his desk. The finger she used to trace a scratch on the beveled edge chapped, the ragged fingernail bitten down to the quick. No way he could find it in his heart to even *verbally* slap that hand. "To my way of thinking, a longshoreman's daughter needs more than words, especially if she don't believe in herself or especially trust you."

"*Dorothea*," Mrs. Meekins interjected.

Roan steepled his fingers and propped his chin atop them, interested. "Actions."

"No flowers or jewelry like most of the devils in the *ton* supply. Not this chit," Elda added, her courage escalating now that he seemed to be listening. "Pardon my way of phrasing it, but she's not like the"—she coughed into her huge hand and did a nervous shuffle—"shallow, bacon-brained coves and addled lady-birds your set is used to. She's like us. Capable and smart. You have to go the direct route. Strip off the title and come down to the level she needs you to. Then you can rise back up together."

Roan stood, sending his chair rocking back, a sense of urgency ripping through him. Yanking his watch from the fob, he checked the time. His carriage was waiting, his duchess fleeing. He needed to *go*. "I thought you and the rest of the staff disapproved of my choice," he said on his way across the room, turning his back on the dilemma, but it could not be helped.

"Oh, no, Your Grace." Dorothea's tone was gentle but chiding, her eyes reflecting pity for his fustian nonsense. "It's your set what can't accept."

"Your Grace, you can't possibly listen to this madness," Mrs. Meekins implored from the dim corner she'd encamped in.

He halted by the coat rack and popped his beaver hat on his head. "Yes, I can because I think they have it."

Chapter Seventeen

Where a Duke Seeks to Rectify a Situation

Roan's first stop when he arrived in London the next day was St. James Street.

Although, his visit to White's ended badly. Or typically, if one knew him well. But his point was taken, and he didn't have to toss anyone in the Thames. He'd simply had to rip out a page from the infamous betting book and enter into a minor fracas with the second son of an earl who'd tried to stop him. Thereby letting the world know that the Duke of Leighton had made the unforeseen gesture of falling in love with his wife.

The sleek black landau pulled to the curb as he sat on the stoop outside White's, nursing a bloody lip and an emotional portmanteau of indecision, wondering how long it would take to summon a hack on Boxing Day as he'd let his coachman go to his family celebration. He needed to change clothing after his unexpected fracas, then track Helena down on the docks. He might admit, if pressed, to dawdling over the fear of rejection. Helena could be a tad mulish when she had an opinion fixed in her mind.

The carriage door opened, and Tobias Streeter's voice wafted from it like London's leaden mist. "The damage is done, I see. Might as well get in."

Roan rocked to his feet, sauntered down the four stone steps, and climbed into the landau. Tobias banged on the roof before Roan had secured the door's latch, and he fell back against the velvet squabs as they shot like a bullet from a chamber down the lane. "I didn't ask you to stick your nose in, friend. How did you even know where to find me?"

Tobias sprawled into the dimly lit corner of the coach, wiggled a toothpick from his waistcoat pocket, and jammed it between his lips. "Macaulay stationed a man outside, the crafty devil. A club that won't accept either of us, a cut we believe you should, for friendship's sake, contest by tossing their membership in their paunchy faces. But that's just me, Romani by-blow of a viscount not welcome in any decent venue in London. You owe me upwards of five pounds, by the by." Nudging aside a scrap of muslin draped before the window, he peered into the haze. "Paying a man double to patrol St. James on Boxing Day."

Roan flexed his fingers with a grimace, kicked his boots up on the opposite squab, and watched with relish as the Romani by-blow's brow puckered in consternation. Dash if Streeter didn't have blue blood running through his veins even if he liked to vehemently deny it. "I don't need your help."

"Tell yourself that if it makes you feel better about botching the task assigned to you. Which is keeping your wife in close view. At least for the first week after the nuptials."

Roan dug a flask from the depths of his greatcoat and took a fast swig. The whiskey—his, Streeter, and Mac's, the finest produced in England—burned as it chased down his throat. "She's in view."

Tobias's gaze made a circuit of the carriage's interior before landing on Roan. "Hate to challenge you on that point, Your Grace, but we are indeed without a wife. Yours, because I know where *mine* is. I was alerted to your departure from Leighton House by the scullery maid with the unfortunate teeth. So here I am, after a rather sudden departure on Christmas Day, no less, hoping to save our charming coterie of lost souls—what does your wife call us, the Leighton Cluster?—from more scandal. Maybe I'll pretend I make an effort because your downfall is bad for business. Although decadent allegations only help us sell more whiskey, according to Macauley."

"Why didn't he come then if he has so many opinions? He's the one who helped her run away!"

"Mac's good in crisis but not in abating gossip. He lights a tinder under hapless debacles and watches them ignite. However, after conversing with your duchess on what was surely the lengthiest ride in centuries on the Great North Road, he agreed we should intervene." Tobias chewed on the bamboo sliver, a habit he'd undertaken to rid himself of cheroots. A practice his wife wished he would cease as she was sick of toothpicks littering every ready surface. "Sadly, I arrived at White's unable to stop what is a force of nature. You and your temper are most predictable."

"I wasn't going to let that bloody page sit in that bloody book, society betting on my *wife*, for another minute. I only had to make it through one son of an earl with a shaky left hook."

Tobias released an annoyed breath, toothpick bobbing. "Let them wager, Ro. Write what they will. Place your own bet for happiness and love. Kiss Helena on the street in full view of society. Let them call you worse than the Defiant Duke. Call her worse than Lady Hell. I'm sure they're creating innovative monikers this very minute in the dead parlors of their souls. Defiant Duchess has a nice ring to it, so expect that next."

"In other words..."

"In other words, *ducal* words, tell them to stick it up their fashionable arses. Show *her* it doesn't matter. Because you can't spend your life defending her. Especially when she's an independent miss, learning how to let you protect her in small measure. A measure you pray will grow. You didn't exactly choose a wilting lily. She's been written about before. All the women we love have been dipped in ink at some point."

Roan whipped a handkerchief from his pocket and dabbed the

corner of his mouth, the edge catching him under the chin, exactly where Helena had taken his skin between her teeth some thirty hours ago. "You should talk. Hildy isn't exactly amenable to husbandly influence, either."

Tobias grinned, the happiest husband in England, damn him. "Oh, my road is littered with ruts of the female variety, shallow and leagues deep. But I want the obstacles. Or better to say, they're worth my time. The woman connected to them is worth every *second* of my time. The *ton* doesn't accept me, and I don't care. My father finally acknowledged me on his deathbed, and you know what? My life remained unchanged. Alleged son of a viscount being sworn as actual matters not. Zero return on the dream. When I'd always imagined hearing him say I was his in front of God and country would be significant. Shocking that it was not."

Roan watched London's gloomy miasma flicker by, the streets deserted due to the holiday, realizing they were tiptoeing into murkier sections of the city. Headed to the docks, Helena's part of the world. Streeter evidently had a plan, like he always did.

"You know I didn't come from an esteemed family. Grew up not far from Limehouse, a stone's throw from you and Macauley, from Wapping and Helena. I can leave this behind. Mayfair. Regent's Park. Primrose Hill. The balls and musicales, the museum exhibitions, the tedious political discussions. Ribbon cuttings and champagne fountains. Unlike you, I never imagined this world"—he knocked his knuckle against the glass windowpane—"was essential. I felt no calling. I merely satisfied an obligation by stepping in when two men before me passed on. I want my fossils, and I want *her*. A family, perhaps, if I'm very, very lucky and not much else. Happiness for my sister. For Theo. They're clear-cut wishes when you sculpt them down to their basic form."

"Does Helena believe this to be true? That you can leave it behind? That they'll let you?"

Roan closed his eyes to the sharp edge of despair, to the sound of air whistling through a crack in the door's casing. He wasn't sure what she believed. Or wanted. He only knew, like most men, what *he* wanted. He was trying hard not to barrel into her warehouse, snatch her up, and make her believe. Like the Cro-Magnon she would then accuse him of being. As Tobias had accurately stated, she was much too independent a chit for that kind of foolish behavior.

Even if the urge to act like a fool fairly overwhelmed him.

"My advice?" Tobias slipped his toothpick free and gave it a strategic tap against his bottom lip.

Roan grunted, shrugged halfheartedly. "Why not."

"Wage war. On her. You like starting fights. Now it's time to end one."

Roan lifted his head and gazed across the ever-darkening interior. It was closing in on sunset, waning streaks of light struggling to muscle through the mist and into the conveyance. His world felt lonely, the twinge in his chest numbing. "I'm listening, although I shouldn't, as you made a hash of it when you were courting Hildy."

"Show her you'll leave this life behind, should she think to make you choose. Which is—"

"Exactly what she's doing," Roan interjected with a blossoming smile that felt feral.

"I feel for the spot you're in, wedged between the duchy and the life you genuinely want. But you can have both. Stray outside the margins for the next week or two, win her over, tell her you love her, that's key, then step back inside. Live life as *you* define it. A dukedom is a powerful persuader. If ever there was a time to wield that mighty power, now would be it. Most will forgive, and for those who don't..." Tobias opened his window and flicked his toothpick into the mean streets with a shrug of indifference. "They can sod off."

Roan banged on the carriage roof. The coach jerked to a halt, and he leaned out the door, relaying his Mayfair address to the driver. When he sat back, it was to find Tobias's keen gaze centered on him. "I have a plan," he mumbled, uncertain now that his certainty had passed. "And it doesn't involve stumbling into Wapping without proper preparation."

Tobias snaked another toothpick from his pocket and anchored it between his lips. "Do you now?"

"It could work. It may." He gave his chest a tap, his breath hitching like it did when he got a little panicked. "It will."

Tobias hummed low in this throat. "I have all confidence, Your Grace."

Roan closed his eyes and let light and shadow play over his lids.

That made one of them.

Chapter Eighteen

Where a Duchess Decides a Duke Doesn't Play Fair

Helena nudged her spectacles high and rocked back on her haunches, her knee giving an indelicate pop. Untangling rope was work she paid others the highest wages on the docks to do. It was late afternoon, her business vacant. Hansard, who'd spent the day surrounded by accounting ledgers piled higher than his head, had finally left for the evening.

Her task was menial but occupied her restless fingers, although it did nothing for her equally restless mind. It brought her back to the days when she'd sat at her father's feet, observing as he built an empire. One of the few ways, the *only*, really, to get his attention. She hadn't been offered another dream, the shipping enterprise landing on her shoulders whether she wanted it to or not. Instead, she'd made every effort to make him proud and learn his business.

And then she'd begun to like it.

Anyway, there weren't many dreams for women aside from being a wife, a mother, a lover, a mistress, a light-skirt, a burden. Watercolors, needlepoint, music, and mindless conversation. She'd had no time for such wasteful pleasures. Or patience, truthfully. She'd been given no choice and thanked the heavens for that most days. Even if the life she'd lived had left her wholly untrained for others that had turned out to be equally possible.

Unanticipated but possible.

A future filled with dukes and duchesses and heirs to a centuries-old kingdom. Building an empire—but one of her very own.

Placing her palm on the chilled planks, she drew a breath redolent of the Thames, raw tobacco, spices, rum. She should have been more comforted when she'd longed for the familiar. But her escape was for naught.

Roan was in London.

The broadsheets had been full of his return without his duchess. And after lying in wait in the alley behind her warehouse, the newspaper rats then realized she'd returned without her duke.

Apparently, he'd caused a disturbance at White's, ripping out a page in that useless betting book, throwing his fist into some bloke's corpulent face. The glow this ridiculous gesture created in her belly was pathetic. More irresponsible behavior from a man known for it. Giving the knot a hard yank, Helena let loose a curse she felt entirely comfortable airing in this space. Tossing aside a length of braided sisal as tangled as her marriage, she rose to her feet.

Perhaps her husband returning to London actually wasn't a surprise, but why had he not sought her out? It had been *three* days. Three days of looking over her shoulder, creeping the short distance to her waiting carriage, peeking around doors before entering rooms. Even once going so far as to glance under her bed. The Duke of Leighton usually got what he wanted. Fought hard for what he wanted. Didn't mind split lips and bruised skin being part of the negotiation. As Macauley had stated, he was a toff but not a coward.

Although she didn't know if he wanted her in the way she *wanted* him to want her. Which was not like he wanted his fossils. This confounding thought made her head ache, although she understood precisely what she meant.

The worst bit, a bit she hated, absolutely bloody hated, was that in the shadowy feminine depths of her mind, she wondered if her impulsive flight from Leighton House had been a test. A test her pupil had woken, in a lonely but tousled bed, unprepared to take.

Crossing to the stack of crates serving as a mock sideboard in the vast space where shipments were received and cargo unloaded, she poured tea from a chipped pot so faded it was unclear if the flowers were roses or lilacs. Then, she stilled as she realized she was unconsciously employing guidance posed to her by the deviously charming ladies of the Duchess Society.

Hold the teapot thusly, pour with your wrist.

They'd been lessons imparted during Theo's tutorials, but Helena had been listening. Too well, she feared. And for all the wrong reasons. To earn a badge from a group of people she didn't even *like*.

How would pouring tea in a certain way help her case at all? Which led her back to her list of wants.

She wanted Roan to feel she was the proper woman for the position when she wasn't and never would be. She wanted him to believe that only she could be the mother of his children; no one else could be right for *him*. If holding a teacup with her pinkie sticking out meant she was fit to love the Duke of Leighton, Marquess of Rothesay, Earl of Holton, share his bed and his *life*, then she would impersonate a blasted lady and stick out her blasted pinkie. She would study like the most diligent of pupils with the Duchess Society until she fooled everyone.

Everyone but Roan. She'd let him see the real Helena anytime he wished to see her. In bed and out of it.

If they could come to an agreement regarding their expectations. If he could accept that in the end, his world *wouldn't* accept her, no matter the role she strived to play to perfection.

Her cat, Rufus, sauntered over after leaving his pile of gunny sacks to circle her legs, begging for food or attention. A lonesome ache settled in her belly. She'd left part of herself with Roan, years ago, perhaps. On a stretch of equally lonesome shore in the south of England.

The voices slithered through a shattered pane on the wharf side of the building, remnants of the latest botched robbery attempt. Her mind didn't catch the meaning behind the words until she realized the men were speaking German. Setting her teacup side, she crept toward the door.

It couldn't be. Not *here*. Conversing with dockworkers and longshoremen in the bitter cold. A salty, misty, gorgeous day on the riverside appreciated by few. Most stayed far away from this locale unless they were retrieving a shipment of whiskey or blood oranges—and then the smartest man seen on the docks was in liveried attire, a centuries-old crest splashed across his carriage door, perhaps. Low man on the pole in Mayfair, a footman, but high in Wapping.

It couldn't be, she reasoned again, her hand finding the dented brass doorknob and giving it a twist.

But it was. The badly accented but adequate German had been his voice.

Helena was on the grimy, pitted dock before she apprehended her state of dress. Trousers. Long knit jumper imported from Ireland that hit her just below the waist. Hessians surreptitiously made by Hoby at great expense covering her slender feet. A sailor's cap she'd swiped from one of her workers and crammed every lick of hair beneath.

And of course, the spectacles she remembered when mist began to blur the lenses, an accessory Roan seemed to like. He'd had her wear them and nothing else that night, for a moment, while she'd ridden him like she rode her mount through Hyde Park.

Then he'd flipped her to her back, deposited the spectacles on the side table, and made her see stars.

Breathless in remembrance, she halted at the entrance of the alley running between her warehouse and the Cock and Bull, the wind ripping off the river, slinging a strand of hair into her face that had managed to free itself. Her fingertips tingled in that *please touch him* way they'd taken to doing the instant she saw him. Her body heated in the brutal chill as swiftly as an iron tossed on an open flame.

Oh, *lud*, she was weak.

And Roan Darlington didn't fight fair.

He'd come without a hint of a duke about him.

Dressed as informally as she'd ever seen him dress, looking like a man of industry, no, of *labor*. An enticement he knew, *knew*, would light her up inside. Tinder to dry birch. Pique her interest, earn her respect, as nothing else could. Bundled up in a heavy woolen coat, rumbled buckskins covering his long legs, Wellingtons that had been through the muck and then some on his feet. A flat cap of indiscriminate origin jammed on his head. Gloves stained. Dark hair dampened with sweat, cheeks flushed, a streak of dirt smeared across his jaw. She cataloged faster than her mind could assimilate, hungry for him.

Hungry and weak.

Weak. Weak. Weak.

A vision of being tangled in his arms, her legs wrapped around him, her fingers plunging into his hair as his hips thrust, rolled through her like a fever.

She could be his in the elemental ways. The begetting heirs promptly ways.

She'd need no Duchess Society lessons for that.

It was then she noted that his left hand was wrapped in a length of cloth, bloodstained at the edges. And because he hadn't recognized her in her working rig, she was to him before he noticed.

"What's this?" Helena reached for his hand, unfurling the linen strip to reveal a jagged but not horrid cut on his palm, while he stood, stupefied, shifting from one boot to the other as he prepared his response. She knew this about him. Roan was impulsive. He met any situation head-on, then he adjusted his strategy as the seconds passed. She tried to ignore the feel of his skin melding to hers, tried to ignore how wonderful it felt to be sheltered in the warmth of his gaze. Even in the leaden, salty mist, she could smell his scent drifting from his skin.

"He's a goot lad," Hans said in a baritone growl, his breath misting the air, "for a snobbish swell. Middling, anyway, and sure to get better with practice. A tad reckless, mayhap. Impatience is never good on the sea. And arriving for work in boots fit for a ball. Skidding all over a slick deck he was." Hans punched his shoulder and grinned when Roan blew out a groaning breath and rocked back on his heels. "Needs to get stronger in the muscle, but his German is not so bad. Makes me"—he placed his gloved hand over his heart and tapped—"sad for home. I only speak with my Martha. I regard the man who goes outside his own for language."

Roan's gaze swept from her sailor-capped head to her custom boots and back. His eyes when they met hers were so outrageously green her knees trembled. His thumb made one languid caress along the band of the ring he'd given her as if surprised it circled her finger still. Like she would ever take it off. "You don't look like a duchess," he murmured.

"You don't look like a duke."

And I like it.

She couldn't say that out loud, in front of Hans. Along *her* stretch of the harbor. But Roan's sizzling stare warmed her beneath layers of knitted wool and muslin, beneath sheets of arctic chill. She had a spare bedroom on the top level of the warehouse. They often had clients who'd traveled long distances and anxiously preferred to stay with their cargo, bondsmen who worked well into the night. The mattress was rubbish, the furnishings sparse, but who needed a bed when she had a sturdy desk? The floor? The wall? Roan had whispered all kinds of wicked suggestions in her ear, ways of making love she'd not imagined possible. Places she'd not imagined.

Caught in his beloved chemistry, they stood in echoing silence, the only two people in the world. Wapping's riverside clamor evaporated like dew on a sunlit petal until only a shimmering fiber of raw need thrummed between them. Carriage wheels striking cobblestones, ships chafing the dock, longshoremen's shouts, seagulls, barking dogs, hawkers selling chestnuts. Everything faded but the light in her husband's eyes, his injured hand still tucked in both of hers. The pulse in his wrist tripped where she held her thumb over it.

Desperately, she wondered how she'd ever thought to live without him. How she possibly could if he decided he didn't want her.

Hans gave Roan a shoulder knock that sent him stumbling into her, then laughed, a booming sound that echoed out to sea. "You'll bloody freeze out here without gloves, both of you. Go let your missus bandage the wee gash. And remember, next time, slice away, not toward the body. I guess your da never thought to tell you this."

His spine stiffening, the smile leaving his face, Roan wiggled his hand from hers and rewrapped the strip of linen with a slight grimace, tucking the ragged ends inside the swaddling. "He didn't think to tell me anything." Avoiding Helena's gaze, he glanced over his shoulder. "Tomorrow, then?"

"Ah, yay, same ship. *The Brennan*. In port for the next two weeks at least. Be here by seven bells, lad. You were twenty past this morn. Don't think I didn't note your dragging arrival. Your marriage into the Astley family, so to call it, only goes so far with this man."

Helena frowned, piecing together the puzzle of Roan's activities. "The *Brennan*? It's in port for maintenance, a crack in the mainmast, if I'm not mistaken. What is His Grace doing on the *Brennan*?"

Hans glanced in Roan's direction, his shaggy brow inching high, beginning to doubt the story he'd been fed by a posturing aristocrat trying to win back his wife. "You sent him to learn the business," he said uncertainly. "Reefing, bracing, hauling rope, polishing brass. You have to know every square inch of a vessel to manage her. Astley has always run on this adage. Like he said, *you* said I should teach him, being busy with the fine duchess life you've been handed and those added responsibilities. I worked him like I would a sailor out of the schoolroom at your direction."

"Like *I* said," she murmured and shot Roan a murderous glare. Then turning, she marched back to the warehouse, knowing her duke would be right on her heels.

"Thank you for the lesson about the igneous rock," Hans called, "and seven bells, lad, not a second later. The next lesson is running rigging."

Helena bumped her shoulder against the warehouse door she'd left partially open, making directly for the hearth and blessed warmth. Her hands were stiff from the cold, but her pulse was a fierce presence beneath chilled skin. "Rock?"

Roan shut the door and leaned against it. Taking his cap from his head, he beat it against his thigh in a composed display. "I showed him your fossil. It's not igneous, by the way." He tapped his coat pocket. "I brought it in the event you'd like it returned to its rightful owner. A woman who denied owning it when I asked her a few short weeks ago. Telling omission, that."

She stilled, her muffled exhalation filling the space. "Quite," she whispered, marveling at her decision-making when she'd left it in

Hertfordshire. Emotional bit of foolishness, it now seemed. A madcap heiress-turned-duchess who'd left behind her sister and her treasures on Christmas day. Lovemaking and hurt feelings combined to make one act irrationally when she'd always been rational before.

Now here they were, back in London but still at cross purposes.

Roan shoved off the door, unwinding his tattered bandage, his smile too unyielding to be genuine. "The parting gift you left with Kieran. Don't you recall? A young man's effort to impress you in Lyme Regis." He paused by the shattered window, dusted his boot through the shards of glass on the floor. They'd done little but stuff the hole with burlap to keep out the winter until a new window could be installed next week. "What happened here?"

She shrugged. "Likely mischief." But she wasn't sure. Astley's newest "employee" didn't need to know the details. Starting out as a humble deckhand, wasn't he?

A pleat settled between his brows as he contemplated the matter, his way of getting involved whether she asked it of him or not. "Didn't you say this happened before?" he asked too casually and dropped his hat on the nearest available surface.

"Once, twice." Maybe three times, which *was* odd.

"Dangerous business, Hellie. You should have guards surrounding this place. But here you are, alone, without protection."

"This warehouse is usually swarming with workers, excise agents, bondsmen, merchants. You caught me at a lull." She shrugged, unwilling to let him make her worry. He was starting to sound like Hansard. Like a father. Or a husband. She picked up a poker and jabbed at the blazing hearth fire. "I have a pistol in my office, and I know how to use it."

He frowned, jaw flexing, then continued his circuit about the room, mumbling beneath his breath. Touching this, poking into that. Searching, snooping. Looking for pieces of her.

Helena followed his progress as he halted by a crate, dipped his hand into the straw, and pulled a jade vase free. "Like the inhabitants of this city need another of these."

"Your comments about my merchandise aren't welcome, Roan. The scuffle at White's. Bribing the broadsheets to keep my name out of them. This dance to make an unsuitable suitable. Why this public display? What are you *doing*?"

"I'm showing you who I *am*," he snapped and let the bloodstained bandage flutter to the floor. "Struggling to break down the walls you've built around your heart by offering mine. It's my grand plan, you see. You won't come to me as I am, so I'll come to you. Gladly."

When he halted before her, it was too much to bear. She dropped her gaze, but he tipped her chin, bringing it back to his. Retrieved the poker from her hand and laid it aside. Slipped the sailor's hat from her head and watched with an arrested gaze as her hair tumbled about her shoulders. A log on the fire popped with a crack that startled both of them. "You're not a quitter. The question is, Helena Astley, Duchess of Leighton, will you accept my offer? Not the title or the responsibility or even the passion, but the *man*. I've been wondering this for nigh on ten years."

Her lips parted as she formulated what to say and how to say it. *I love you. I want to try. I want to be fearless. You're perfect.* When of course, he wasn't. But he hadn't said he loved her, not outright. What if he didn't mean *love* exactly? What if he—

"Dammit, Hellie." He cut off his speech, seized her lips beneath his, passionate and angry. "You're my duchess," he whispered against them, his appeal sliding into her throat to thaw her heart. "You're the woman I want. The woman I need. The woman I *love*."

Leaning into him, Helena looped her arms around his neck, fingers spearing into his hair. His lashes were dark crescents as they slid low over his eyes, his expression tormented. Nerves scampered along her skin, followed by rampant desire. He left her nowhere to hide, to run.

The kiss was fury, assertion, a plea for understanding. Confusion, ire, velvet madness. Two souls negotiating the contract of life.

With a groan, Roan stumbled, and they hit the wall, his back against it this time. His moist breath caught her cheek as he slanted his head, diving deeper, his hand coming to her jaw to still her as he took control—in the one area where she let him lead.

Changing speed, devilish persuader, he gentled the kiss, coaxing her tongue into a delicate dance. Devouring her lips as if this kiss was their last, as if he was expiring of desire for her. He tasted of mint and tea, river brine and purpose. He was broad in her arms, more than she could handle, even when she knew she could handle him. He dared her with a whisper, a gentle nip to her bottom lip, his fingers sinking into the tender skin of her hip.

Frantically, she bounced up on her toes, drawing his broad body against her aching breasts, fingertips pressing into his scalp. He was varied textures. His skin was hot, the tips of his hair moist from the river's vapor. Soft, hard, rough. His shaft was a solid presence against her hip. No longer afraid, in possession of him as well, her hand traveled down his chest, his belly, moving beneath his greatcoat to trace the rigid outline of his sex.

He made a ragged sound, his arm going beneath her bum, lifting her off her feet. "Come here," he whispered as if she had a choice and hoisted her high, her legs instinctively circling his waist.

Ease of movement in her current attire. *Brilliant.* She felt inspired.

"I like you in britches, *hell's teeth*, I do. But I don't want another man to see your round arse displayed like this, the material hiding nothing. I thought to rip them off you on the docks in front of all of Wapping and set my teeth to your creamy skin."

"To prove I'm yours," she whispered against his shoulder, his possession melting her.

"That would be it, sweetheart. Because you are mine. And I'm *yours.*"

Breathless kisses followed, gasping encouragement, delight.

"We're alone?" Releasing her lips, Roan rested his forehead against hers, his fevered breath batting her cheek. His hand clenched around her hip and dragged her greedily against his hard length. "Because I'm about to combust."

"Alone," she whispered and pressed her teeth into his shoulder, his groan of surrender curling her toes, turning her body to liquid pleasure.

They were alone, and she was going to have him.

Shakily, she reached to unbutton his close while he unbuttoned hers, his speed impressive, though it was a task he completed for himself every day. He slipped his fingers inside the slit in her drawers, one digit sinking into her in a single, demanding thrust. Her head fell back, and he swooped in, his lips, teeth, tongue setting to the nape of her neck and working her into a frenzy.

"Look at me," he growled, pumping his fingers in a slow, delicious rhythm. He liked to watch. Wanted her to watch. She had not forgotten.

His eyes were midnight promise. Flecks of amber and gold in a sea of green. Long lashes fluttering as he tunneled another finger inside her. Her body throbbed in response, an ardent appeal. Answering it, she marched into battle, rounded her hand around his shaft and stroked once from base to crown. She wanted him to be unable to watch, gone, absent, lost. Shattered. Destroyed by their passion.

Determined, she touched him as he'd shown her, her grip tight. Sweeping her thumb over his swollen head, she drew him back into the kiss while they fondled each other, clumsy but enthusiastic handling. Almost adolescent. Nothing choreographed or orchestrated. Raw, uninhibited yearning. She melted in his arms, her core damp, slick against his fingers. He shifted and, with a curse, set her on her feet. Ripped his greatcoat from his body and tossed it to the floor. Then they were there, crouched atop it, on their knees, hands roaming, speech unintelligible as they bit and scratched to get at each other. She nibbled his earlobe, the curve between neck and shoulder. Tasted his skin, his salty, glorious essence, drank him into her soul.

She was as spellbound as she'd wanted him to be.

Her vision blurred until she was forced to close her eyes or tumble.

"That's it," he encouraged and laid her back, the velvet collar of his coat kissing her cheek as she turned her face into it. He palmed her breast through the jumper they'd not thought to remove in their haste. Thumbed her nipple and took her moaning acquiescence between his lips. Surrender. Moving frantically now, he yanked her drawers and trousers to her knees, swept his hand over her bottom with an appreciative sound, his fingers skimming her thigh, teasing her moist folds. "I'm wholly entranced by you. Like nothing I've ever experienced, Hellie. All my dreams laid out right here."

She quivered as he worked his shaft into her, gradually, preciously, when she wanted wild abandon. She arched her hips, begging.

He laughed wickedly, slipping into her in gentle degrees. She pulsed, contracted, and he groaned, his lips going to her brow. "You're going to have me over the edge, sweetheart, in seconds."

He lost his control. She lost hers. He went deep as she spread her legs, accepting everything he had to give. They began to move in a frantic tempo, the sound of their merging bodies ringing through the warehouse. A primal, dull slap of skin. Curving in and over her, he took, his hips rolling his shaft into her until she receded in a state of aroused yearning.

She felt claimed. Challenged. Overwhelmed as he moved atop her, stretching her, touching every part of her.

This was different from before. Impassioned hunger with an edge. A piece of himself Roan hid from most. A piece of herself she showed everyone.

There was nothing delicate about the encounter. No feather mattress or the scent of lavender clinging to silk sheets. Her world smelled of turmeric, tobacco, dust. Of Roan. A lazy gust from an open window. The sounds of the Thames slapping the seaside matching their sensual rhythm.

The uneven planks were merciless beneath her as he thrust, and she only wanted *more*. Harder, faster. Which caused his movement to stutter when she told him. She snatched at his shirt, wanting to feel the crisp hair on his chest. Their clothing was a hindrance. And a reminder. Of how taken they were by and with each other. How consuming passion such as this could be. His breath was hot in her ear, in her throat as he seized her lips in a blinding kiss. His hands cupped her breasts, tangled in her hair, cradled her head to protect her when the storm began to sweep them under.

She wrapped her hand around his hip, splayed her fingers wide, and recorded the shift of muscle beneath her palm as he thrust. Directed his movement, guided when he got close to where she needed to be. Her words were whispers against his skin, impassioned directives. He braced his arm by her shoulder and hung his head, closing in on his release.

"Now, Hellie, *now*," he growled, slowing the pace, making her cry out, pleading.

Desperate to find her release, she worked her hand between them, not to touch him but to touch herself.

He lifted his head, his eyes fever-bright. "Oh, my greedy duchess. Just when I think you can't surprise me."

"I want you," she murmured and watched his body tremble with the admission.

Thunderstruck, he gave up the battle to continue teasing her, his lids sliding low, his lips closing over hers. His thrusts increased in speed, the end near. Reaching, he shifted her leg high on his hip, sending him deeper. She groaned at the invasion, arching her back, meeting him with every stroke. A wave of pleasure waited offshore, and she was racing into the sea.

It was enough to record his release, enough to satisfy, but everything else staggered her.

His touch. His kiss. His fever. His *need*.

The origins of their lovemaking closed ranks to slay her.

Chapter Nineteen

Where a Duke Seeks to Rectify a Situation, Part II

T he night began to dominate the city, shadows slithering down the wall to pool about their tangled bodies. The call of a calming harbor and a low tide rippling like a wave through the dwelling. The hearth fire had died, and a chill chased her lazy caress over his chest. She seemed unable to stop touching him; he was unable to stop touching her. Such was their powerful connection and the intensity of what had occurred this eve.

Roan was relatively sure Helena's pocket watch had tumbled free during their adventure and was now wedged under his hip. The warehouse planks were as unforgiving as marble. He had a cramp in his thigh. He'd long ago lost sensation in the hand he'd injured splicing rope on the *Brennan*, a wound he felt sure would hurt like the devil when sensation returned. He suspected his duchess had left a bite mark on his neck. A spot below his ear burned, a pain-pleasure throb.

As Tobias had eloquently stated, wives were worth every scrape, every moment of indecision or angst. Helena was indeed worth his time, his investment of love. He'd never been as sated in his entire life.

Heart and body. Never wanted anyone this much. Never expected to feel *connected* after tupping. Emotional even.

He thought that only happened to women.

Now, he simply had to make her believe.

"I can't breathe," she squeaked and shifted, trying to untangle her leg from beneath his thigh.

With a muffled laugh that whispered through her hair, he rolled to his side, propped his chin on his hand, and let his smile float free. Mirroring his pose, her lips curled in a satisfied, slightly cunning smirk, eyes glittering in the narrow strip of light that had found its way through a slit in the dirty windowpane. Her cheeks were flushed. What little clothing she wore was in utter disarray. In his enthusiasm, he'd ripped her jumper at the neck.

She seemed blessedly unconcerned. The wistful look on her face was adorable and priceless. He knew at once, if he'd ever doubted it, that he loved her. There was fear in the admission but also a sense of rectitude.

Or more accurately, relief.

"I wonder at the meaning behind that smile." She reached to trace the scar on his lip, an altercation at university in payment for reckless behavior. A lifetime of hiding behind a menacing façade. He was quite tired of being that man. "Look at you, my working man," she whispered and, with her thumb, buffed away what must have been a streak of grime on his jaw.

Turning his head into her hand, he kissed her palm. He might as well tell her all his secrets. They were bursting to get out. "My father wasn't killed by someone he owed money to, though he owed most of London as the broadsheets proclaimed he did. He died by his own hand. There was a witness, a boy on the docks who watched him jump into the river. A betrayal, even if our relationship was horrendous and he assumed he had nothing to live for, that I've had trouble moving past. Forgiving him for. Leaving me with Pippa and debts piled higher than my head at every merchant in the city." He waved her off when she went to speak, her gaze going a misty lavender that sparked a salty sting in his own. "The incident at Cambridge, my expulsion, was in reaction to a comment that was closer to the truth than any I wanted to hear about him."

"That's why you don't trust anyone," she murmured with a shiver that shook her slender body. "Roan, I'm so sorry. You never told me this. That's why you reacted to Hans's comment about your father teaching you to handle a knife. I wondered at that silence, the bleakness that entered your gaze. And this is..." She brushed a stray lock from his brow then let her touch linger. "When we first met, I couldn't understand how a man that seemingly had everything could look so despondent. Your eyes filled with loneliness. Now I know."

He reached to draw his rumpled coat over her waist, an ineffectual task but one that allowed his gaze to leave hers for the telling. "I try not to think of him often. But you have it wrong. It's why I *require* the trust of the few in my circle, not so much I can't give it. My father tossed us out like rubbish in his negligent way. Then he showed himself the same courtesy. Leaving a young man to assume responsibility for his distraught sister when the young man was distraught himself. I suppose that changes a person, shifts his perspective. You see, I'm not interested in half measures. From my friends, my colleagues, or my wife. No business agreements are going to carry us through. It's love or nothing for me. You have mine, you always have, but I must have yours in return. Or I can't do this, Hellie. I can't."

Her lips parted, and he placed his hand over them, begging her without words to let him continue.

"We met by chance, a random occurrence that never felt random to me. It felt like the gods conspiring to give me someone of my very own, a thunderbolt that shook me where I stood on that seaside crag. My person set before me. Forcing me to shove myself in your path whether you wanted me there or not. A courtship I handled poorly as neither of us realized I was courting.

"But I'm stubborn in that I acknowledged the challenge of you. Leading me to the inevitability of discovering love on an unassuming day on a deserted stretch of sand. It sounds poetic when I'm no poet, but what I feel for you"—he captured her hand and placed it over his wildly beating heart—"is like what every paleontologist I've ever studied struggles to predict and quantify. The why. It all comes down to the *why*."

Tears glittered on her lashes, and she dipped her head to hide her reaction to his words.

"Don't," he whispered and leaned in, pressing his lips to her brow, her cheek. "Don't hide from my feelings for you. I've unlocked a chest that will remain open. Fear isn't going to have me slamming it shut. Not anymore. I have only myself, and a title you don't want, to offer. A sister in Pippa. I can't promise you that society will welcome us, and I don't *care*. The men I respect most aren't welcomed. I'm happy to join them in exile. I love you with everything I am, everything I have. It's there for life, this love, should you choose to take it. But I won't accept half measures, Hellie. I cannot. Not from you. If you can't match this, can't assume it—"

"I love you too," she exclaimed against his hand.

He blinked, his arm falling to rest on the floor. "Repeat that, please."

Her laugh was gentle and naughty, knowing. "I love you, too, Roan, and I think I always have. Would I have kept the fossil if the man who'd given it to me didn't mean the world?" She covered *his* lips with her hand when he started to speak, her eyes shining brightly in the dim light. "My turn, Your Grace. I've never had a family, never had anyone truly. Until you. Until Theodosia. And Pippa." A tear trailed her cheek, and she brushed it away.

"I'm trying to let you into a heart I've guarded well. Too well. We've spent years apart when we could have been together. If only I'd thought to listen to your repeated apologies and understood they were coming from *your* heart. Trusted you even a little. Or better yet, trusted myself. I don't desire anyone else. I will never desire anyone else. So be patient because you're my future. I'm not the proper choice, a fitting choice, but I will do my best. I don't care about the title, but I need the *man*. I want to help a duke sell his unwanted antiquities to the highest bidder to fund his tenancies and build a new school in his village. Help him find a physician who thinks giving birth is worth the medicinal effort. I want to be the eighth Duke of Leighton's mother."

He swallowed hard and held up three fingers.

She tilted her head, confused.

"Three wise men. Three witches in Macbeth. Three children."

Helena slipped her hand over her midriff, her gaze bemused. *"Three."*

"Let's start now." Roan went to kiss her, remembering the plank floor was unforgiving—but not so much that he couldn't make use of it —when he heard the sound. Breaking glass and an urgent discussion drifting in from the alley behind the warehouse.

He was on his feet immediately, the hair on the back of his neck prickling. Wrenching his drawers and trousers to his waist, he buttoned his close with determined speed. "Get dressed. Then slip behind those crates until I see what's going on."

Yanking on his boots, he gestured to a dark corner, his harsh expression daring her to argue. From his pocket, he produced a knife that, like her pistol, he knew how to use. "Not a peep, Helena. Not one word. *This* is where you let me in. Let me be your husband, your protector, for one bloody second."

She thought to argue, second nature to Lady Hell, and he saw the rise in color on her cheeks. Then she rolled to a sit, adjusted her clothing, following his orders without comment.

For the first and perhaps last time in their marriage, she offered no argument.

Although his heart turned over in gratitude and love, he wasn't kidding himself about the constancy of her agreement.

After giving her another telling glance, Roan crossed to the alley side of the warehouse. He was, in fact, standing beneath the damaged window when a polished Hessian popped through it, a long body following, gloved fists holding the metal and jagged glass edge with care. He stepped back but not far, his blade glinting, at the ready.

Reginald Norcross gasped when he turned, his curse echoing off the wood and steel of beams of the structure. His hair glimmered in the light thrown from the sconce, all shades of gold.

"Norcross," Roan murmured, resting his shoulder against a wooden pillar while he folded his blade, hiding the weapon in his pocket. "Interesting to find you breaking into my wife's warehouse."

Like a valiant soldier, Norcross straightened his spine in acknowl-edgment of defeat. "So, it's true. The broadsheets spill honest ink for once. I should have known by the way you looked at her at Epsom that she wouldn't be unmarried for long."

Roan rubbed his chest, counting to five to soothe his ire and the need to give an asthmatic cough. He always got that pinch when he got angry. However, this was a situation he needed to unravel without his temper or his fists. Or his childhood fragility rearing its ugly head. "Why would a knight of the realm break into a shipping facility in Wapping? Repeatedly, if I'm to believe the coincidence. Can you help me understand this before I beat you to a bloody pulp?"

Norcross yanked his beaver hat from his head and dragged his fingers through his tousled hair. His jaw was stubbled, his eyes blood-shot. The man was near the end of his lead. "I wanted her to feel she needed to finally take a husband. A man to protect her business, protect *her*. A partner, if you will. I asked twice and was rejected cleanly, so I'd hoped to enhance my chances through some harmless trickery. I never counted on her blocking me by falling for a duke."

Roan settled in, crossing his feet and praying Helena would stay in her hiding place for at least another minute, if for no other reason than to save this poor sod's dignity. Norcross had asked her to marry him *twice*? "How bad is the situation?"

The man didn't try to lie, which marginally elevated his status in Roan's mind. "My eldest brother was a wastrel if you've not heard the outrageous tales about him. He tore through London like a demon, leaving smoldering opium wrecks in his wake. Rumored to have shared a pipe with King George. I returned from war to find buckets of debt, a deceased brother, and an ailing mother. Tenant's homes in disrepair.

"Our estate, tiny compared to anything connected to a duchy but one that has been in my family since the 1600s, falling down around me. There are fruit orchards and quite the most gorgeous parkland to be had in England. I'd thought to have my children grow up there." With a sigh, he slumped back against the window ledge, running his hand along his downcast jaw.

"Not much of a plan, I realize. Desperation and all that. I was a better battlefield strategist. Before signing any agreements, I would have told Miss Astley, um, Her Grace, about the debt. But I simply thought, she's alone and needs protection. I'm a soldier. Protecting people has been my employ since I was nineteen years old. The only suitable profession I've been trained for in actuality." His gaze found Roan's, his smile self-disparaging. "And she's lovely. Spirited. Intelligent. Not a hard agreement in the end, as you well recognized."

Roan laughed softly, amazed how love was changing him. "I have contacts within the highest levels of the East India Company. They require capable men in various positions in their trading houses. You'll need to be comfortable hobnobbing with Parliament as the company has a renowned lobbying effort. Some say bribery. I'll stick with calling it business. If you're seriously considering marriage, though I cannot believe I'm offering it, my partner, Tobias Streeter, well, his wife has an enterprise for such things."

Norcross grinned, his dark eyes sparkling. Tunneling inside his greatcoat, he snaked a flask from an inner pocket. "The Matchmaker. The Countess Society. I've heard of them. Like most. A lot of incorrigible females, all told."

"Duchess Society, but you're close enough. I'll arrange an introduction. Then the ladies will put you through the matrimonial paces. They only accept honorable men, I should tell you, so you'll have to rise in the moral ranks a bit." Roan shoved off the pillar, extending his hand for the flask. Damned if he didn't need a drink after this day where he'd gone from deckhand to lover to savior. The whiskey was excellent, flowing down his throat without a hint of discord. He wiped his mouth and gave the flask back. "Is this my brew? I'm a silent partner with Streeter and Macauley in the whiskey venture."

Norcross shrugged, indifferent. Another enterprise for a duke wasn't exciting news. "It's the best, isn't it?"

"Might be a position there too. We're opening a new distillery in Shoreditch. May have a spot managing security if you can adjust how you handle burglaries. Although, I'm guessing you wanted these to be discoverable."

"I have an armed man outside to ensure no one came in behind me to create real havoc. A former colleague in the field. My intent was to save myself by being... useful, I suppose. Rescuing the damsel in distress or some such trite nonsense. I don't know why we grow up thinking we can be heroes. It must be the books we're read as children."

Roan dipped his head, his laugh floating free. "You merely made a miscalculation with my girl. But I've made many with her myself. We'll discuss the situation tomorrow, my townhouse, eleven sharp."

Norcross tucked the flask away, his expression slightly bewildered. "Why are you helping me?"

Roan kept himself from glancing over his shoulder. He could feel Helena's gaze burning into his back, but she remained silent. Her tolerance was admirable. And surprising. "Perhaps I want to share my good fortune at finding her first. Too, I remember that scramble to climb the hill of respectability after being abandoned by my family. No man should lose the loveliest parkland in England without a hard-fought battle to keep it."

They spent a few moments talking, then Sir Reginald Norcross exited through the door, his visage lighter than it had been upon his entry through a smashed window. He'd never know his discourse had been aired before the Duchess of Leighton.

Roan sighed when Helena's arms circled his waist, her cheek pressing against his back. "You're generous of soul, my darling duke."

His hands covered hers where they lay atop his belly. "I'm going to foist him off on Macauley."

"You devil. How cunning. I love that about you."

Unable to deny himself, he turned in her embrace, setting his lips to hers.

The kiss was a duke's promise to his duchess.

The forever kind.

Epilogue

Where a Duchess Finds a Family

Leighton House, Hertfordshire
Nine Months Later

Helena crossed the sloping lawn, her gaze on Roan as he led Kieran through a riding tutorial along the winding gravel footpath bordering the parkland. The boy was outfitted in new boots, buckskin breeches, and a coat with overlong sleeves that hung past his wrists. But he looked the dapper gentleman, like his instructor. The estate grounds were still luxuriant from summer, stalks of grass as green as her husband's eyes dusting her ankles, bright crimson and gold leaves from the maple trees a delicate crunch beneath her slippered feet. The slight chill in the air and the hint of woodsmoke brought hearth fires and hot cocoa, holidays and home to mind.

Family.

Helena halted, her hand going to her midriff and the baby that would arrive in a few short weeks. She thought it was a girl, Roan wagered a boy, and the village physician, a lovely gentleman who'd wished to leave the bustle of London for a quieter existence, thought it might be twins. Her little secret, the only one she planned to keep from her duke ever again.

Kicking at the grass, she restarted her waddling trek across the lawn, her mood effervescent. Roan had proven to be an adorably apprehensive expectant father. The thought of two babes enough to send him off the proverbial ledge, while the thought *delighted* her. Her grandmother had been a twin, so the possibility was genuine. She grinned. She'd left that part out to save him from sleepless nights.

Kieran giggled at something Roan said and punched him lightly in the shoulder, an action he wouldn't have dared do even two months ago. The boy had blossomed under Roan's care, her care, but mostly her husband's. He was so good with children, patient and... *kind*.

Roan was temperamental, stubborn, and argumentative. But he was also generous. Impartial. Droll. The most intelligent man in any room, a truth he never, *ever* dangled like a carrot before a horse. She hadn't thought to have a husband who cared for his friends, family, or tenants with all his heart. One willing to listen to his wife's suggestions with factual interest. They often spent the breakfast hour in deep discussion about shipping routes, excise taxes, and plans for expansion.

They were becoming partners in not only life but business.

The broadsheets had taken to calling him the Duke of Labor, a moniker he liked, although he hadn't admitted it. Not that the *ton* meant it solicitously. He'd found he enjoyed working at the shipyard, prowling the docks, managing physical aspects of Astley Shipping that were, even if she was loath to admit it, more easily governed by a man. Combined with his parliamentary responsibilities, the duchy, the fossil symposiums for which he was building a revered reputation, he'd created a full life. A happy life.

The Duke and Duchess of Leighton *were* invited to fewer balls. Although there were more than enough with the ones they were asked to attend. There were cuts on the street, one on Bond outside her modiste the week before, in fact. The Countess of Ainslie had refused to return her greeting, and Helena had had to pinch Roan to keep him from defending her. *Ignore it, darling*, she'd said and kissed him in full view of society.

For one moment, she transported him to the place where it was only the two of them. Soon to be three with the babe. Or four, she thought with a soft smile.

It didn't matter. Because she, like Roan, didn't *care*.

They had their friends. Hildy and Tobias, Georgie and Dexter. The incorrigible Xander Macauley. Even Reginald Norcross, who was a pleasant but faintly bewildered man, it turned out. Although the Duchess Society had yet to find a wife for him, they were looking. Moreover, he'd proven to be an able head of security for the expanding distillery enterprise.

They had their growing family. Theodosia, Pippa, and now, little Kieran, sleeping in a bedchamber next to the nursery. A more significant part of their lives than anyone had planned as he moved from the position of groom to son. Roan's constant shadow. Even Patience, who had settled quite gracefully into the role of aging duenna to a duchess.

They had Leighton House, a place to escape when London's walls closed in too tightly.

A thankful respite, as this was where she wanted to raise her children.

Roan glanced up, catching her protective hold on her stomach. He was before her in five brisk strides, winded from the sprint. "Are you well? You shouldn't be out here, tromping around in the chill. Shall I have Doctor James sent over?"

Helena caught his jaw in her hand, love spinning her heart like dice in her chest. "Roan. I'm fine. More than. Continue your lessons. The boy needs to know how to ride safely and well. The tumble he took last week took seconds off your life."

Roan squirmed under her scrutiny and stepped out of reach. His attachment to Kieran and Kieran's obvious attachment to him hadn't been expressed by either party. She thought it the sweetest thing that her husband loved deeply but *shyly*. He gave his entire heart, but he gave it after judicious contemplation. And always while looking over his shoulder. It was no wonder it had taken him ten years to tell her he loved her.

With wifely concern she loved exhibiting, she dusted a bit of straw off his sleeve. "When is the Leighton Cluster arriving?"

Roan shaded his eyes and glanced at the sun, gauging the time. "In another hour or two. Though I'm not sure you should be entertaining so close to the babe arriving."

"It's Pippa's birthday, my darling duke. A young lady needs a celebration on such an occasion. You only turn twenty-two once. Besides, Theo has had the best time decorating for the party."

Silent on the topic, he sighed and scrubbed his hand along the back of his neck. He was worried about his sister. Pippa was entering the next season as if she was being escorted to Newgate's gallows. The Duchess Society had recommended she wait out the last, due to what London had taken to calling the "ratafia incident." Appearances weren't the problem; Hildy and Georgie had prepared her well. She seemed a lady from every angle. But there was a haunted look in her eyes. Secrets, Helena guessed, the opinion of a woman who'd been good at keeping them. Added to Roan's concern was Pippa's mutinous threat to become the *ton's* most renowned wallflower. She vowed to disappear behind potted ferns at every ball and never come out. Not even to waltz, a scandalous dance she loved.

Helena was worried too. Lady Philippa Darlington had, in the time Helena had known her, been good to her word.

Helena straightened his cuff, more unnecessary touching. "You could try to talk to her again."

Roan grunted without comment.

"Maybe the children arriving will brighten her mood. Pippa enjoys having a full house. A little joy before being tossed back into society's foul pond might not be a bad idea."

"You know how many tots are *arriving*, don't you? The Duke of Markham's litter. Is it three now or four? Tobias and Hildy with their two, the latest only a month old, so you know he'll keep us up when we have few nights left to sleep before our darling is born. Plus, Streeter won't leave London without those damned cats. Last time, they got into the pantry and tore through all the cheese on the estate! I found Nick Bottoms sleeping on my bloody pillow. He fights with your boy Rufus every time, fur flying."

"I find it charming. The Rogue King of Limehouse and his felines."

Roan grunted again, this one with less vigor. "I suppose it's mildly charming."

"Macauley?" she asked, knowing this was a touchy subject. Their friend had been absent more than not since their wedding for reasons unexplained. Roan was beginning to take it personally.

Shrugging, Roan glanced over his shoulder, gestured to Kieran to wait a moment for him. "He declined, but he sent a gift. He's busy with that gaming hell he and that wild Scot, Lachlan Campbell, are restoring. Anyway, I left it with Pippa, which somehow seemed to make her angrier. Women," he muttered hotly beneath his breath. "I don't even know what it was. Something appropriate, I hope. You never know with that scoundrel. I likely should have opened it first, but it's *her* gift!"

"Let's take this season one step at a time. Pippa doesn't have to get married. Now or ever," Helena reminded him, her constant refrain.

He turned to her, his temper flooding his eyes. They'd made it almost all day without him getting mad. Near to a record. "Do you think I'd push her into a union she doesn't want? But she's a duke's *sister*. She has to wade through this mindless muddle of balls and musicales, the ones we still get invited to when I wish we got invited to none, the same as you and I do. I can't change what our life has become, her responsibilities. I can only protect her. If she's not out in society, how is she to meet him? If a man is lingering in the shadows of her life?"

Helena stepped into his arms, giving him no alternative but to wrap them around her and pull her in close. "How about destiny? Fate? Meeting him on a blustery day on a deserted shore in southern England? This last one sounds perfect to me."

"Magical," Roan whispered in her ear, a tickle that fluttered past her heart. "I can only wish that for Pippa."

"Magical," Helena agreed and nestled into his body.

Home. Family. Love. As she'd always desired.

Pippa Darlington placed the gift on the bed as if the contents would detonate upon opening. Then, crawling atop the mattress, she crossed her legs and stared at the small wrapped parcel with angst, indecision, and anticipation. X.M. was scrawled on the back in elegant script, taunting her. As if she'd not known *immediately* who it was from.

Careful, Little Darlington, as you navigate these treacherous waters.

Xander Macauley's words rolled over her like a wave, as they seemed to do at least once a day. Sometimes at night, alone in her big bed, which was the biggest secret out of all the secrets a duke's sister was forced to keep.

Along with the memory of their stolen moment in the gaming room came the *feelings*.

Heat thrumming through her limbs. Through her head like champagne. Pulse skipping, heart bumping against her ribs. She felt drunk. On a *man*.

Why, why, why did it have to be him?

Roan would never allow it. Xander Macauley would never ask it. He thought her a bothersome fly buzzing about his face. Less than a fly, an ant he smashed beneath his boot. He had his choice of every lifted skirt in London. Why would he want her? Unsophisticated sister of his best friend?

She refused, simply *refused*, to be bothersome. A burden. A nuisance. When she married, *if* she married, the pitiable sod would be absolutely besotted, out of his head, *gone* for her. Tripping along behind her like her brother tripped along behind Hellie. The Duke of Markham with Georgie. Tobias Streeter with Hildy, perhaps the worst case of lovesick behavior she'd ever seen.

Gads, there were men, hundreds, to choose from on her side as well. Duke to baronet, solicitor to vicar. Her heart didn't have to set its sights on the most unreachable in status and demeanor. A confirmed, nay, *sworn* bachelor. A man born in the rookery of all places. A blackguard. A scoundrel. A *rake*. Hildy Streeter had done it, of course, married a rogue who'd climbed from the pits of the slums then gone on to love him with all her heart and more.

Nevertheless, even after observing these beautiful relationships,

Pippa wouldn't follow their examples merely because of a fickle attraction.

She had a sister, two of them now, and the eldest, the powerful Duchess of Leighton, said she didn't have to marry if she didn't want to. But she'd also said she had to *try*. Make it through another season, for her brother's sake.

She was going to be the grandest wallflower who'd ever *lived*. Fade into every room she entered like mist. Prop up columns and disappear behind shrubbery brought into the ballroom for the event. They would not even know she was *there*. Her only spot of despair was missing out on the waltzes, but miss out, she would. Signing her dance card would be the most challenging feat to accomplish in England.

Pippa caught her tongue between her teeth and touched the package, traced her index finger over the twine wrapped twice around it. Simply presented, like the man himself.

Echoes from carriages arriving on the front drive fluttered through her open window along with the crisp evening air. Fall was upon them in gorgeous measure. She heard the children first, shouts of bedlam after hours of forced containment. She loved when Leighton House's hallways rang with mischief and merriment. They'd not been so lonely, she and Roan, since he'd allowed all these interesting people into their lives. Since he'd opened his heart finally and let Helena into its protected confines.

She fiddled with the package for another minute, then sighed and tugged on the bow, the twine unraveling in her hand. The paper, similar to what would be wrapped around meat delivered from a butcher, fell open to reveal a small, bejeweled knife. Not contained in any fancy box or packed with additional trimmings. Just the knife. Tiny enough to fit in a fob pocket. Or in her boot.

With a laugh she wouldn't have been able to contain had the man who'd given her the gift been sitting in the chamber, she picked it up and brought it close to her face.

An inscription was etched in the silver edge.

To help navigate the waters.

Pippa flopped to her back, the present clutched in her fist. It heated against her skin like an ember plucked from the fire. With a vulgar growl the Duchess Society had said she must *not* utter in public, she punched the mattress in frustration and awe. Xander Macauley remembered their stolen moment as well as she. She'd not imagined his breathless wonder, the bounder.

This would be the best gift she received for her birthday, the most personal. She just knew it. Damn and blast. Somehow, he'd seen her for one brief moment. The real girl.

Closing her eyes, she wondered how she would ever forget that fact.

THE END

Come along for Pippa and Macauley's tempestuous romantic adventure in *The Wicked Wallflower!* Next in the Duchess Society series!

In the meantime, have you read Hildy's and Georgie's story in *The Brazen Bluestocking* (book 1) and *The Ice Duchess* (prequel)?

THE DUCHESS SOCIETY SERIES

While waiting for book 3, check out other books by Tracy Sumner or dive into one of WOLF Publishing's latest release: The steamy and witty Regency romance series by Charlie Lane: The Debutante Dares Series!

THE DEBUTANTE DARES SERIES

Also by Tracy Sumner

The Duchess Society Series

The Ice Duchess *(Prequel)*

The Brazen Bluestocking

The Scandalous Vixen

The Wicked Wallflower *(coming April 2022)*

League of Lords Series

The Lady is Trouble

The Rake is Taken

The Duke is Wicked

The Hellion is Tamed

Garrett Brothers Series

Tides of Desire: A Christmas Romance

Tides of Love

Tides of Passion

Southern Heat Series

To Desire a Scoundrel: A Christmas Seduction

To Seduce a Rogue

Standalone Regency romances

Tempting the Scoundrel

Chasing the Duke

About Tracy Sumner

Award-winning author Tracy Sumner's story-
telling career began when she picked up a
historical romance on a college beach trip,
and she fondly blames LaVyrle Spencer for
her obsession with the genre. She's a recipient
of the National Reader's Choice, and her
novels have been translated into Dutch,
German, Portuguese and Spanish. She lived in
New York, Paris and Taipei before finding her
way back to the Lowcountry of South
Carolina.

When not writing sizzling love stories about feisty heroines and their
temperamental-but-entirely-lovable heroes, Tracy enjoys reading,
snowboarding, college football (Go Tigers!), yoga, and travel. She loves
to hear from romance readers!

Connect with Tracy: www.tracy-sumner.com

facebook.com/Tracysumnerauthor

twitter.com/sumnertrac

instagram.com/tracysumnerromance

bookbub.com/profile/tracy-sumner

amazon.com/Tracy-Sumner/e/B000APFV3G

Made in the USA
Middletown, DE
10 June 2022